PRAISE FOR THE TEXAS KINGS SERIES

Cowboy Take Me Away

"The playful banter between tough cowboy Chase and sassy veterinarian Hope is the highlight of Lane's latest in her Texas Kings series. Lane's strong, contemporary writing, genuine, relatable characters, and steady pacing will draw readers into the story. With Chase and Hope's passionate connection at the center of an engaging plot, this story is a sexy, charming Southern read."

—*Romantic Times Book Reviews*

"*Cowboy Take Me Away* is recommended for any folks who love second chance stories with secret complications thrown in, stories about hardworking men and ladies who are good at their jobs, and love stories that conquer tons of miscommunications." —*Fresh Fiction*

The Devil Wears Spurs

"It's no gamble to bet on cowboy Ryder King. Soraya Lane's *The Devil Wears Spurs* is hot as a Texas summer. It's a wild ride you don't want to miss."

—*New York Times* bestselling author Jennifer Ryan

"Watch out, the Devil has met his match! Sit back with Soraya Lane's *The Devil Wears Spurs* and enjoy the sparks that fly between champion bull rider Ryder and Chloe, a barmaid with a few aces up her sleeve. You won't want their story to end!"

—Laura Moore, bestselling author of *Once Tasted*

Also by Soraya Lane

The Devil Wears Spurs
Cowboy Take Me Away

I Knew You Were Trouble

Soraya Lane

St. Martin's Paperbacks

This is a work of fiction. All of the characters, organizations, and events portrayed in this novel are either products of the author's imagination or are used fictitiously.

I KNEW YOU WERE TROUBLE

Copyright © 2016 by Soraya Lane.

All rights reserved.

For information address St. Martin's Press, 175 Fifth Avenue, New York, NY 10010.

ISBN: 978-1-250-06010-5

Our books may be purchased in bulk for promotional, educational, or business use. Please contact your local bookseller or the Macmillan Corporate and Premium Sales Department at 1-800-221-7945, ext. 5442, or by e-mail at MacmillanSpecialMarkets@macmillan.com.

Printed in the United States of America

St. Martin's Paperbacks edition / July 2016

St. Martin's Paperbacks are published by St. Martin's Press, 175 Fifth Avenue, New York, NY 10010.

10 9 8 7 6 5 4 3 2 1

For Hamish.
I think it's about time you started reading
your wife's books!

Acknowledgments

This series was so much fun to write, and it was very fulfilling to write longer books with a bigger cast of characters. I'm sad to leave Nate, Chase, and Ryder behind, because in my mind those heroes are still very real.

Thank you so much to Holly Ingraham for letting me turn my ideas into reality. I appreciate all the time you have spent editing each story with me, and I hope to keep working with you in the future. You're the kind of editor authors love, because you embrace each story's characters and plot, suggesting changes that serve to make the book so much stronger.

I also need to thank my agent, Laura Bradford, for her fantastic advice and helping to make this series happen in the first place. I would be lost without you, and five years on I'm still so happy that you're in my corner.

As always, I have to make special mention of Natalie Anderson, Nicola Marsh, and Yvonne Lindsay—amazing authors and even more amazing friends. Thank you for your daily encouragement and support. I also receive incredible daily support from my family, and I couldn't write any book without "grandma & granddad" childcare. My boys are so lucky to have grandparents who adore them and spend so much time with them. We all appreciate it!

Thank you to all my wonderful readers—every email, tweet or Facebook message means the world to me. As an author, it's the reader correspondence that helps on days when the words just aren't flowing as fast as usual.

And lastly for my husband, Hamish. Many years ago he told me that once I was published he'd read my books, but five years on and almost thirty books later, he's got a lot of catching up to do!

Chapter 1

NATE KING winked at the beautiful blond flight attendant as she stood near the entrance, hands behind her back, as she watched him exit the plane. It had taken every inch of his willpower not to react to her blue eyes and pillowy lips during the flight, but staying in control was something he was trying to teach himself. Gone were the days of racking up points in the mile-high club with sexy flight attendants on the family's private jet, and in were the days of behaving like a man in charge of an empire. If his grandfather stayed true to his word, Nate's future was going to involve a whole lot more business, and a whole lot less pleasure.

"Bye, Nathaniel," she purred.

He stifled his groan as he checked her out one last time. "Bye, sugar," he replied, eyes slowly traveling up and down her body.

Nate paused for a slow second when her hand slipped into his back pocket, and met her sultry blue gaze. But when he closed his fingers over her wrist, it was to remove her hand, not encourage it.

"Call me," she whispered.

He smiled, giving her a final nod before taking his sunglasses from his inside jacket pocket and sliding them on. The sun was hot, just how he liked it, and he pushed up his shirtsleeves as he crossed the tarmac and headed for the terminal. The blonde had been sexy as hell, so maybe he would call her, but right now he had business to attend to. In less than fifteen minutes, he would be back in his car and headed toward the ranch, and after a week away he was happy to be back in Texas, even if it was going to take him days to catch up on work.

Nate pulled his iPhone from his pocket as it started to buzz, smiling when he saw his brother's name on the screen.

"Hey, Chase. I've just landed."

He picked up his pace and walked through the hangar building, emerging out the other side and waving to the valet. The young guy waiting there ran off to retrieve Nate's vehicle as soon as he saw him.

"I was just driving past your place and you have a visitor."

That got his attention. "Who is it?" *Who the hell would just drop by unannounced and be waiting?*

"Well, she's kind of your type, so I didn't want you to waste time at the airport, if you know what I mean."

Nate chuckled, relaxing when he realized it was a woman waiting. "Who is she?"

"Dark hair, olive skin, bangin' body, kind of looks like a young Eva Longoria . . ."

Faith. There were plenty of beautiful dark-haired

girls in Texas, but only one in particular sprung to mind. Or at least only one who might turn up at his place—he never took women back to the house, but he'd always made it clear to Faith that she was welcome. And there was only one woman his brother would enjoy teasing him about.

"Don't talk to her. Just leave her waiting," Nate said, trying to keep his voice level so Chase didn't do anything just to annoy him. "I don't—"

"Chill, big bro. My bed's already taken, but I do have one of the ranch hands with me right now. She's pretty gorgeous, always has been, though, right?"

There was only one woman who had always gotten under Nate's skin, and he knew Chase got a kick out of teasing him. But Nate wasn't going to take the bait that easily.

He had a reputation as bad as his siblings' when it came to the opposite sex, so he knew exactly what they'd think, if they ever got too close to her. *Even if they were both taken, he didn't like the idea of them even thinking about Faith like that.* He'd knock every one of Chase's teeth out if he dared let the ranch hand go near her, too. Nate clamped his jaw shut, thinking about that long, almost-black hair tumbling over her shoulders, slender body and full breasts that teased him every time he saw her. Hell, keeping his eyes and his hands off her had been one of the biggest challenges of his life when he'd been younger.

"Just keep away from her, okay?" he muttered, wishing he'd just stayed on the jet with the blonde. At least he would have avoided this entire conversation. "I'm on my way home. Now."

"Maybe she's looking for the housekeeper's job you've been advertising. Any takers for Mrs. T's old job?"

"Don't you have some work to do? Like, oh, I don't know, running our goddamn ranch?"

Nate growled and hung up to the sound of his brother's laughter. He would kill him—he would actually kill him. Nate's best friend Sam's little sister was strictly off-limits, and he would— The throaty rumble of his Ferrari caught his attention and distracted him as it pulled to the curb. The valet jumped out and Nate opened his wallet to tip him, before throwing his bag in the passenger seat and getting into the car. He closed his eyes for a second, hands on the steering wheel, before pushing down on the accelerator and heading for home. The car always relaxed him, and the drive to the ranch would keep him calm until he could wrap his hands around his brother's neck. *And his fist into the ranch hand's face if he was so much as drooling over her.*

Nate forced himself to slow down as he turned into the wide gravel driveway, the big wooden sign announcing the King ranch swinging in the wind as he passed it. He'd driven like a madman from the airport, but now that he was here he needed to settle down. The driveway was over a mile long, stretching past endless post and rail fields where they kept their horses, large oak trees making shadows in the long grass. It was a hell of a place to call home, and he never failed to appreciate the property he'd grown up on every time he came back. And it wasn't just his childhood home—it was the place he'd live until his dying days, just like his grandfather had. There was nowhere else Nate would rather be, and there was nothing he wouldn't do to preserve the property that had been in his family for generations.

He drove past the first house and scowled, hoping that Chase wasn't in there. Nate's brother had just built a new home closer to the front of the property with his wife, and as annoyed as he was with Chase right now, he did admire the architecture of the place every time he came up the drive. Although he was going to give Hope full credit for the way the house had turned out.

Nate slowed as he approached the garage to the original homestead, the house he still called home, glancing around to see where this mystery woman was. The more he'd thought about it, the more he'd convinced himself that it couldn't be Faith. What would she be doing at their ranch, anyway? Maybe Chase was just trying to get him fired up.

He jumped out of the car and walked from the garage, crossing the gravel to the front door. Sure enough, there was a brunette sitting on the front steps, head down, and even better, there was no sign of his brother.

"Faith?"

Nate grinned when she looked up, because there was no mistaking the brown eyes that met his. Her gaze was warm, her eyes were darker than the richest chocolate, her smile lighting up her face, as she walked toward him.

"Hey, Nate."

"What are you doing here?" Nate ran up the steps and pulled her in for a hug, taking her slender body into his arms. It took every inch of his willpower to keep his chest half an inch from hers. But Faith had other ideas.

She hugged him tight, stepping closer against him so that he could feel every part of her.

Nate forced himself to step back before he ended up with a hard-on, holding her at arm's length. And as soon as he did, he knew something was wrong. She didn't meet his gaze, and Faith never usually had a problem staring him straight in the eye.

"You've never just turned up to say hi before, so I'm guessing there's something going on. Is it Sam?"

She shook her head and tucked a strand of long dark hair behind her ear, the look on her face making her appear . . . *vulnerable*. Faith had been the little sister who'd always tried to keep up with her brother, who never showed a sign of weakness. Right now the look on her face was making Nate's protective instincts go into overdrive. He wanted to fold her back in his arms and protect her, find out what the hell had upset her and make sure it never happened again. He cleared his throat, impatient, waiting for her to respond.

"Sam's fine; at least he was the last time I saw him. I just . . ." She sighed. "I'm in over my head and I needed somewhere to go."

"What happened?" Nate asked, hating that he couldn't just think of her like his surrogate sister. Heaven knew he'd tried.

He followed Faith's glance toward his door, and it was then he noticed two large suitcases sitting together, like they were waiting to be invited in. The look she gave him was one he'd seen her use on her brother countless times, and he wasn't finding it easy to ignore. Usually puppy dog eyes wouldn't have worked on him, but Faith somehow managed to pull it off.

"Faith?"

She cleared her throat and stared back at him, lips tipping up into a smile that made Nate uncomfortable. *Hell no.* He was about to be talked into something; he just knew it.

"I heard you've been advertising for a housekeeper," she said, "and it just so happens that I'm perfect for the job."

"No, you're not," he replied. "If you need someone to talk to, then come on in, but I'm not hiring you. Besides, you're way overqualified." And the last thing he needed was to be tempted by Faith bloody Mendes in his own home.

"Yes, you are," she insisted, hands on her hips. "And no, I'm not. I haven't even graduated with my master's yet."

"Faith, your brother is my best friend. I'll help you, but he'd never let you take a job with me, let alone one that involved you being in my home." If he so much as looked at her the wrong way Sam would have his head, and there was only one way a man could look at Faith. She was pure sex appeal, no other way to describe her, all long limbs, bronze skin, and deep-brown eyes, not to mention that hair that she always wore loose and tumbling over her shoulders and down her back.

Nate sighed and looked out to the fields. He'd kept his distance from her for so long, and having Faith in his home working for him wasn't something he was going to let happen.

"Nate, I need somewhere to stay and you need someone to look after your house. It's the perfect arrangement."

"Stay? Now you've definitely lost your mind," he muttered. "I don't recall at any point advertising for a live-in housekeeper. And besides, all applications were supposed to go to my assistant. Maybe I should give you her number."

"Please, Nate? I wouldn't ask you if I wasn't desperate."

Nate tried to look away, tried to ignore her, but when her hand found his and she blinked up at him he was powerless. Never in his life had he found it hard to say no to anyone. Hell, he did it all the time. But Faith? There was something about his friend's little sister that made it impossible for him to walk away. And the older she became, the harder it was to remind himself that she was off-limits, especially when she looked at him like that. That mouth of hers alone was pure torture, because every time she spoke, hell, every time she moistened her lips with the tip of her tongue, there was only one thing he thought of. And it was wicked the things his mind could come up with.

"Nate, I have nowhere else to go."

He sighed and moved past her, refusing to acknowledge her bags on the porch and pushing open his front door.

"Fine, you can come in. But that doesn't mean I'm saying yes, you hear me?" He'd hear her out, find out what was wrong and what kind of a predicament she was in. Then he could figure out what to do with her.

Faith settled into one of the oversize outdoor sofas on the patio of the King homestead and gazed out at the land. She'd only visited the property a few times when she was younger, but never for a second had she forgotten how beautiful it was. The fields seemed to stretch endlessly into the horizon, the only intrusion the massive barns and stables a few hundred yards from the house. It was easily the most beautiful place she'd ever seen, and when she was a child it had been the kind of home she'd fantasized about. Horses to ride, trees to climb, places to hide . . . and now here she was seeking refuge, still looking for that place to hide away from reality. Everyone always talked about the King ranch being the most sought-after real estate in Texas, but it was more than that. There was something about the place that could just make a person forget everything else, and Faith could see exactly why it had been in the same family for so many generations.

"I was going to offer you a beer, but I decided a coffee was probably more appropriate."

She looked up when Nate appeared, his big frame filling the doorway. It didn't matter that she'd known him her whole life—he still managed to make her stop and stare. His shoulders were broad, body big and muscular, and those eyes . . . she'd never managed to match his warm, chocolate-drizzled gaze without smiling.

"I've been legally allowed to drink for quite a few years now," Faith told him with a laugh. "You're not going to get in trouble for giving me alcohol anymore."

He passed her the cup of coffee and sat down on the other sofa, a hint of a smile bracing his mouth.

"You know, you always were a pain in the ass when you wanted something."

Faith grinned as she reached for her coffee. Nate had been her brother's best friend since before she'd started elementary school, which meant she'd had a lot of practice at convincing both of them to do things for her. The only difference was that today she actually did need help, and Nate was one of the few people in the world she knew she could count on. She might have had a crush on him throughout all of her teenage years, but right now she wasn't interested in being with *any* man, and it wasn't like Nate had ever treated her as more than an honorary little sister. Although she could see how he managed to lure so many women into his bed—even the way he stroked his fingers across his coffee cup made her wonder what he'd be like between the sheets.

"So does that mean you've decided to let me stay?" she asked.

He shook his head, jaw fixed like steel as he stared straight at her. "No. But I'll call Sam for you."

"I don't want you to call him, Nate. I need to deal with this on my own."

His laugh was deep, like the rumble of a volcano. "And by on your own, you mean with my help?" He stared at her, eyes never leaving hers. "You haven't even told me why you're really here."

She sighed, glancing away. "I don't expect you to understand."

Now Nate looked annoyed, the scowl on his face impossible to ignore. She watched as he took a sip of his coffee and looked out over the land, before taking a deep breath and turning to face her again. If she hadn't known him for so long, she might have been intimidated by the dark expression on his face and the way he leaned forward, elbows on his knees as his body came closer to hers.

"Tell me what the hell's going on, Faith!" he demanded, words as cool as ice. "I can't help you if you don't talk to me, and you're not staying here unless you give me a damn good reason."

Faith met his gaze and leaned forward to put her coffee down again, knowing what she had to do, that the only way Nate was going to let her stay was if she opened up to him. Right now she needed to be here, needed time and space to figure things out. She took a deep breath, then stood, lifting the hem of her T-shirt and holding it just high enough to show him her stomach, shivering as she bared herself.

Faith forced herself to meet his gaze, watching his mouth open like he was about to protest before he clamped his jaw shut again. It only took a second, a moment for him to look her in the eye and then focus on her skin again, before the darkness in his face exploded around them.

"Who the fuck did that to you?" Nate's voice was so quiet, so menacing, that it was more terrifying than if he'd yelled.

Before she could answer, he stepped into her space, so close to her that she could hardly breathe, his big body the only thing she could see as he towered over her.

Faith glanced down at herself, saw how ugly the purple bruise looked against her skin. Nate was peering at her stomach, his eyebrows bunched together and his fists clenched at his sides.

"I asked you who did this, Faith? Was it that scumbag boyfriend?"

She watched Nate clench his fists into tight balls, and

one glance up at him told her she'd managed to make him angrier than she'd ever seen him before. It was just Nate, though; she knew he'd never hurt her, that he'd always look after her. Faith gulped, wishing he didn't look like he was about to hurt *something*.

"Yeah, it was," she managed.

Nate stepped back, running a hand through his hair before folding his arms across his chest.

"I'll fucking kill him, Faith," he murmured, words almost too quiet to hear. "I'll make him wish he'd never laid a goddamn hand on you. No one hits you and gets away with it, you hear me? *No one.*"

She took a deep, shaky breath, wrapping her arms about herself, not sure what else to do. Maybe she shouldn't have come here, shouldn't have been honest with Nate about what had happened. Something told her that he maybe was capable of doing what he'd just threatened, and she didn't need that on her conscience. Just like she didn't need to be faced with violence right now after what she'd been through.

"I was just so sure Sam was wrong about him," she said, instinctively touching where he'd hurt her. "I guess he was right, though, huh?"

Nate stepped forward and touched her hand, guiding her top down, before putting his palms on her shoulders and staring hard into her eyes. He was easily a head taller than her, but he'd angled his body so they were almost level, his decadent brown eyes so full of unexpected kindness that it almost made her cry. But she wasn't ever going to shed another tear again, *not where any man was concerned.* She'd done the one thing she'd always sworn she'd never do, and that was fall for the same kind of man her mom had. But Faith sure as hell wasn't going to make the same mistake twice.

"I *will* make him pay for this, Faith," Nate muttered. "Sam told me he was a jerk, but I figured he was just being overprotective. Seriously, I'm going to make him regret *ever* laying a hand on you, and that's a promise."

"No, you're not Nate, but I like the fact you want to protect me. If I told Sam he'd just lose it, and the last thing I need is you or him ending up in jail trying to look after me."

"There's one thing I'm good at, Faith, and that's keeping my word. He won't ever hurt you again, you hear me?" His low chuckle sent a shiver down her spine. "And don't worry about me going to jail. I might be hot-headed, but I'm also careful."

Faith let Nate tuck her against him when he tugged her forward, relaxing into the warmth of his body. His cologne smelled like citrus and she just shut her eyes and inhaled, knew that he would never turn her away now. Nate's big arms held her tight, his torso hard against her chest. His embrace was firm yet soft, her frame snug against his in a hold that she knew would be so easy to never pull away from.

She knew what everyone said about him, that he was Mr. Love 'Em and Leave 'Em, but she didn't care. Nate might have bedded half the women in Texas, but he'd always treated her with respect, and right now that respect went a long way. But there was something dangerous about him, something that made her think he just might try to kill her son of a bitch ex. And right now, as much as she was loath to admit it, the idea was kind of comforting. She might not want him to actually commit murder, but the fact that Nate was prepared to do anything to protect her was kind of comforting in a weird sort of way.

"Tell me what happened, Faith. Tell me everything," Nate said when he finally let go of her and pulled away. "I want to know exactly what he did to you, every last detail."

She sat down, this time on the same sofa. She'd shown him her bruise and that meant Nate expected answers.

"It's been getting worse for a while, drinking, all the usual stuff. But this time he got so drunk and I couldn't get out of his way when I realized what was about to happen. I just still can't believe that after all the years of counting down to get out of Dad's house I went and fell for the same kind of man." She took a big breath and looked out at the horses that'd come closer to the house, needing the distraction as she was forced to relive what had happened. "He punched me hard in the stomach, and then pinned me by the arms. He just kept on yelling that he'd seen me with another guy, that I was a bitch, that he'd make sure no other man would ever want me. He'd never laid a hand on me before, and I wasn't going to hang around for him to do it again." She took a big breath, needing a moment to gather her thoughts. "Nate, you have to believe me that I never would have moved in with him if I'd thought he'd hurt me. I honestly thought we had a future together."

Nate took her hand and squeezed it, but the softness of his touch wasn't matched by the look on his face. His eyes were as dark as a thundercloud.

"Screw what your brother thinks," Nate muttered. "If you want to stay here, you're welcome for as long as you want. But you need to tell him what happened, because if you don't, I will." A smile played across his lips. "Or maybe I'll tell him *after* I make that asshole pay for what he did," Nate said in a low voice.

"I'm scared of what he'll do if he finds out. Sam's not like you; he could just freak out and do something stupid. You know how he is when it comes to me."

Nate's laugh was ice-cold. "Sugar, I'll make sure Sam keeps his head. When I tell him that I've got it under control, he'll trust me."

"Really?" It meant a lot to her, having Nate in her corner. He had a reputation for being fiercely loyal to the few people close to him.

Nate put his boots up on the low table and smiled over at her. "You don't have to be my housekeeper to stay, Faith. I made a promise to your brother years ago that I'd always look out for you, and that I'd, ah, well, never . . ." He laughed, shaking his head. "Let's just say he made it very clear that his little sister was off-limits. To me, anyway."

Faith shook her head. All those years of trying to make Nate notice her and he'd made a vow not to touch her? Typical. It sure as hell would have been nice to know that particular fact when she was seventeen. Instead she'd wondered what the hell was wrong with her that Nate King didn't so much as look at her when she'd tried so damn hard to catch his eye.

"I appreciate the offer, but if I'm staying here I want to earn my keep." It wasn't like she wanted to work as a housekeeper, but she was short of cash and it was the only way she could pay her way.

"You're sure about that?" The slight upturn of his lips

told her that he found her offer amusing, and it annoyed her—she wasn't afraid of hard work and she'd prove him wrong if that's what he thought.

She turned to Nate, smiling straight back at him. "Oh, I'm sure. I fully intend on making everyone in my life proud one day, I've got big dreams, and I want to know that I stood on my own two feet to get there."

"There's just one condition, then," Nate said.

"What's that?" she asked.

She could see exactly how he managed to bed so many women—that dimple alone was probably enough to get some girls stripping their clothes off. If she didn't know him so well, she'd have thought he was making a move just with his stare alone, the way he was sitting too close, hard thigh brushing hers. Or maybe he just didn't know how to turn the sex appeal *off*.

"If my brother Chase so much as looks at you, feel free to give him a bloody nose. You'd be doing me a favor."

Heat flooded her body, warmed every inch of her. Because for a moment there, she'd wondered if he was going to suggest an entirely different type of condition.

"Aren't both your brothers married?"

"I still don't trust them. Not one damn bit."

Chapter 2

NATE signaled for his secretary to enter his office. He slid her a considering look. She was an attractive woman, no doubt about it. For weeks he'd been ignoring the way she fluttered her lashes at him, but now he was starting to wonder if she'd be a good distraction. He needed one. *Bad.* He didn't usually like to mix business with pleasure, but he needed to do something about the hard-on he'd been fighting ever since he'd held Faith in his arms. The more he told himself she was off-limits, the more he seemed to want her in his bed, and now that she was staying in his house he wasn't convinced his willpower alone was going to keep him from doing something he'd regret. Or at least he'd regret it if her brother ever found out.

"Any word on the Landcorp acquisition?" The company Nate was now CEO for had been in his family for three generations. The Kings were the biggest landowners in Texas, and since Nate had become more involved he'd expanded their commercial holdings in New York and Las Vegas.

Right now he was negotiating a big deal on a new acquisition, and he wanted it closed and done.

His assistant shook her head. "There were no calls while you were out, except for Alison Roberts, who asked—"

"Tell her I'm away on business." It didn't seem to matter how clear he made it that he was only interested in sex, not a relationship—women like Alison just kept on trying to talk him into something more serious. "And get Wilson at Landcorp on the phone."

"Yes, Mr. King."

He grimaced at the title—it was bittersweet. His grandfather was Mr. King, and now Nate was sitting in his granddad's office and taking over the role he'd held for almost forty years while he battled for his life. Nate was proud that he believed in his eldest grandson enough to let him take the reins, but if it had meant keeping his grandfather at his side, Nate would have happily stayed second in command for a whole lot longer. They were a close family, and the thought of it being just the three of them without their granddad was a tough pill to swallow.

Nate's direct line lit up red signaling his assistant had the Landcorp associate on the phone, and he picked up immediately.

"Do we have a deal yet?" he demanded.

"We're close but—"

Fuck. "Fifteen million, Wilson. It's our final offer, take it or leave it. If you say no to me now I'm moving on to something else."

There was silence at the other end and it made him smile. He fucking loved this. The land was worth at least a few million more, but he had them over a barrel and they knew it. He loved the adrenaline rush of closing a deal, the feel of his heart thumping hard, blood rushing through his body.

"Done." Wilson sounded a bit strangled but said, "It's a pleasure doing business with you, Mr. King."

Nate grinned, knowing that the man hated dealing with him. He'd personally seen the look on Wilson's face when he'd been in New York. "Send the documents over. I'll have them signed as soon as they arrive and the funds will be deposited immediately."

He hung up and reached for his iPhone, still smiling as he dialed a number that he'd hardly ever had need to look up, one his grandfather had always kept on file just in case they ever had a serious problem that needed to be dealt with. Nate flicked through a few papers that he almost knew from memory as he listened to the phone ring, poring over the oil-drilling information as he waited.

"Nathaniel?"

Nate dropped the papers, his focus shifting. "I have a situation that I need you to handle. You have someone for the job?"

"We talking a hit? 'Cause that ain't something I can organize quickly."

Nate leaned back in his chair, took a deep breath as he thought about the bruising on Faith's otherwise flaw-less golden skin. *Tempting.* It would be all too easy to just have that asshole taken out, permanently, but Nate needed to keep his head. And besides, he never went for the easy option. If he was going to do something physical about her ex, Nate would be doing it with his bare hands, because he wanted to look him in the eye before he beat the shit out of him, and make sure he never touched Faith or any other woman ever again.

"I just want someone to tail the guy," he said, keeping his voice low. "See what he's up to, find out where he goes, what he does, if he's been in trouble with the law before. I want to handle the rest of it myself." Nate gave him the details of Faith's ex. He knew where he worked, which meant it wouldn't be hard to find out more.

"I'll be in touch."

Nate dropped his phone onto his desk and crossed the room to pour himself a whiskey. He looked out at the view and downed it. Sometimes he got so caught up in what he was doing that he didn't take time to appreciate what he had and the role he'd stepped into. And besides, he needed to take a few minutes at this time of the day. Once he was done it was time for his daily visit with his granddad, and then Nate was going to have to practice that little thing that he'd been lacking since puberty called self-control.

Faith poured herself another glass of wine and turned up the music. She had the house to herself while Nate was at work, and she wanted to have something nice cooked for dinner when he returned. She hadn't expected him to say yes to her staying so willingly, and she wasn't going to give him an excuse to go back on his word. When she'd offered to be his housekeeper, it hadn't been an empty promise—she was going to work hard to prove that she deserved the job, not to mention the roof over her head. Her dream wasn't to be cleaning and cooking for someone else, but she hadn't finished school yet, so it wasn't like she could be picky.

She walked into the massive pantry behind the kitchen, flicking the light and looking around. It was bigger than most kitchens, but that was the only impressive thing about it. There was hardly anything in there, except for a heap of empty containers and some canned goods. Faith walked back out to the main kitchen, poking her head inside the fridge. It wasn't much better in there—a lot of alcohol, some basics, and very little else.

Given the fact that she didn't have a car, she was kind of stuck. They were going to end up eating a couple of cans of baked beans if she didn't figure out a way to come by some ingredients. She wondered if Nate would mind if she borrowed one of the cars to run to the store. There were several sets of keys on hooks beside the door in the kitchen, and she doubted he'd give a damn about her taking anything for a spin.

"I'm home!"

Faith grinned as Nate's deep voice boomed down the hall. *Saved by the rancher.*

"When you said you urgently required a housekeeper, you weren't kidding," she said as she listened to his footfalls on the timber floor.

"Is the place that filthy?"

"No, it's that empty," she replied, her smile widening when she saw what he was carrying. "Pizza?"

He set the box on the counter. "Granddad was asleep when I went to the hospital to visit, so I decided to grab some dinner instead. You like pizza, right?"

"Is that even a real question?" Faith put down her wine and opened the fridge. "You want a beer?"

He nodded and sat down at the counter, opening the box and pulling out a slice of pepperoni. She glanced at him as he undid the top two buttons of his shirt, revealing tanned skin and a sprinkling of dark hair. She turned away. There was no doubting she'd always been attracted to Nate, but after what had happened she didn't even want to think about being intimate with another man just yet.

"So when you said the place was empty . . . ?" Nate asked.

Faith returned with a beer and leaned forward to take a slice. "I'm guessing you eat a lot of takeout, because there's nothing in the fridge or pantry. How long has your housekeeper been gone?"

"She retired a couple of months ago. Mrs. T did all my cooking and cleaning for me, so I eat out a lot now. Or I order in. Either way, it doesn't involve me in the kitchen."

"Well, I wanted to cook something nice to say thank you, but when I couldn't find enough ingredients for anything I was starting to contemplate taking a car and heading to the grocery store." Faith took another bite of pizza as she watched Nate's face, but he didn't look surprised. "Am I right in thinking you wouldn't have minded?" she asked when he didn't say anything, guessing he couldn't care less.

"Depends which one you'd taken," he replied with a grin. "I'm kidding. They're all insured, so help yourself. You want to head to the store tomorrow, take the Range Rover."

Faith laughed. She was used to driving a beat-up truck—and still would be if it hadn't just broken down on her—and tomorrow she'd be able to cruise around in a vehicle that probably cost more than the house she'd grown up in.

"Thanks for all this," Faith said, reaching for her wine and toying with the stem of the glass. And it wasn't just being able to stay that she was grateful for. Knowing that he was protecting her was comforting, and she liked how safe she felt at his house.

"It's just pizza."

His throaty laugh sent a chill down her spine and she couldn't help but smile back at him.

"Look, I've known you since you were a little girl, and there's nothing I wouldn't do to help you or Sam," Nate said. "I just don't want to cause a rift, because we both know that your brother will flip when he finds you came to me instead of him. But I think of you as a sister, Faith. I always have."

For years she'd tried to get Nate's attention, and nothing had worked. When she'd been younger, it had upset her that a man with such a bad reputation where women were concerned wouldn't so much as look at her, but she'd convinced herself that it was because he thought of her as a little girl instead of a young woman. Given their history, she doubted Sam would be *that* upset. Nate hadn't stepped out of line once where she was concerned, no matter what she'd done to show him that she was all grown-up. She was the one who'd had a problem with the boundaries between them.

"You know he's living at his girlfriend's place, don't you?" she asked Nate.

He took a sip of his beer and leaned over for another slice of pizza. "The cute blonde, right? He's kept her kind of hidden away from me."

"Ha-ha, I wonder why?"

Nate just winked at her, the tilt of his mouth in one corner telling her that he didn't give a shit that even his best friend was worried he might steal his girl. Faith just shook her head, forcing herself not to laugh. *Arrogant son of a bitch.*

"I'm sure she would have let his little sister stay," Nate said, suddenly more serious. "If that's what you were worried about?"

"He moved in with her less than a month ago. I'm not convinced she would have been happy with me landing on her doorstep so soon."

"You moved in with your guy around the same time, right? I remember Sam telling me that you weren't living at home anymore."

She sighed, not wanting to go back to that place in her mind even for a second. Bad decisions weren't something she was used to making, and she sure as hell wasn't going to make the same kind of mistake ever again.

"Can we make a deal that we don't talk about either of them again? My dad or my ex?"

Nate nodded, his eyes softening around the corners as he did so. He'd been sexy before, *tempting* before, but the way he was looking at her right now was something she could start to crave. Because now he wasn't just turning on the sexual charm—now he was looking at her like he truly cared, and she liked it. Liked the feeling of being looked after right now without having to give anything of herself in return.

"Sure. But if you want to talk about it . . ."

"I won't," she insisted.

"That's settled then. So I guess we should just eat pizza and get drunk?"

She groaned, pleased that he'd changed the subject. "Does that line work when you're trying to get lucky and take a woman home with you?"

He shrugged, smiling before taking a bite of pizza. "Sugar, I never bring women back here."

Faith burst out laughing before she realized he was being serious. He was staring back at her without that trademark grin. "You're full of shit. You're hardly chaste."

He shrugged again, leaning forward slightly, his body coming into her space. Faith inhaled, loving the scent of his citrusy cologne, tempted to lean that bit farther toward him. But she didn't.

Faith glanced from her glass of wine to his face, not wanting to stare at him. The truth was, she was jealous of the women he bedded—being the sole focus of Nate's attention in the bedroom was something she'd fantasized about plenty in the past.

"Who said anything about being chaste? I don't like sharing this place with just anyone, and it's way easier to just rent a room if I need to, or use my apartment in town. I keep my private life separate from my . . ." He raised an eyebrow, reaching for his glass and taking a long, slow sip, leaving her staring at his mouth, waiting for him to finish his sentence. "Sex life."

Okay, then. Faith swallowed as a shiver ran through her body, not answering him straightaway. What she needed was to stop thinking about Nate naked, and talk like this wasn't helping. Part of her still simmered for him, probably always would, but there was a difference between a fantasy and reality, and part of her was scared at the thought of being with any man, even Nate, right now.

"Too much information?" he asked.

Faith shrugged, not sure what to say. She'd asked and he'd told her straight. "I'm not some underage virgin who can't deal with hearing about your naughty escapades, Nate. It's not exactly a secret that you've slept with every woman in this town."

He met her gaze, stared her straight in the eye. When he spoke, his voice was lower, husky. "I haven't slept with you."

She swallowed, hoping he couldn't read her mind and tell just how many times she'd wished she was one of his conquests.

"I'm starting to see why my brother kept me away from you," she managed, pretending like nothing was wrong, like she wasn't coping with how intense he was.

"Sam is going to kill me when he finds you here. You do know that, right? He's going to go all soldier crazy, pull his army shit or something."

"You really think that he'll make some crazy-ass assumption that we're together because you've let me through the front door and lifted your no women in the house rule?"

Nate glared at her, his patience obviously waning. "Look, Sam is like family to me. He's the one person aside from my brothers that I like to keep firmly on my side."

"I was only teasing. Besides, I'll be the one he lays into, not you."

"So are you actually planning on being my housekeeper, or do I still need to keep running that ad? Because this place is going to go to complete shit if I don't find a replacement for Mrs. T soon."

Faith put her hand over her mouth, in danger of laughing out her mouthful. This was what she wanted from Nate, just plain old fun and friendship. "I can't believe you had that lovely old lady working here for so long. She must have been like eighty when she retired."

Nate winked and Faith tried to relax. Nate wasn't the one who'd hurt her; he wouldn't lay a hand on her without her okaying it. There was nothing wrong with having fun with him, chatting and laughing.

"I think keeping this house added at least twenty years to the poor old girl. The three of us were kind of a handful."

Faith finished chewing and made herself look back up at Nate, not sure why things suddenly felt so different between them. Or maybe she was just being more sensitive given what had happened. He'd never shown her any interest, but now that she was in his kitchen she was certain he was coming on to her, and . . . he seemed a whole lot more dangerous than before. Those dark eyes, his full lips, the confidence that as good as dripped from him. She'd be lying to herself if she didn't admit to wanting to know what it would be like to let those experienced hands of his pleasure her. And he was huge, his shoulders as wide and big as a quarterback's.

Faith cleared her throat. "I'm deadly serious about

working for you, Nate. I'll keep this place tidy, handle the groceries, and take care of the meals. You just ask and I'll do it."

They stared at each other for a minute, the silence deafening. Faith was the first to look away, trying to stop her hand from shaking as she reached for her glass. *All those thoughts she'd once had about her brother's best friend were back tenfold, no matter how hard she tried to fight them.*

"Well, okay then," he agreed. "But it's only short-term, until you find your feet."

She wasn't ready to be close to a man, wouldn't be for . . . she didn't know how long. Right now her hands were shaking just at the thought of Nate touching her skin.

Nate shut the door behind him and walked in the dark toward the closest field. Faith was inside busying herself in the kitchen, and he'd made up an excuse about needing to check on a pregnant mare. It was a lie, his brothers dealt with all the livestock on the property, but he'd needed some space. Staying in the house a second longer would have been a mistake, because he was dangerously close to losing control.

When he'd told Faith that Sam had always warned him off her, he hadn't been lying. But just because he wanted to protect her didn't mean he hadn't noticed how goddamn beautiful she was, and the trouble was, her brother knew it. Christ, Nate was hard just thinking about her now, let alone when he was looking into her warm brown eyes and seeing her body up close and personal. And having her in his kitchen, drinking in the low-cut T-shirt and skintight jeans . . . it had been almost too much for him to resist. *Almost*. Right now he was barely in control.

Nate leaned on the fence and let his eyes adjust to the fading light, watching the horses graze. He hardly ever thought about the day that Sam had thrown a punch at him and shoved him to the ground, but seeing Faith today had brought it all back

He wanted her. He wanted her so damn bad. No matter how much he tried to tell himself that he should be acting like her brother, it wasn't even close to working.

He'd promised Sam he wouldn't touch her. He'd sworn he'd never go there. And yet now . . .

Even if he screwed everyone in his little black book, he doubted he'd get Faith out of his head. Because it was her he wanted in his bed, her body he wanted naked and glinting with sweat beneath him, and he wanted her right fucking now.

His phone rang, breaking the dead silence on the ranch and scaring the shit out of him.

"Hello," he said without looking at the caller ID.

"You've been hiding away, Brother."

Of course, it had to be Chase. Again. "Just training my new housekeeper." Two could play at this game.

"A hot live-in one? I should have gotten me one of those when I was single."

Nate clamped his jaw and refused to be baited. "Look, she's Sam's sister and she needed a place to stay, so I gave her the job. End of story."

"She always did drive you crazy, huh?"

Nate didn't want to talk about it. "Just keep all the guys away from her. She isn't the type to be toyed with and we both know that's their specialty."

"Fuck you," Chase said good-naturedly. "You're the love 'em and leave 'em king; what do you care?"

But Nate knew she was more in danger of him toying with her than anyone else right now. Even her hair had been a temptation, falling over her shoulder every time she'd leaned forward to reach for a slice of pizza, hiding the delicate skin of her neck and making him want to sweep it back and press his mouth there. He wanted to strip her naked and see exactly what that lush body looked like bare, preferably bent over his kitchen table.

Damn it! She'd been roughed up by her ex; the last thing she needed was Nate wanting to rip her clothes off.

Nate shook his head and hitched his heel on the rail in front of him. *She was driving him insane.*

"You've got to admit that she's hot, though, right? I mean—"

"Enough," Nate ordered. "Just be nice to her if you see her."

"Yes, sir," Chase said. "I had no intention of being anything but. You do know I'm married, right? Or have you forgotten all about the fact you have another sister-in-law?"

Nate said good-bye to his brother and stared at his phone. Just his luck Sam would call him next, and then Nate would be forced to lie to his best friend. For a guy who'd decided to keep his head down and stay out of trouble now that he was running the King empire, he sure wasn't doing very well at it. Not very well at all.

He jumped when his phone buzzed again, his concentration lapsed, but the ID told him it was a call he wanted to take this time.

"Yeah," he answered.

"Nothing unusual going on with the guy, not that we can see, but we'll keep tailing him." The man cleared his throat. "And we have a man for the job, if you decide not to take care of it yourself. Seems to me that it won't be hard to take him, if you know what I mean."

Nate took a slow, deep breath. He knew it was wrong to want to hurt another human being so badly, but teaching this guy a lesson was something Nate was starting to look forward to. "You just get me the info I need; I'll take care of the rest."

Nate shut the phone. It was time Faith's ex had a taste of his own medicine, and learned the hard way that it was never okay to hit a woman. The easier thing would have been to pay someone else to do it, but getting other people to do his dirty work wasn't the King way.

Faith hadn't often woken up in a house that wasn't hers, but there was something liberating about being at Nate's place. She'd been guilted into looking after her dad for years, until she'd finally realized she didn't have to pay for her mother's mistakes for the rest of her life. Her mom had walked out, and Faith's dad was a drunk, and for years she'd felt she owed it to her dad to stay with him.

When she'd moved out she'd been so determined not to repeat the mistakes she'd already lived, not to ever let a man treat her bad or not respect her. At least she'd left as soon as he'd hurt her, though—for that she'd be forever proud, even if it had been scary. She wasn't about to repeat the mistakes her mom had made, letting a man break her heart and stifle her dreams.

Faith ran her hand along the banister as she walked down the stairs, loving the smooth texture of the timber beneath her palm. It was early, too early for Nate to be up, and it was a nice feeling to just pad around his luxurious house and enjoy her freedom.

Faith crossed the hall and peeked into a room she guessed was Nate's office, before heading for the kitchen. She was thinking of making something simple like an omelet for their breakfast, because she knew he at least had fresh eggs, but then—

"Oh my god! Sorry," she gasped.

Faith forced her mouth to shut and tried not to stare, but it wasn't easy. Nate was standing in just a pair of running shorts, bare chested, a carton of juice in one hand. He had sweat dripping off him, chest slick, and way too much skin on show for her to be admiring.

"I didn't expect you to be up already."

Ditto. She wouldn't have come down in her tank top and boy shorts if she'd heard so much as a noise to alert her that she wasn't going to be alone. But Nate, half-naked and gorgeous before 6:30 am? Now that was enough to make her pulse ignite, even if she was trying not to think about him like that. Hell, she doubted there was a heterosexual woman in the world who'd disagree with her.

He set the juice down on the counter. "I run for an hour before sunup every morning. Did I wake you?"

Faith shook her head, still struggling to raise her eyes from his impressive abs and the arrow of hair that ran from his belly button down to his . . . She swallowed and met his gaze.

"I was just coming down early to grab a coffee and figure out what to make for breakfast," she managed.

"Sounds good. I'm off to hit the shower."

Nate walked past her, T-shirt slung over his shoulder, and all she could do was stand and wait for him to pass. What the hell was wrong with her? It wasn't like she hadn't seen a bare-chested guy before. But Nate was, well, *built*. There was nothing about him that didn't scream sex.

Except she wasn't going to go there. If she wanted to ogle half-naked men, she could do it on the Internet. Although there was nothing quite like the muscles and warmth of a real-life body. . . . Faith shook her head. She was crazy. Looking was one thing, looking was okay; it was the thought of actually being vulnerable again that was what scared her.

What she needed was a strong coffee, black and sugary, and then she'd head back upstairs to put some clothes on. Clothes that didn't show off *her* half-naked body, and make it way too easy to imagine what it would be like to be in this house with Nate for another reason entirely, instead of just being his platonic housekeeper.

The one thing her mom had taught her, before she'd left them and disappeared, was the importance of understanding a person's place in the world, and Faith knew she and Nate were from different worlds. It didn't mean she couldn't admire him, but it gave her another reason to remember why it was one thing to look and another thing entirely to act on those thoughts. She'd

already made a mistake with one man, and she wasn't
about to do it with another.

   She filled the kettle with water, flicked the switch, and
found the coffee. Today was about making herself use-
ful, and thinking about what the hell she was going to
do with the rest of her life. Today she was starting over,
stepping out from the past and making her own way in
the world. She just had to figure out what she wanted for
once, instead of trying to please everyone else. And
remember that Nate was a friend and nothing more.

Chapter 3

NATE had stayed in the shower way longer than usual. He'd blasted it so hot that it had almost taken his skin off, and when that hadn't erased the mental picture tormenting him he'd turned the faucet to cold. All that had managed to do was piss him off, and he was still remembering just how goddamn hot Faith had looked in her nightwear. Tiny little shorts that showed off a hint of butt cheek, a tight top that displayed the perfect silhouette of her nipples, and her hair all tousled and messy, like she'd been rolling around between the sheets before coming downstairs.

He groaned as he pulled on his jeans, wishing he wasn't still so goddamn hard. *This* was why he shouldn't have let her stay. Hell, now that he'd had time to think about it, he could have put her up in a nice hotel or somewhere else indefinitely, anything to help her without having to directly involve himself. Instead he'd as good as invited the lamb into the wolf's den.

What he needed was a night out, somewhere with

plenty of single women. Maybe if he distracted himself with enough sex, he'd stop thinking about Faith like that. *He laughed.* With Faith it was more than just physical, it always had been, which was why nothing helped him to stop thinking about her. Never in his life had he been told he couldn't have something if he wanted it bad enough. It didn't mean he was handed everything on a silver platter; he'd learned to work hard to get what he desired, but at the end of the day he always figured out a way to get it. Faith was in an entire category of her own, and the fact that he couldn't just screw her and get her out of his system was starting to seriously piss him off.

The doorbell rang, followed by some loud thumping, and he grabbed a shirt and headed for the stairs. Enough with thinking about Faith's legs wrapped around him and her ass pressed to the glass in his shower. He had work to do and he needed to get her the hell out of his head.

"I'll get it!" he called out.

It was probably one of his brothers or a worker come to ask him something, and he didn't need any of the guys copping an eyeful of Faith if she was still wearing her itsy-bitsy outfit. If he had barely any willpower when it came to her, the ranch hands would have zero.

Nate hurried down the stairs, pulling the shirt on and leaving it open as he unlocked the door and opened it.

"Sam?" *Fuck.* "Hey," he said. *Double fuck.*

Sam ran a hand through his hair before hooking his thumbs into his jeans. "I know this is going to seem weird, but I—"

"Did you get the door?"

Nate stifled his groan and stepped back, not seeing any point in concealing her when Sam had just heard his sister call out. His morning had just gone from bad to goddamn terrible.

"Faith?"

Sam looked as surprised to see Faith as she did to see him, but she didn't linger in the shadows. She walked straight toward him and gave him a big hug, her arms locked around his neck.

"Hey, Sam," she said. "Before you say it, I know I should have called, but I didn't want to worry you."

Nate breathed a sigh of relief, even as Sam glared at him over her shoulder. As far as Nate could tell, he'd dodged a bullet by the simple fact that she was wearing jeans now, even if she was barefoot and looking way too at home.

"What the hell are you doing here?" Sam asked. "I came here to get Nate to help me track you down, and—"

Nate stepped back and motioned for them both to follow. "Come on; I need a coffee." Or possibly a whiskey depending on Sam's reaction.

Nate walked into the kitchen and hesitated when Faith moved in front of him, touching his arm and shaking her head like she was way too comfortable with him.

"I'll get it," she said. "I need a second to think."

Nate glanced at Sam and saw the darkness in his gaze, knew how pissed his friend was right now. He kept his own mouth shut, letting Faith take over instead of adding to the scene.

"I called you a dozen times last night and this morning," Sam said, sitting down at the table, gaze still leveled on Nate even though he was talking to his sister.

"I went past your work last night and they said you'd quit, and then—"

"Sorry, I turned off my phone," Faith said, interrupting him. "I didn't want Cooper trying to get in touch."

"Sam, I was going to call you this morning on my way into the office," Nate said, smiling as Faith set their coffees in front of them.

"And what exactly was it you were going to tell me, huh?" Sam said, making it clear how pissed off he was. "Explain why my little sister is in your fucking house at this time of the morning?"

Nate leaned back when Faith came over to the table to join them, pleased she hadn't heard her brother's low words. He might have been thinking dirty things about her all morning and half the goddamn night, but still. Surely they'd been friends long enough for Sam to give him the benefit of the doubt?

"Faith turned up here yesterday needing a place to stay," Nate said. He was going to let Faith explain the rest.

"And you came to *him* instead of me?" Sam asked, shaking his head as he first glared at Nate, then watched Faith.

She was nursing her cup of coffee, but her gaze was strong as she stared back at her brother. Nate admired her strength, that she wasn't intimidated by either of them. He'd sensed she was a whole lot more vulnerable than she usually was, which he fully expected after what she'd been through, but she was still strong and he admired that.

"I needed somewhere to go and I came here. You always said we could trust Nate no matter what, and I did," she said. "What's the big deal?"

Nate tried not to laugh. There was no way Sam was going to ask outright if something had happened between them, not a chance.

"Your asshole boyfriend wouldn't even open the door when I went around there, and Dad said he hadn't seen you. How the hell did you think I'd react? And no, it's not okay that you chose him over me." Sam took a sip of coffee and rose out of his seat. "Look, if that dick laid a hand on you I'll fucking kill him, so just tell me."

"You were right about Cooper," Faith said, her voice low. "He hurt me and I left, end of story. There's nothing else you need to know."

Nate watched as she wrapped her hand tight around her cup, the other in a small fist at her side. His anger started to simmer again, thinking of her beautiful skin being marked by some guy who thought it was okay to rough up women, remembering her bruise.

"He what?" Sam's voice was barely audible.

"He hit me, Sam," Faith said calmly. "It could have been a lot worse, but I left and now I'm here. I just needed some time away from everything."

"Tell me we're going to do something about this, Nate." Sam slowly lowered himself back down into his chair. "I'm not going to let anyone get away with hurting my sister."

"He hit her, I took her in, and the guy who did it will soon know that he messed with the wrong people," Nate said, noticing that Faith was staring out the window now. His instinct to protect her kicked into life, but he didn't want to scare her by getting into details while she was listening. She was probably sick to death of even thinking about what had happened, and reliving it right now probably wasn't helping.

"And you two?" Sam asked, staring him straight in the eye.

"There's nothing going on here other than me looking out for your little sister," Nate said, thankful that Sam couldn't read his mind. He raised an eyebrow, daring his friend to accuse him outright of screwing her. Sam was pissed right now and Nate didn't know what to expect. "Hell, Sam. She's been through enough without you acting like there's something"—Nate cleared his throat—"*inappropriate* going on here."

"Tell me what happened," Sam seethed, his hands in fists on the table. "I'll deal with him myself if I have to."

"I'd say get in line, but we both know better," Nate cautioned.

"You know what? This is none of your business, Nate."

He wasn't going to lose his temper, not with Sam, but the look on Faith's face was telling Nate that his and Sam's arguing wasn't making the situation any easier for her. Nate took a deep breath to calm himself the hell down.

"You've been my business my entire life, Sam. Don't forget that this is where you came every time you had to get away, too, when it was your dad." Sam had always been welcome in the King home, no matter what time of the day or night he'd turned up, and Nate wasn't going to take the rap for being the bad guy, not for this. He hadn't done anything wrong and Sam needed to be reminded. "And Faith became my business the moment she turned up on my doorstep. You know you can trust me when I say that I'm handling it."

Sam sighed, staring back at Nate as he opened his palms, obviously trying hard to diffuse his anger. "I'm not going to say I told you so, but Faith, seriously? The guy was a dickhead from the start."

"Falling for him wasn't my smartest move," she said, smiling at her brother. "I just wish he hadn't been my boss, too. It was only waitressing, but it was okay money."

Faith's low, soft voice somehow settled them both. Nate wanted to do something to comfort her, but he also knew better than to touch her in front of Sam. Hell, he didn't even know if she'd want him to touch her.

"You sure I can't deal with him?"

"I'm sure," Nate said, staring hard at his friend. "Just think of Faith visiting you in jail, and get those kinds of thoughts out of your head."

Sam nodded, but he was focused on Faith now. "Why didn't you come to me?" His voice was softer than it had been before, his gaze intense as he stared at her.

"I just wanted to deal with this on my own for once, instead of running to you for help."

"So you ran to Nate for help instead?" Sam asked, glowering at him.

Nate shrugged and leaned back in his chair crossing his legs at the ankles and folding his arms across his chest as he watched them. It was a fair question—he'd asked her the same thing himself.

"I didn't want you to find out," she finally said after an awkward stretch of silence. "When it comes to me you overreact, you always have, and I didn't want you losing your temper and doing something crazy. I'd be the one who'd have to live with that, and I needed some time to think without having you to deal with, too."

Sam looked pissed, but Nate had to agree. Sam wasn't exactly easy to simmer down when he was angry, and if it was to do with Faith then he was entirely unpredictable.

Faith reached for her brother's hand and squeezed it. "You always said coming here made things better for you, when we were younger, and now you're finally happy. I just wanted to deal with this and move on without putting you in a position like that." She smiled over at him and Nate returned it. "I trust Nate, and it felt safer coming here than one of my girlfriends' places, in case he tried to find me."

Sam suddenly angled his body toward Nate, pointing his finger at him. "Wolf in sheep's clothing, that's all I'm going to say. He won't hurt you with his fists, but you *do not* want to go there, okay?"

"Leave my clothes out of it," Nate said with a grin, lazily doing one of his shirt buttons up and leaving the rest open. He would have done them all up, but he wasn't opposed to pissing Sam off just a little more. What Faith had said had hit home, made him feel like a jerk for thinking such unbrotherly things about her, but he also got that Sam wouldn't want to talk too much about his feelings and what Faith had done. He wasn't good like that.

"Nate has been an absolute gentleman," Faith said, reaching out and patting Nate's hand. "You should be thanking him."

Sam made a face, changing it only when Faith swatted at him. Nate was just relieved she'd taken her skin off of his—contact like that was not something he needed from her. Keeping his mind off sex was hard enough without her goddamn stroking him, and that soft hand against him was like torture. Pure fucking sexual torture.

"Don't you have work to go to?" Faith asked her brother.

Sam stood up and Nate did the same. "Speaking of work . . . ?" Sam asked.

Faith chuckled. "I'm Nate's new housekeeper. For the meantime, anyway."

"You're kidding me?" Sam groaned, shaking his head.

It took all of Nate's willpower not to snigger at the disgusted look on Sam's face, but he kept his expression impassive. "Come on; I'll walk you out."

They left Faith in the kitchen, and Nate headed for the door. "I'm sorry you had to find out like this, but nothing's going on."

Sam blocked the entrance, arms crossed over his chest. "You so much as lay one fucking finger on her and you'll be the one I go to jail for."

"There's nothing going on," Nate repeated. "She's your little sister; I get it. But she has a point about you not being good at controlling yourself when it comes to her."

"Seriously, Nate. Don't even . . ." Sam turned and opened the door. "Just forget that she's even a woman, okay? Just forget it."

Nate watched him go, braced against the doorjamb. *Forget Faith was a woman?* That was like telling an addict to forget they'd ever tasted their drug of choice.

He loved women, and Faith? Hell, she was like Viagra wrapped up in extrashiny packaging, and he could no more pretend she wasn't what she was than a lion would forget its prey.

But he could stop himself from acting on his thoughts. He needed to keep practicing that little thing called self-control that his grandfather kept drilling into him. If he was going to prove that he could singlehandedly step in and run the King empire, this was a good way to start, by proving to himself that he was able to control every single facet of his life. Starting now. Not to mention the fact that he needed to think more about protecting Faith. He had no idea how she was feeling after what that asshole had done.

"Hey, what do you say to a night out?" Nate called out to Sam as he was about to get into his Chevy.

"When?" Sam had his hand up to shield his face from the sun, leaning against the vehicle.

"Tomorrow night. We can all head out, have a few drinks, catch up. I've been away so much lately we haven't had time to hang out."

Sam looked a whole lot more relaxed than he had a few minutes earlier. The lure of a big night out had always been enough to put a smile on his face, and Nate needed a chance to let off some steam, too.

"You're on. Meet at The Den? Usual time?"

Nate gave him a wave. "See you there. And bring that gorgeous girl of yours." He would have preferred to go to Joe's and rough up Faith's ex, who managed the place, but the last thing Nate needed was Sam with him when he confronted the asshole.

Now Nate had a heap of work to get through, starting now. And the faster he got out of the house and into his office, the better.

Faith was tidying up the breakfast dishes and keeping an ear out for Nate. When she finally heard the front door slam shut she let out the breath she'd been holding and wandered out to look for him. She had some apologizing to do, and she needed to do it now. So much for growing up and not needing anyone to help her—she'd just had her brother and Nate arguing because of her, and it hadn't been fair to either of them. Just because she was a muddle of thoughts and feelings didn't mean she could just expect Nate to come to her rescue and come between her and her brother.

She stepped into the hall and caught Nate about to walk up the stairs.

"Nate?"

He stopped, turning when she spoke. His expression was warm, but he also looked . . . She couldn't put her finger on it but there was something different about the way he was watching her. Maybe he was feeling guilty about flirting with her, about having her to stay when he'd told her all along how annoyed Sam would be about the whole thing.

"I'm sorry about what just happened. I should have called Sam and told him I was here. I should have trusted that he wouldn't act out, but to be honest I'm not so sure he would have held back if I'd gone straight to him."

Nate smiled, but he looked a million miles away. "It's fine. We both knew he was going to be pissed; I just didn't expect him to turn up here so fast."

She stared into his eyes, wished she wasn't so

conflicted over how she felt. Cooper hitting her had done more than dent her confidence. She backed down a step, needing to put some distance between her and Nate. She'd wanted him close, but the thought of him actually closing the distance between them . . . Her palms were sweating and her heart was beating overtime.

"You two aren't the only ones with daddy issues, Faith. For what it's worth, I get it."

She'd never heard a lot about Nate's dad, except that he'd been out of their lives for a long time. "Well, I just wanted to say that I really appreciate you letting me stay, and for sticking up for me. It means a lot."

He nodded and looked away.

"It's no problem." He glanced at his wristwatch. "Look, I have a meeting at ten so I have to go, but keep tomorrow night free."

"Tomorrow?" *What's happening tomorrow night?*

"I thought a night out would do us all good. Sam's game, so we're heading to The Den at eight."

Nate moved to turn and Faith almost ran to him, wanted to touch him, to press a kiss to his freshly shaven cheek. But she didn't.

"Thank you," she whispered.

Nate stared at her, long and hard, their eyes locked. "You're welcome."

He was everything she liked in a man—strong, sexy, capable of protecting her—but she wasn't ready to even think about being intimate again. Cooper's fist slamming into her replayed through her mind when she least expected it. The way he'd thought he could lay his hands on her made her stomach turn. She was stronger than he'd thought, though, and there was no way she was going to let what he'd done to her hold her back.

Faith smiled thinking about Nate. He was trying so hard to be the perfect gentleman, and she doubted that came easy to him. As much as she'd always liked him, she knew what happened when a girl like her became involved with a rich and powerful man like Nate. Which was why he'd only ever been her fantasy date, the guy she'd want in bed but not have any other expectations for.

Her own mom had spent her entire life mourning for the man she'd loved, a man who'd ended up marrying a woman his family had deemed more appropriate for him, and besides, Faith wasn't looking for anything more than a fresh start and a fun time.

Which meant she had to forget all about how good Nate looked half-naked. *Or what it would be like in his bed.*

Chapter 4

NATE sucked in a deep breath and gripped both hands tight on the steering wheel, waiting for Ryder to pick up the phone. He'd been happy and relaxed surveying the parcel of land he'd earmarked for oil drilling, but that mood had quickly disappeared the moment he'd gotten back in the car. He'd had an irate message from his younger brother and a call from work, and Nate could already feel his blood pressure rising for the day.

"Hey."

"Hey," Nate replied, easing off on the accelerator a little.

"Whatever the hell you've done to piss Sam off, I need you to deal with it."

Nate groaned. He guessed his brother needed Sam to work a problem horse, which was why Nate was getting the blame for his mood. "What did he say?"

"Nothing. Except to mutter that you were a fucking asshole and he wanted to smack his fist into your face about now."

"You do know I've done nothing wrong, right? His sister turned up on my doorstep needing a place to stay and—"

"Whoa, she what?" Ryder roared with laughter. "You have *Faith* staying in your house?"

"Yup." His brothers had always loved giving him shit about her. He hadn't exactly done a good job of pretending not to be attracted to her, because she'd *always* managed to rile him up the wrong way. Or the right way, depending on which way he looked at it.

"So you need to convince him that you're a goddamn monk where his sister's concerned, okay?"

A monk? Now that would be an impossible task. "Why?"

"Because he just walked off the job before, *Brother*. And if we don't get these three-year-olds started under saddle soon . . ."

Nate had no idea Sam had been scheduled to work on the ranch. They'd used him in the past when they needed him, but Ryder and Chase dealt with anything ranch related. "I'll deal with it." *Fuck.* "He'll cool off soon; it just surprised him, that's all. He's probably around seeing Faith again now that I'm gone." He didn't know if that was a good idea or a very, very bad one. As much as he hadn't wanted Faith staying in his house, the thought of her going pissed him off, too.

"He'd better be just letting off some steam. We haven't been breeding these horses just to have them as goddamn paddock ornaments, and I need his help. I need him here yesterday, so whatever the fuck you have to do to get him back and focused, do it."

"Don't lecture me, Ryder." Nate was getting pissed

off. "I've got an appointment now, but I'll call you later."

They said good-bye as Nate pulled into the entrance to the hospital. Every time he arrived it scared the crap out of him. Give him a raging bull, an unbreakable horse, a husband whose wife he'd screwed, hell, there was nothing on this planet that really scared him shitless, but looking up at the hospital looming in front of him . . . He pulled into the lot, parked his car, and took a sip of his now lukewarm coffee. *Hell.* Clay King had summoned Nate to his bedside, told him not to tell his brothers, and now here he was about to face the one man in the world he admired above all else. No amount of bravery was ever going to prepare him for losing his grandfather, and the fact that he'd called for him, rather than just waited to see him that evening, told him something was wrong.

Nate locked the car and stuffed his hands in his pockets as he walked. He entered the building, nodded at the receptionist he passed on his way in, and headed for the elevator. Within moments the doors were opening on the correct floor, and less than a minute later he was standing outside his grandfather's private room, the suite that was as comfortable as any hotel room now that they'd spent time making it feel like home for him. But it was the fact that it might be the last room he ever saw that always sent a gut-deep stab of pain through Nate.

The staff on this floor all knew him well, which was why he'd been able to pass through the hall undisturbed. If he had it his way he'd have them reporting directly to him, but Clay wasn't ready to be babied and hadn't allowed it.

"Granddad?" Nate said his name quietly, not wanting to startle him in case he was sleeping. The room was filled with sunlight, more like a pretty bedroom than a hospital space, with flowers and photos adorning almost every surface, a lamp from home on the bedside table for him to read under at night if he had the energy.

A hand rose in the air, slowly but surely, followed by a croaky voice. "Nate."

He took another deep breath and crossed the room, reaching to help his granddad sit up in the pillows. It only seemed like yesterday that he had been coming home for a week here and there in between treatments, proud as hell to be meeting Ryder's wife and then even attending Chase's wedding. His brothers had sure made the old man happy when they'd settled down. Clay loved the way his granddaughters-in-law fussed over him, too, seemed to enjoy the extended version of their family.

"How you feeling today, Granddad?"

"Like I need a damn strong whiskey. You have one for me?"

Nate settled on the big armchair beside him and leaned forward, slipping his hand into his jacket pocket and taking out a small silver flask. Chase and Ryder might not have been so forthcoming, but Nate didn't give a damn.

"Here," he said, unscrewing the lid and raising it to his granddad's lips for him to take a sip. "Just a little."

"Good boy." The words were strained, his grandfather breathless even on oxygen.

"The others would kill me, but who the hell am I to deny you, huh?" Nate couldn't see the point in not letting the old man have a little of his favorite drink. He had weeks or less to live now that the cancer had spread like wildfire through his body—what would a few sips do now?

"Glad you're here, son." Clay reached for Nate's hand, his movements slow, but Nate clasped it and held on tight. A lump formed in his throat, one he was unfortunately getting used to, and he swallowed it away.

"You're getting ready to leave us, aren't you, Granddad?" His voice sounded deeper, huskier, than usual, the emotion almost choking him as he tried to stay strong.

"I haven't got long now, son, and I . . ." He stopped talking, breathing heavy. "I want you to see my will. I went over it one last time with our attorney today."

Nate glanced over his shoulder when his granddad inclined his head, seeing a wad of papers stacked on the low table. "This it here?"

Nate reached for them, took a cursory glance over the top copy. "You don't need to show me this. Whatever you've decided, it's up to you, Granddad. We'll all respect your wishes."

"I'm proud of you, Nate. Proud of all of you . . ." Nate cringed as he listened to his grandfather's struggle with his breath again. "But you're the one I want in charge. You're the one, Nate. Always have been."

Nate frowned. It wasn't that he wasn't proud as hell that his grandfather put so much trust in him, but he didn't want to cause a rift with his brothers. Blood ran thicker than water, and he wasn't going to jeopardize their relationships for anything. He was already taking over as CEO of the company that owned all their landholdings.

"We've all inherited our thirds of the ranch already, Granddad. You don't want to change that, do you?" Chase had already built his new house, was happy with Hope and running the ranch on a day-to-day basis, and Ryder had finally settled down. He was married and he'd transitioned from superstar rodeo rider to producing some of the nation's top rodeo bulls faster than any of them had imagined. They were all happy with their own success and what they were achieving, and Nate didn't want to ruin that.

"There's a reason you got the main house and more land than the others, Nate."

"Because I'm the eldest. You always said you wanted the eldest to inherit the main homestead."

"I wanted you to have it so you could keep drilling for oil, son. You're going to make this family even wealthier than I have, Nate; I know it."

That made Nate chuckle. "Impossible. I'll work damn hard to make sure we keep growing the business, but I'll never accomplish what you have. I've stepped in at just the right time, so all I have to do is make careful decisions to keep growing what we have."

Clay squeezed his hand, his fingers around Nate's weaker than they'd ever been, but the meaning in his touch crystal clear.

"You make smart decisions. You're impulsive but not hotheaded. You know what you're doing because it's in your blood."

"Because I've learned from the best," Nate murmured, wishing they weren't having this conversation, wishing he had another decade before he had to be faced with losing the old man.

"You're my heir, Nate. You will run the business, you will have the homestead, you will . . ."—he coughed and wheezed—"drill for oil, and you will have the final say regarding all of our property and businesses."

Tears welled in Nate's eyes, spilling over onto his cheeks as he stared into dark eyes the exact same shade as his own. It was like looking into a mirror, only one that showed him the man he'd be in fifty years' time.

"If that's what you want," he said, quickly brushing the tears away, refusing to let his granddad see him break down, "then I'll honor your wishes. I'll keep all of our income the same, because I don't deserve any more than my brothers, but the majority of the company's earnings will be reinvested into property, into growing our portfolio." They all received a significant payment each quarter, and would for life, but Nate was more interested in building the business than taking more than he needed.

Clay's eyes were filled with tears, too, the old man looking so weak in the hospital bed, nothing like his former big, imposing self. The long conversation had taken what little strength he had. "Your brothers are good, capable men, Nate, but every family needs a leader. Someone with vision and passion."

Nate nodded and let go of his granddad's hand, settling back into the armchair and feeling like he'd been hit by a ten-ton truck. Now that they'd settled business, it was time to make the old man laugh.

"You wouldn't believe what happened to me today, Granddad."

His eyes lit up. "A woman?"

Nate laughed and passed him the flask again. "It sure as hell was."

Faith had spent the morning cleaning the house, which she didn't want to admit wasn't exactly her forte. Cooking? Sure. She didn't even mind getting groceries so long as she had enough cash to buy what she wanted, but she wasn't exactly used to wielding a mop and bucket. Give her a collection of art to admire—that's what got her attention and held it.

"Hello?"

Faith sat bolt upright, fingers tightening around her cup of coffee. It was a woman's voice, one she didn't recognize, and she rose to walk out into the hallway.

"Hello? Anybody here?"

"Hi!" Faith called back, locking eyes with a beautiful brown-eyed blonde. She had a toddler on her hip, with hair as blond as her mother's but eyes the brightest blue.

"Sorry, I saw someone was here and I thought Nate must have been home."

Faith tried not to bristle, hated how jealous she was over the gorgeous woman standing in the hall who'd walked in as if she knew the place well. So much for Nate not bringing women into his home.

"I'm, ah, Nate's new housekeeper," she said, turning to walk back into the kitchen to put her cup down. "Do you want to leave a message for him?"

The woman had followed her, her daughter on her feet now and tottering off unsteadily. "No, I'll catch him later. I was going to ask him over for dinner, but now that he's got you I guess he won't be so desperate for a home-cooked meal. Don't tell him I said it, but he's been a lost soul without Mrs. T looking after him!"

Faith smiled as the child climbed up onto the sofa. "Your daughter is beautiful." Faith hated that she was bristling over the thought that the child could be Nate's.

"She loves her uncle Nate's house, that's for sure." The woman smiled. "Sorry, where are my manners? I'm Chloe." She held out her hand.

Faith took it, relief hitting her like a train head-on. *Nate was the girl's uncle?* "Faith," she said. "So you must be . . ."

"Ryder's wife," she said, going over to unsuccessfully grab the little girl. "And this is Rose."

"Poor girl, having an uncle like Nate to keep all the boys away when she's older." Faith smiled. "I can just see him with his brothers, all lined up on the porch with shotguns."

Chloe laughed. "Maybe, but right now she has both her uncles wrapped around her little finger, and her daddy, too. She's lucky to be the only girl."

"Can I get you a drink?" Faith was suddenly a whole lot more relaxed.

"You having a coffee?"

"I've just had one, but if it means I don't have to clean for a bit longer then I'll have another." Faith was already starting to warm toward Chloe, especially now she knew she was Nate's sister-in-law and not her competition.

She turned to put on the kettle again, pulling another coffee mug down.

"Do you work at Joe's sometimes?" Chloe asked.

Faith grimaced. "Yeah. Well, I used to. Have I served you there?"

Chloe shook her head, a smile bracketing her mouth, eyes suddenly dancing like she was about to burst out laughing. "Not really, no. But I've just put two and two together. You're Sam's sister, right? Ryder pointed you out to me a couple of times."

"Guilty as charged." She raised an eyebrow. "Why?"

"I just can't believe you're in Nate's house when he's usually so . . ." Chloe shook her head. "It's none of my business. I shouldn't have said anything."

Faith looked up, coffee forgotten. "Say it, what you were about to tell me. What is it?"

Chloe sighed and rescued Rose from the sofa where she was flapping her hands wanting to get down. "It's just that he's always kind of twisted in knots over you. Chase and Ryder like having him on about it."

Now it was Faith laughing. "Nate all twisted up over me? Don't be silly. I think you have the wrong girl."

"I'm not," Chloe said, leaning in to retrieve her coffee and grinning at her like they were co-conspirators. "And I shouldn't have said anything; he'd kill me if he found out. But it's true. The big, indestructible Nate King all in a knot over you. We all laugh about one night when we were out and he caught sight of you. Talk about rustling his feathers."

Faith flushed; she could feel the heat hit her cheeks, and wished that she could believe what she was being told. "I don't believe you for a second."

They sat in silence for a moment, both blowing on their hot coffee and taking little sips while Rose kept herself entertained pottering around the living room that adjoined the kitchen. She'd pulled out some toys that Nate had obviously stashed away for her.

"So what's it like living in paradise every day?" Faith asked.

"Here?" Chloe smiled. "I guess it *is* paradise. I thought I'd be practicing as an attorney and spending most of my time in the city, but then Rose came along and there's no way I could leave her. Not yet."

Faith loved the way Chloe looked at her daughter, had always wished she'd had a mom who gazed at her so adoringly. "When did you graduate?"

"About a year before she was born," Chloe told her. "So I worked in Dallas until I was about ready to pop. Nate's been great in involving me in some work for the family, though, so I've still been able to keep my head in the game. Long may it continue." She laughed. "And before that, I worked at Joe's, and that's where I met my husband. It must have been before you started."

"I've only been working there over summer vacation," Faith said.

Faith grinned as Rose came toddling over, arms outstretched and looping around her mom's neck when she gathered her up and lifted her to sit on her hip.

"And that's my cue to go. She's probably ready for her nap," Chloe said. "Thanks for the coffee."

"My pleasure." She was still stuck on the fact that Chloe had some crazy idea that Nate liked her. "Maybe I'll see you again soon."

"Yeah, if Nate doesn't flip out having you in his house before I come past next."

Faith couldn't help grinning. "So you'd find it even more amusing if you knew I was living here for a bit?"

Chloe clamped her hand over her mouth, making an indecipherable noise. "You're kidding me? Please tell me you're kidding."

" 'Fraid not."

"Now that's the funniest thing I've heard all day. Wait till Ryder hears."

Faith leaned on the doorjamb until Chloe had disappeared from sight, staring out into the bright sunshine bathing over the surrounding fields. So maybe she wasn't imagining the spark between her and Nate. She didn't believe Chloe for a second that Nate was twisted in knots over her; hell, he could have *any* woman he wanted, so why the hell would he be all hot under the collar for her? But it was a nice thought, to think that he felt a simmer of something.

She shut the heavy front door and laughed to herself as she went back into the kitchen to tidy up. *Nate into her?* She'd seen the way he looked at her sometimes, the heat in his gaze, but there was a difference between that and what his sister-in-law had said.

Faith felt a pang of desire, a hum through her body, but stamped the flame out. Could she let him touch her? Was she ready to have a man's hands on her after . . . She gulped. She'd crushed on Nate all her life, *trusted* him with her life, but it was just too soon to go there.

"Faith!"

She groaned, standing dead still, hoping her brother wouldn't notice her. He must have seen Chloe leaving and spotted Faith. Given the fact that she'd never even managed to evade him with her expert hiding when they were kids, hiding in plain view and hoping she was a statue probably wasn't going to work.

"Faith!" he called out again, banging on the front door this time before pushing it open. *Damn!* If only she'd thought to turn the lock. "Faith?"

She turned, forcing herself to smile. Sam was her big brother, and he'd always been great, if just a little too overprotective. She couldn't exactly ignore him.

"Hey."

"Didn't you hear me calling you?" he asked.

"I was just coming to the door," she lied.

"Huh." He kicked off his boots and folded his arms across his chest, his eyes narrowing as he gave her a look that spelled lecture. "We need to talk."

"Come on then," she muttered. "I'll make us coffee." By nightfall she'd be bouncing off the walls with the amount of caffeine she'd consumed.

"Nate coming back anytime soon?"

"Not sure; I don't exactly have his schedule on me," she said dryly.

"We're talking about Nate King; you know that, right?" Sam grumbled. "You haven't thought this through; he's—"

"What?" she asked, spinning around to face Sam, planting her hands palms down on the counter. "Your best friend? The guy who always looked out for you when things were shit at home? The very same guy who's always treated me with respect and never, *ever* tried anything inappropriate with me?" She sighed. "We're talking about the same guy, right? Because that's the guy whose house I'm crashing in, Sam. I'm here working for him; that's it." She didn't point out that it was Nate who'd always kept him from doing anything stupid, like hauling him out of fights before things went too far.

"You think he's so damn respectable, you wouldn't know the half of it," Sam scoffed. "Let's pack your things up and you can come stay with me."

"No." She placed her hands on her hips, not about to be bossed around by her older brother. "I'm not a child, Sam; you can't just snap your fingers and tell me what to do."

"Nate's . . ."

"What?" she demanded.

"He's a womanizer. He's used to getting whatever and whoever he wants."

Faith laughed. "Oh, and suddenly you're Mother Teresa just because you've been in a relationship for a couple of months? Cry me a different song, Sam. You've got a history of leaving women high and dry just like Nate has, so don't go trying to make out like he's the bad guy and you're not."

"I'm your brother, goddamn it, and I want to keep you away from him." Sam stalked around and poured his own cup of coffee, his face like thunder. "Is it so bad that I care about you?"

Faith sighed, shoulders falling as she looked into her brother's eyes. She nudged him with her arm as she scooped a spoon of sugar and dropped it into his cup. "I love that you care about me, Sam; I do. But I need to stand on my own two feet."

He grunted and slung an arm around her. "Running into the arms of Nate is not standing on your own two feet, sweetheart."

Faith tried not to bristle, knew that Sam was trying to look out for her. "How many times do I have to tell you that I'm here working? It's a hell of a lot better than the bar. And let's not start on how well you deal with guys doing wrong by me." She laughed. "Not that any of them have been deserving of being roughed up before now."

Her brother made a growling noise and she pushed away from him and jumped up onto the counter, staring down into eyes the exact same shade of brown as hers.

"So there's nothing going on between you?" he asked, sipping his coffee, then grimacing at the heat. "I didn't walk in on anything this morning when I showed up?"

"For the last time, *no,*" she insisted, hoping her cheeks didn't flush. A couple of months ago, hell, *a week* ago she'd have stripped her gorgeous boss down to nothing at the first opportunity. But that was before. Nate had flirted with her, but he hadn't so much as touched her inappropriately since she'd arrived. "I needed somewhere to stay; he needed a housekeeper. It was a win-win situation for both of us."

Sam leaned forward, arms on the counter across from her. "Just be careful around him, okay?"

"You've already warned him off me, Sam," she said, wondering if she was pushing it by admitting what she knew. "I know he wasn't allowed to come near me when I was a teenager, that I was the one girl he wasn't allowed to try his luck with, and he seems pretty sure that the rules of not coming near me are still in place."

"It was for your own good," Sam muttered, but he didn't meet her gaze, was obviously embarrassed at being caught out. "And it still is."

"Well, now I'm all grown-up, Sam, and I can look out for myself. You don't need to tell me who I can and can't be with." The way he was acting he was almost pushing her toward Nate.

"Like you did with Cooper? After what that asshole did to you—"

"Nate would never lay a hand on a woman," she said, interrupting him. "Don't you ever compare him to Cooper."

Sam shook his head, coffee cup braced in one hand. "He won't break your bones, Faith, but he will break your heart. I know he will, and seeing you like that would hurt me more than seeing you with a bruise on your stomach. It'd kill me, because that kind of pain doesn't just disappear in a week like an ugly bruise that fades to nothing."

Faith's belly flipped, both from the reference to the blow she'd taken the day before and from just thinking about Nate, about the power he could have over her, how hard she could fall for him if she let herself. But she wasn't going to. Getting into his bed was one thing, but she would never let him close enough to break her heart.

"I'll be fine, Sam. I promise."

"And you're sure you don't want to stay with me?"

"Three's a crowd," she told him, jumping down and pressing a fleeting kiss to his cheek as she took his cup from him, put it in the sink, and then grabbed his hand, hauling him down the hall. "Now it's time for you to go. I have work to do, and I'm guessing you do, too."

"Just be careful."

Faith laughed and pushed him out the door once he had his boots back on. "You say that like I'm about to go on an African safari without any protection from the wild animals."

He groaned. "That's exactly what you're doing."

She just shoved him and then shut the door behind him. Sam was wrong; she wasn't in danger of Nate or any other man breaking her heart.

She was going to finish her master's degree, work hard over vacation to save money, and then make her own way in the world. Carve out a career from what she loved. Now was the time to let her hair down, have fun while she planned out her future. If her sexy rancher boss wanted some no-strings-attached fun, one day she might consider it. But not just yet.

Chapter 5

NATE stepped inside and resisted the urge to call out, "Honey, I'm home!" Instead he chuckled to himself and walked down the hall, pausing only to drop his work-bag to the floor. It was weird how much he was looking forward to seeing her, given how desperate he'd been to get out of the house and put some distance between them earlier in the day.

"Something smells incredible."

Faith appeared, barefoot and dressed in skintight jeans and a loose blouse. He sucked in a breath when his eyes traveled up, the blouse unbuttoned just low enough for him to see too much of her breasts. Ordinarily he would have appreciated it, but with Faith it was the last thing he needed, to be distracted by her gorgeous body.

"I went shopping," she said. "The fridge is full and I have my secret tomato sauce just about ready." Faith smiled as she spun back around to what she was stirring in a big pan. "I'm hoping you like spaghetti and meat-balls."

Nate shrugged out of his jacket and threw it down over a chair. He could get used to this way too easily, and he wasn't just thinking about the cooking. Seeing Faith all barefoot and cute in his kitchen was kind of a turn-on.

"I thought you were part Latino," he joked, raising an eyebrow as he crossed the room and made for the fridge. He needed a beer—it had been a long day—and he also needed something to distract him from Faith.

"Just because I'm Latino doesn't mean I can't cook Italian," she joked back, glancing at him over her shoulder. "I took an Italian cooking course a while back, when I decided that I actually had to get my ass into gear and learn how to create a few culinary masterpieces."

He grinned. "Well, now that you've told me it's a culinary masterpiece . . ."

Faith laughed at him without looking and it annoyed him. He'd anticipated the flash of her eyes, the warmth in her gaze, and he craved it.

"My Mexican is good, tacos and comfort food, but this was me expanding my skills," she continued. "I can't say my father appreciated it. . . ."

"But I will," he said gruffly, feeling protective over her.

"I bet Mrs. T cooked amazing food for you all the time."

Nate grunted. *Yeah, but she never looked like that when she was doing it.* "She always had something waiting for me."

"Come try this."

He took a long, deep pull of beer, not answering straightaway. Was she trying to seduce him or did she actually have no damn idea? He stifled a groan. He was going with no damn idea.

"I . . . ," he started to protest.

"*Please,*" she said, holding up the wooden spoon and grinning at him. "I need you to tell me if it's any good."

Nate met her gaze, stared straight into eyes that he couldn't decide if they were innocent or the complete opposite. He hauled himself up, leaving his beer and walking toward her. Faith held out the spoon, her eyes widening as he leaned closer and opened his mouth, letting her feed him. The sauce was incredible, full of flavor, but it was the light in her gaze and the wide smile she gave him that nearly took his breath away.

"It's amazing."

"Really?"

Nate knew he should have taken a step back, should have put some distance between them, but he was like a magnet drawn to metal. He'd resisted her for so long, stayed away from her, not let himself even think about touching her like he'd wanted to, and now . . . He reached out and brushed a strand of hair from her face, knowing he shouldn't have, but the urge to touch her was suddenly unbearable.

When she jumped at his touch, pushed back like she was scared, he backed off fast.

"Yes, really," he finally responded, giving her some more space. "It's great."

She didn't say anything, the spoon still hovering. "Well, ah, good."

He watched as she took a big breath and moved back closer to him.

Nate closed his hand over her wrist, slowly lowering the spoon and placing it on the bench. Faith was staring at his hand, looking up under hooded lashes when he tightened his hold, only just enough for her to notice. He could see she was breathing hard, but he had no idea whether she wanted him to back off or the complete opposite.

"Are you trying to seduce me?" he asked, his voice barely a gruff whisper.

He watched her swallow, noticed her cheeks turn a soft, tempting shade of pink. He'd never actually seen her blush before, and he liked it.

"No," she croaked, shaking her head.

"I've never had a woman try to seduce me in my own kitchen before," he told her, releasing her wrist and turning it over in his palm until her hand was facing up so he could trail his fingers across her soft skin. Her hand was trembling. "So, accidental or not, you're doing a damn fine job of it."

Faith made a noise that was hard to decipher. "I don't think I'm even capable of *seducing* anyone, let alone you. Especially not right now."

"After what happened?" He felt like shit. "That was seriously insensitive of me, pushing you like that. I'm sorry."

She slowly took her hand away from his. "I'm not exactly a *seductress* when it comes to men, Nate. And yeah, what happened has me kind of shaky still. I don't feel like me again yet, if that even makes sense."

"I get it." He stared into her eyes. "I'll let you come to me next time."

Her smile was sweet as pie.

"You know, you're even more tempting because you actually have no goddamn idea," he said as he took another step back. She definitely didn't know the effect she had on him. "Any other woman, I'd think this was all just a clever plan, but you?" Nate chuckled. "I actually think Sam's been so good at keeping most of the male population away from you that he's actually stopped you from realizing the power you have over men."

Faith laughed. First it was a shy giggle; then she was actually laughing. "I thought you were being serious for a moment."

She turned her back on him and went back to stirring her sauce, like nothing had happened between them, like she hadn't managed to tease him and tempt him with her damn Italian sauce.

"Do you want a glass of wine?"

Faith looked up. "I'd love one. A pinot would be great with this dish."

Nate raised an eyebrow. "And just like that you're running my household," he said dryly.

Faith paused, like she was unsure what to say. "Is that why you're so scared to have a woman in your house, Nate? Because you don't like the idea of losing control?"

He didn't even bother answering, just went through to the wine cellar and pulled out a bottle, stopping to check the label before returning to the kitchen. He uncorked it and decanted it before pulling out two oversize wineglasses.

"If we're going to drink a red, we may as well make it a good one," Nate told Faith. "If I'd known I would have got you to put it out to get to room temperature a few hours ago."

Faith nodded and checked the spaghetti, bumping shoulders with him when she turned to drain the water off. "How about you put the wine on the table? I'll have dinner served up in a few minutes."

Things were strained between them, suddenly strange, and Nate didn't like it. One moment they'd been easy; the next it was . . . He cleared his throat, refusing to feel uncomfortable in his own home. He was never *uncomfortable,* never not in control, especially when it came to the opposite sex. So they'd had a moment. So what? Nothing was going to happen, especially not after hearing how shaken up she still was. He'd been so busy thinking about how to deal with her ex, Nate hadn't thought about how rough she must be feeling still.

"Anything interesting happen today?" he asked, settling down at the table and stretching his legs out as he tried to make easy conversation. He glanced at a book she had open and reached for it. "Or were you too busy tidying up this pigsty?"

"It was hardly a pigsty."

Nate flicked through a few pages. The artwork was interesting, but it wasn't his area of expertise. "You've been studying?" he asked.

"No. It's a new book on contemporary artists. I was just doing some reading for pleasure."

He watched as Faith tipped spaghetti into an oversize white serving bowl as he undid the top button of his shirt and then the one below. He wore a shirt every day and a suit sometimes, relentless about his appearance given the types of clients he was dealing with and wanting to make sure they realized how seriously he took his role. But even the fact that his closet was full of Dolce & Gabbana and HUGO BOSS didn't mean he liked wearing fancy clothes when he could be in jeans and a tee at home.

"You do realize the whole brainy-student thing is kind of sexy, right?" Nate laughed as he said it, wishing he'd just kept it to himself.

Faith glanced at him and raised an eyebrow before spooning the meatballs and sauce on top of the spaghetti. "I'm not that brainy, but thanks." She smiled and shook her head, like he'd embarrassed her. "I met your sister-in-law," she said, changing the subject on him.

He leaned back, beer in hand. "Yeah? Which one?"

"Ryder's wife."

Nate grinned. "Ah, so you met the lovely Chloe."

"Yes," Faith said as she lifted the big bowl and walked toward him. Nate went to jump up, but she just smiled and shook her head, carrying the bowl and placing it down in the center of the table. She'd already set their place mats, and when she sat across from him he leaned forward and poured her wine, doing the same for himself now that he'd finished his beer.

"And what did Chloe want?" he asked, smiling as Faith served up one plate and then passed it to him. "Bet she was all twenty questions trying to figure out what you were doing here."

"She was just coming by to see you," Faith told him.

"During the day? I don't think so." He chuckled and

waited for her to finish serving herself so he could start. Now that the food was in front of him he was starving. "She knew damn well there was a woman here and she wanted to come be all nosey. I'd put money on it, and that's saying a lot where Chloe's concerned."

Come to think of it, Chloe had given him some serious shit about Faith when they'd been drinking at Joe's one night. Heaven help him if she figured it out; she'd give him hell. *If she hadn't already.*

"Well, she seemed lovely, anyway. Once I realized she wasn't your girlfriend, that is."

Nate paused with his fork midair, about to twirl his first mouthful of spaghetti. "I don't have a girlfriend. You think I'd have you here if I did?"

Faith frowned. "What difference would it make?"

Nate fought the urge to laugh at the innocent expression on her face, but he couldn't help his mouth kicking up into a grin. "If I had a girlfriend, hypothetical of course, there's no way she'd let me have a woman like you working for me in my home, let alone staying." He reached over to touch her hand, meaning to pat her but instead ending up tracing his fingers over the back of her hand, wishing to hell he hadn't touched her soft skin again. "Sweetheart, you're way too beautiful for another woman to ever trust you with her man. Believe me."

Faith stared at his hand for a moment before retracting hers, twirling spaghetti covered with sauce around her fork, and taking a bite. Nate watched her, transfixed by the way she ate, the tiny bit of sauce on her lower lip. He cleared his throat and looked at his own dinner, suddenly more hungry for a certain woman than food.

"Sam came by."

"Again?" Nate had his mouth full now, the tomato sauce like an explosion on his taste buds. "Damn, this is seriously good." When she said she'd learned how to cook he hadn't exactly been imagining something this incredible.

"He wanted to warn me off you one last time." Now it was Faith with her mouth kicked up into a curve and he had to resist the urge to wipe the smile straight off her face. *With his lips.*

Brotherly, he reminded himself. He was supposed to be brotherly with her.

"And what did you tell your big bad brother?" Nate asked her.

"Something along the lines of the fact I can look after myself," she muttered. "Although given my recent track record that didn't go down so well. But still, I gave it to him straight."

"I went to school with a guy, was friends with him for years," Nate said, pausing to take another forkful of spaghetti and meatball and finishing it before continuing. "Anyway, he had a bit of a temper, and one day after we lost a baseball game I came around a corner and caught him kicking the shit out of a dog."

Faith's cheeks lost all color. "You're serious?"

"Deadly." He grimaced. Just because he didn't mind talking with his fists when he needed to didn't mean he'd ever hurt an animal. *Or a woman for that matter.* "The point is, I'd known him since we were in junior high, and I'd never realized he was capable of doing something like that. He was kicking this poor defenseless dog and she didn't have a shot of getting away from him, let alone defending herself."

Faith had set her fork down now, was dabbing at the corners of her mouth with her napkin. Nate was thinking he should have waited to share this story until after they'd finished eating, especially given how pale she was suddenly looking. It had probably brought everything about the other night back to her.

"So what happened?" she asked.

Nate hoped she'd like the ending. "I was with Chase, and it just so happens that neither of us likes to see an animal get hurt. Let's just say it wasn't long before that guy was the one howling in pain and promising never to lay a hand on a dog again."

She sighed and picked up her fork again, absently pushing food around on her plate. "You're telling me this because you want me to know you're going to beat the crap out of Cooper?"

"No, Faith, I'm telling you because we all make bad judgment calls sometimes." He took a sip of wine, the red smooth as he swallowed it. "Do you remember that old dog Molly we used to have here? You probably saw her when you visited with Sam years ago. She always came out to greet anyone who arrived."

Faith's eyebrows pulled together. "I think so."

"Well, that was her. We scooped her up that day, found she had a couple of pups in the alley with her that she'd been trying to keep concealed, and took her home with us. Chase found new homes for the puppies once they were bigger, and she lived out her days here. We couldn't have loved that old girl more if we'd tried."

Faith took another mouthful, eyes suddenly bright

again. "You come off as this tough guy, Nate, like you wouldn't give a damn about anything other than yourself or your family, but it's not who you are, is it? I've always seen past that bravado."

He arched an eyebrow. "Oh really."

"Yes, really," she replied. "You wouldn't harm any animal and you couldn't say no to me when I turned up on your doorstep. You might frighten the crap out of grown men, but you don't scare me."

"Well, I should," he grumbled, placing his fork down so he could lean closer to her. "I *should* scare you, Faith."

"I'm not scared of you, Nathaniel King," she insisted, but her voice was wavering, no longer as strong and full of confidence as she had been a second ago. He didn't want to scare her, but he didn't want her thinking she was safe with him. Not from everything.

"When Sam said you were the lamb in the wolf's den, he wasn't lying." Nate held her gaze, didn't take his eyes off her for a second, never giving her a moment to break their connection, showing her why. "You shouldn't be here with me, Faith. You might not be scared of me, but it doesn't mean that you're safe with me."

"Are you going to hit me?" She was staring at him intently.

He frowned. "No."

"Hurt me?"

"Never."

"Then what?" she asked. "What should I be scared of? You've never done anything to make me think you'd hurt me."

Nate gritted his teeth, fisted his palms under the table.

"Don't push me, Faith, because if I have you in my arms for even a second, I might never let you go."

Faith ran her fingers down the stem of her wineglass, refusing to give in to the feelings she was having for Nate. She wanted him, she couldn't ignore the way she was feeling, but she also wasn't going to be made to feel like a girl. Nate was everything she liked in a man, *everything she'd always desired.* Trouble was, she wasn't sure if she was ready. *Yet.*

"You need to stop seeing me as Sam's little sister," she said, keeping her voice even, taking a slow, determined sip of wine, pushing away the voice in her head telling her to stop.

"And what should I see you as, Faith?" Nate's voice was raspy, husky as hell.

"A woman," she said. "All grown-up and fully capable of making her own decisions, especially when it comes to men." She knew how that sounded, but she'd left her ex the first time he'd laid a hand on her and she wasn't going to let that one bad experience scare her off the opposite sex for life. She was stronger than that.

"And what is it you want from me, Faith?" If Nate's voice had been raspy before, it was husky and dragged over gravel now, like pure sex if ever she'd heard it. "Or is it another man you're talking about?"

She tried to laugh, but it ended up sounding more like a choke. "Maybe it is another man." It was a lie, but she wanted to knock Nate down a peg, didn't want him to constantly have the upper hand. His cockiness was endearing sometimes and frustrating as hell at others.

"Well, if it is," he said, leaning back and away from her as he twirled the stem of his glass, "don't be inviting him back here."

"And why's that?" she asked, wishing she had the confidence to laugh in Nate's face and tell him that two could play his silly games.

"Because I'll kill any bastard that tries to touch you while you're under my protection, Faith. With my bare fucking hands if I have to."

Silence was like a cloud above them, hanging immobile, as if about to strike with thunder and lightning.

"You're starting to sound a lot like my very overprotective brother," she said pointedly, once she realized Nate wasn't going to say anything else. "The one I thought was incapable of dealing with my current situation without being a douche bag."

"Believe me, sugar, my thoughts about you are anything other than goddamn brotherly. Never have been."

She sucked in a breath, took another sip of wine for something to do, dinner long forgotten. "Maybe we should have just sat and eaten our spaghetti. Not said a word."

"So you could seduce me with your culinary skills rather than your bedroom eyes?" His voice was almost cruel now, predatory.

"So we could enjoy delicious food and more convivial company, actually," Faith told him. "I think I already made it clear that I have no powers of seduction, regardless of what you might think." She also wasn't sure she was up for bantering with Nate unless she was certain she was ready to go there. Which she wasn't.

"Then let's eat," he said, picking up his fork again and attacking his food with gusto. "The meatballs are incredible. You're a great cook."

"Thank you," she said, accepting the compliment, wishing she wasn't thinking that food was the way to a man's heart. Because she didn't want or need to go messing with any hearts, hers included. Maybe what she needed was some fun between the sheets, to loosen up a little. Get over what had happened and prove to herself she was as strong as she kept thinking she was. And wasn't as bad in bed as Cooper had insinuated.

"How about we start over?" he suggested, leaning forward for another helping, even though it had started to go cold.

Faith watched as he served himself, deciding that she might as well finish her food, too. She'd been chopping and stirring for what had seemed like hours at the time, so it seemed a shame to let it go to waste.

"What do you suggest?"

"How about I start by telling you about my day? Or maybe I should confess my sins to you?"

Faith shrugged. "Sure." She started to eat as Nate piled his plate high.

"You know, I don't like anyone to sense any weakness in me, Faith, which is why you rattle me. You turn up and I turn into a goddamn pussy, letting you look at me with your puppy dog eyes." He shook his head, ran a hand through his hair. "And now I'm about to lose the most important person in my life, my grandfather, and I'm afraid it's going to cut me off at the knees without me being able to do a damn thing about it. So I guess that makes two of you managing to dent my tough-guy armor."

She gulped. Maybe she should have been more encouraging when he'd suggested he just tell her about his day.

Nate headed out the door and crossed the field as a shortcut to the barn. He was pleased to get out of the house. After finishing dinner, talking way too much to Faith, and then helping her with the dishes, he needed to get away from her. He'd avoided her for so long, but the walls he'd invisibly erected between them were being ripped down. And fast. He was just pleased he'd already arranged to meet his brothers for a beer.

"Hey!" he called out to Ryder, seeing him turn over a few feed buckets for them to sit on. The lights were on, the interior of the barn flooded with light.

"Hey!" Ryder called back. "Chase is on his way."

"How's everything going?"

"Good. I got Rose to bed; she wanted three stories tonight. Honestly, Nate, I have no damn idea how I'm gonna cope when she starts to bring guys home. . . ."

"She's two," Nate said dryly. "You've got a lot of years ahead of you before you have to start worrying."

"I know. I just can't believe how much I love that little girl. It kills me. And if some bastard hurts her? Damn, I'll lose it. Seriously."

"You know I love hearing about Rose, but I was actually asking about work before, not your home life," Nate joked, taking the beer Ryder passed him. "How're those big bulls of yours?"

Ryder took a long pull of his beer, elbows resting on

his knees as he sat on the upturned bucket. "All good. Bruce is turning into a fucking superstar."

Nate laughed. They'd all made fun of Bruce the bull, because of his name and the fact that he had an attitude to rival a diva, but Ryder had managed to prove them all wrong with his new business venture. Not to mention his impeccable taste in livestock. "Good. You miss it, though? Actually being out there and riding?" Ryder had given up the rodeo after one big fall too many and after meeting his wife, but as happy as Nate was that his brother wasn't riding two-thousand-pound bulls anymore, he knew it must have been hard for him.

"I miss the thrill of getting up there, climbing the rails and gripping the rope. Listening to the crowd cheering," Ryder said, his eyes lighting up just talking about his glory days. "But when I look at my girls? It's a no-brainer. I had my fun, but after those falls I had, only an idiot would have kept riding. One more fall and I could have ended up a vegetable or dead. Isn't that why you were always busting your nuts to get me to stop?"

"Damn right."

"You reminiscing about the rodeo?" Chase called out as he entered, grabbing a beer and dropping down to his makeshift seat.

"Yeah," Ryder said. "It hurts not being a current champ at anything, not bringing home any new title belts. But Bruce is gonna become more famous than I ever was!"

They all laughed. Nate sipped his beer, always relaxed when he was hanging out with his brothers. They fought heaps, usually over stupid shit, but the worst they did was throw a punch. They were close and it was just the way he liked it. And even though they all had their own places now, they still always met up in the barn where they'd spent their youth sneaking beers.

"So how you getting on with Miss Universe staying over?"

Nate took another pull of beer. He was usually pretty sensitive when it came to his brothers talking about her or giving him shit, but he could hardly argue with what Chase had just said about her.

"I'm walking around with a permanent hard-on; that's how damn well I'm doing," he told them honestly.

His brothers howled with laughter. Nate scowled as Ryder slapped his hand on the bucket, he found it so amusing.

"I know I'm risking a black eye here, but have you thought about just scratching that itch?" Chase asked.

"Fuck you," Nate muttered.

"Would it be so bad to corrupt her? She's not exactly a child, Nate. She's a beautiful woman, and if she feels the same . . ." Ryder didn't finish his sentence.

"She's Sam's little sister. Enough said."

"Every woman has a brother or a father, Nate," Chase reasoned. "And since when do you let someone else tell you what you can and can't do?"

"Since that someone was Sam," Nate told them, too confused to be pissed with them. "He's the only person outside of this family I've ever truly trusted, and he's always been there for me. I'm not gonna screw that up just because I'm all hot under the goddamn collar for Faith." He sighed. *"It's Sam."*

"So tell her to find somewhere else to stay," Chase said. "Get her out of the house and off your radar."

Nate groaned. "I can't."

His brothers laughed again.

"You're between a rock and a hard place then." Ryder passed him another beer. "All I can say is good luck."

Nate ripped at the label on the beer bottle, trying to push Faith out of his mind and failing badly. "Women aside, I need to talk to you both about Granddad."

The atmosphere immediately turned somber. This was why Nate had wanted to see them.

"What's happened?" Chase asked, eyebrows drawn tightly together.

"Nothing, but he called me in this morning and I don't think we have long. He's been seeing his attorney, has everything in order. He's preparing to say good-bye."

"Anything we need to be concerned about?" Ryder asked.

"No," Nate replied, turning the bottle around in his hand, not sure whether to tell them everything or not. "Unless you guys have a problem with me amping up our oil drilling. Nothing will change with anything else on the ranches, you have my word, but I have to honor the promises I've made him." Oil excited Nate, made him feel alive and amped about earning their family empire more money, but his brothers never had the same burning desire like he did. It wasn't that they weren't supportive; they just had other interests.

"He wants you as his successor, Nate. We've always known he would, so you don't have to sugarcoat it." Chase shrugged. "You're already CEO, so it's not like anything's going to change."

"Let's face it," Ryder said. "You've been running the business alongside him for years now. I never saw that changing, and it's only logical that you'd be heading the family and the businesses. The last thing we need is too many chiefs, right? Just don't cut our share of the profits and you won't hear any complaints from me."

Nate studied his brothers, looking at first Chase, then Ryder. "So we're good?"

"I'm not gonna argue with anything Granddad wants. It's his legacy, and that makes it his decision. So long as you don't try to start interfering with how I run this place or oversee the other ranches."

"All the ranches are yours to run, except for the oil-drilling component," Nate confirmed. "I'd never step on your toes when it comes to the day-to-day running."

"Just let me do my thing with the bulls," Ryder said. "And the horses, too. I'm not giving up running our bloodstock program, okay?" He chuckled. "Besides, it's not like our head horse trainer will want to work with you, anyway. And our horses would be nothing without Sam's help. So all that shit I said before about just going for it with Faith? Forget it."

Nate grimaced at the reference to Sam. He just needed to keep his hands off Faith and he wouldn't have a problem.

"How about we toast Granddad?" Nate suggested, holding his beer bottle up in the air. "To the man we owe everything to."

His brothers held their beers up, too. Nate blinked away tears, refusing to break down. He never cried, and he sure as hell wasn't about to give in to his emotions before his granddad was even cold. Nate owed it to him to stay strong, and that was exactly what he was going to do.

And then he had to decide what to do with Faith. Asking her to head out with them the following night might not have been his best ever idea.

Chapter 6

NATE felt like he was waiting for his date to the prom. Faith had called out that she'd only be a few minutes, but he was counting down already and it hadn't even been sixty seconds yet. He checked his watch again for something to do, then decided to go pour himself a drink, needing a whiskey.

"Hey."

He just about spilled the liquor straight onto the counter instead of into his glass. Nate finished the task, telling himself not to react no matter how damn good she looked, turning slowly as he put the cap back on the bottle of Wild Turkey.

Damn. "You look," he said, unable to stop his eyes from roving all the way up, then down her body, "amazing."

She smiled and shrugged, like she hadn't made a special effort, but Nate knew otherwise. Faith always looked great, but tonight she was more than a distraction to him; she was dynamite. Only he was the one in danger of exploding.

"You don't look so bad yourself," she said, checking something in her purse, then zipping it back up.

Nate took a small sip of whiskey before deciding it would be best to not drink before getting behind the wheel. He glanced down at his jeans and shirt. "I'm just happy not to be wearing a suit, but you?" He shook his head. "Sam's gonna flip."

She looked confused. "Why Sam?"

"Because every goddamn guy in a twenty-foot radius of you is going to stare, which means he'll know exactly what thoughts will be running through my head."

Faith tucked her purse under one arm and reached for him, smoothing her fingers across the collar of his shirt like she was pressing it for him. "And what thoughts would they be?"

He chuckled and expertly moved out of her reach, not about to struggle with his self-control now before the night had even started. She was flirting and she knew it. Once they were out of his home, away from his territory, maybe he'd find it easier to stop wanting her so damn bad.

"Sweetheart, if you could read my thoughts you'd be running. Fast." He shook his head, refusing to let his feet walk back toward her, resisting the urge to run his fingers through the silky locks of her hair. "In the opposite direction."

Her hair was usually straight and smooth, but tonight she had soft curls, curls that he was aching to tug out. She was wearing a pretty dress that showed off long tanned legs that . . . Nate cleared his throat. *Maybe he*

*should have finished his drink after all and just ordered
a cab.*

"Nate, I keep telling you that you don't scare me, so
lighten up," she said, chin tilted in defiance as she stared
at him. She hadn't been lying when she'd said she was
all grown-up—there was something in her eyes that told
him she was a whole lot more worldly than either he or
Sam had ever wanted to realize.

"And I keep telling you that you damn well should
be," he replied, fetching his key from the hallstand and
marching to the door. He hauled it open and waited for
her to pass through, sighing when he got another eyeful
of her pert butt and endlessly long, golden-brown legs.
Her skin was flawless and it made him want to trace
across every inch of it. "There's an old saying about not
taunting a wolf unless you—"

Her laughter interrupted him, infuriated him, and
pleased him at the same time. "Enough of the wolf talk.
I think of you more like a big Labrador, Nate," she said
as she opened her own door and looked over her shoulder at him. "You can be scary when you need to be, but
really you're just a big softy."

Nate was stationary, staring at her, wondering what
the hell had just happened to him. He'd made a reputation for himself mirrored on that of his granddad,
demanded respect from everyone he worked with. No
one spoke to him like he was someone's goddamn
Labrador!

"You're gonna get yourself in trouble with that mouth
one day, Faith."

She just laughed and slipped her legs into the car.
"Yeah, right."

What the hell had gotten into her? "Yeah, well you haven't spent much time around me, have you?"

Nate stormed around to the driver's side, equal parts furious with her and so fucking turned on he didn't know what he wanted to do to her. The one thing he was certain about was wishing they weren't about to meet her brother for drinks. An intimate dinner date, just the two of them, followed by cocktails in a private booth . . . now that's the kind of evening he wanted with Faith. *And it was exactly what he'd never let himself do with her.* Because if they were drinking and alone? His self-control would be gone . . . as if he'd never had any in the first place.

"So do you normally go out looking like this?" he demanded once he'd pushed the keyless GO button and started backing around.

"Like what?" she asked, arching an eyebrow and clearly amused at the line of questioning. "Looking all dolled up? Wearing a dress?"

He sighed, impatient. "Like no man should be let near you because he couldn't be trusted."

Faith laughed and placed a hand on his thigh, her touch gentle. He shifted, wishing she'd keep her hands off him and then regretting his thoughts the moment she removed it.

"You're just sensitive about me, that's all," she said. "It's a summer dress, Nate. I'm not even showing a lot of skin."

"Oh really? I'm sensitive about you, am I?"

"Like a bear with a thorn in his paw," she murmured.

"Yeah, well, if I've got a thorn, Sam's gonna act like he's a bear with a bullet lodged in his ass."

"You're overreacting," she said, wriggling in her seat to face him. "Now tell me how your granddad was today?"

Nate gripped the steering wheel a little tighter. "He seemed good, considering what he's going through. But then he's always been good at making us boys think there's nothing wrong with him."

"And did he say anything else about the reading of his will?"

He grunted, wishing he hadn't divulged something to Faith before telling his brothers. Keeping things to himself wasn't usually a problem for him, but in this particular instance he'd almost needed someone else to talk it through with. Usually he could have turned to Sam, but he wasn't going out of his way to seek his friend out right now.

"He keeps telling me not to worry, that nothing will come as a surprise to them, but I just don't want to cause a rift. I told them a lot, but I didn't tell them that he wanted a formal reading of it while he was still . . . here." Nate pumped the accelerator a little harder. "My brothers mean more to me than anything. No amount of money or power in the world would be worth sacrificing our relationship."

"It must be nice always knowing that they have your back and vice versa."

Nate glanced across at her. "Yeah, it is. And now that they have wives, our circle has grown a little. Meaning I have even more people I love to protect."

"You have a lot riding on your shoulders, Nate," she said, her voice low. "You can give yourself a break sometimes and just be you. Around me, anyway."

Her words made him laugh. "I've never had any trouble letting my hair down and partying, Faith, if that's what you mean."

She smiled, but she didn't laugh back at him. "Fair point. But I think we both know that's not what I meant."

"So would you usually dress like that to head to Joe's?"

"Enough with what I'm wearing, Nate!" She play-punched him in the arm as she laughed. "And we're not going to Joe's, so I'm hardly gonna be overdressed. I told some of my friends to join us, said it was a good excuse to put something nice on and go out, so it's not just me in a nice dress you'll have to worry about."

He ground his teeth together, jaw like steel. "I don't give a damn about your friends, darlin', only you."

"I'm a big girl, Nate," she reminded him.

"Yeah, so you keep saying." So why was it he alternated between wanting to strip her naked like the big grown-up girl she kept claiming to be and fighting the urge to wrap her in cotton wool and protect her from the world the rest of the time?

"So will we be dancing?" she asked coyly, as if she knew exactly how her teasing affected him.

"No, there'll be no goddamn dancing," he muttered. "At least you won't see *me* dancing."

"We'll see." Her voice was sweet as pie, and if he hadn't had his hands on the steering wheel he would have grabbed her by the shoulders and kissed her like she'd never been kissed before. He didn't know what the hell had happened to her, but it was like she was on a mission to ruffle his feathers tonight, and she'd sure as hell succeeded.

* * *

Faith had no idea what the hell had gotten into her. She'd gone from being timid around Nate to being desperate to push all his buttons just to get a reaction from him. And every time she got a reaction from him it only spurred her on all the more. It was like she was playing a part, wanting to stand up to him, to prove that she wasn't the little girl he seemed to see her as still, and to make matters worse, she was liking it. *Loving it.* And best of all, she hadn't thought once about her douche-bag ex. With Nate, she knew she was protected, didn't need to look over her shoulder.

"Do you come here much?" she asked as Nate parked the car.

"Sam and I used to come here all the time," he said. "Not so often these days."

"What do you think of his new girlfriend?"

"She seems nice," Nate answered before turning off the ignition and unclipping his seat belt. "But then I've only met her a couple times, so I can't really say."

Faith watched as he got out of the car and seemed to stalk around to her side. She kept telling herself she wasn't ready for anything to happen between them, but if they took it slow . . . She swallowed. She wasn't sure if Nate did slow, but if he did . . . Faith adjusted her dress, made sure she wasn't showing more than she wanted to, and clasped her purse. She'd be lying if she said she hadn't dressed for Nate tonight, and she wanted him to notice. When he opened her door she stepped out, her heels clicking on the pavement as they walked side by side toward the bar.

Nate cleared his throat as they walked, glancing at

her. She just smiled back at him, pleased she'd gone with her highest heels so that she wasn't at a complete disadvantage to his six-foot-four frame. He still made her feel tiny, in a Thor to Natalie Portman kind of way, and it wasn't so much that she didn't like it; she just wanted to be able to look him in the eye instead of having to crane her neck.

"You do look beautiful tonight, Faith," Nate said, his brown eyes warm when they connected with hers.

She breathed deep, lost every inch of the self-confidence she'd been so full of earlier. "Thank you."

"Now let's get inside and deal with your brother."

Faith watched as Nate nodded at the doorman, following close behind him. The place was already busy, full of people trying to talk over the music, which at least meant no one heard her gasp when Nate reached for her hand, his warm palm jammed against hers, fingers strong and firm as he led the way.

"Stay close," he murmured in her ear, sending a ripple of goose pimples down her back.

Faith took her chance to do exactly that, her body skimming his as she pressed a little closer to him. Everything about him was overtly masculine: his cologne, the hardness of his body, the sheer size of him. And she wished—

"Hey, little sister." A firm hand closed over her shoulder and she quickly let go of Nate, feeling lost and vulnerable the moment she broke the connection between them.

She turned and found herself face-to-face with her brother, and based on the look he was giving her, she was certain he'd noticed her holding hands with Nate.

"Hey, Sam," she replied, leaning forward to press a kiss to his cheek.

Nate must have turned at that exact moment, as the smile on Sam's face hovered straight into a frown.

"Nate."

"Hey, Sam."

Faith tried not to laugh; the expression on Nate's face was hilarious. Her brother and her boss, staring at each other like two male lions about to fight for leadership rights of the pride. Ordinarily it wouldn't have been so funny, except for the fact that she was used to them being the best of friends. She didn't ever remember them having a falling-out through her entire childhood.

"You guys remember Kelly?"

Faith smiled at her brother's girlfriend, calling out a hello. Nate stepped forward to kiss Kelly's cheek, making Sam look even more pissed off, until Nate suggested they grab a drink, which seemed to settle him.

Nate's hand slid across Faith's back as he indicated for her to walk ahead of him and she felt a familiar shiver run the length of her spine at his touch.

"What do you want?" he said the words, so close to her ear she thought his lips were about to brush her skin.

You. The word was on the tip of her tongue, but she swallowed it. No matter how brave she was feeling around him, she wasn't going to say it. Not yet. Not until she knew whether she could go through with it or not.

"How about cocktails?" she replied, glancing at him as she spoke.

"Martini? Mojito?" He laughed and dipped his head close to hers again. "Cosmopolitan?"

Faith laughed straight back. "Mojito. How about you?"

"Whiskey, sweetheart. It's always my poison of choice."

He was seriously too cool for school, and she would have told him exactly that except she didn't want to sound like a silly girl for saying it. She was twenty-seven, but for some reason she still felt young beside Nate. He wasn't that much older than her, thirty-two maybe, but everything about him had always made him seem so experienced, so worldly.

They ordered, her brother insisting on paying for her drink instead of letting Nate cover the bill, and then they headed off to find somewhere to sit. She kept glancing around, looking for her girlfriends, and just as she started chatting to Kelly two of her friends appeared.

"Hey!" She smiled and hugged Anna and Cara, trying not to laugh as they both glanced at Nate. "You know Sam, and this is his girlfriend, Kelly. And Nate, a friend of my brother's."

Anna boldly shook Nate's hand and said hello, Cara waved, and within moments he was on his feet and heading to the bar to buy them drinks. Faith couldn't help watching him as he strode through the crowd of people.

"So let me get this straight, you're working for this guy?" Anna asked.

Faith turned back to the girls. "Yes." She'd never mentioned Nate to them before, never needed to. She hadn't mentioned Nate to *anyone*. "I'm just doing some housekeeping for him, cooking and stuff."

"Hmmm, what type of stuff?" Cara asked, winking and making them all laugh. Faith might not have said anything about him before, but that wasn't fooling her friends; they knew her too well. Besides, they knew her ambitions went further, that it wasn't like her to want to cook and clean. They all talked about moving away, making it in New York, working in beautiful art galleries or for big auction houses.

"Nothing like what you're thinking." She reached for her cocktail and took a sip, loving the tangy taste. "Not that I haven't thought about it."

Anna touched Faith's arm, leaned in close like someone might hear them despite the loud music. "How are you feeling, after Cooper? I can't believe the asshole actually hurt you. Sure had us all fooled by his nice-guy routine."

She'd told her friends the truth about what had happened when she'd invited them out, and the truth was she could have turned to them if she'd needed to, could have stayed on their sofa in the little apartment they shared. But after Cooper she'd needed to feel safe, like he couldn't get close to her again even if he'd wanted to, and going to Nate had seemed like the right thing to do, especially when she hadn't wanted to involve her brother.

"I haven't seen him since," she told them. "He tried calling a couple of times, then a few texts, but I've just ignored him completely." The last one he'd sent had been him pissed that she hadn't shown for a shift, as if she was just going to turn up for work and forget about the fact that he'd hit her. He was just lucky she hadn't called the cops.

"You're better off without him," Anna said. "Asshole."

"My thoughts exactly," Faith muttered.

"Ladies." The deep voice from behind them sent a familiar lick of anticipation through her, and she turned to make way for Nate to pass the girls their drinks. They both smiled and thanked him, and Faith had the sudden urge to stake her claim, make it clear that he was off-limits. Only when Nate turned and looked into her eyes, his gaze wicked as he winked at her, she realized she didn't have to. He'd been polite and charming to them, but the only one he was paying real attention to was her, and it would have been impossible for her friends not to notice what was going on between them. Whatever the hell that might be.

"You've slept with him already, haven't you?" Cara hissed when Nate excused himself and sat back down across from Sam.

Faith laughed. "No. He thinks of me like a little sister; nothing is going to happen."

"I call bullshit," Anna said, draining almost half of her drink. "You two are eyeing each other up like a kid looking at candy."

Faith sipped her drink for something to do, wishing she didn't feel so guilty. She did want Nate. Bad. Always had, always would. And there was no way she could hide it from her friends.

"Let's just say that Nate has always been my fantasy guy," she admitted, keeping her voice low. "It's not something I ever thought I'd act on, and after Cooper?" She shrugged. "The idea of his hands on me is kind of scary."

"You know who my fantasy guy is?" Cara asked.

Faith and Anna shook their heads.

"Johnny Depp. The difference is that he'll never know I exist and yours is ready to rip your clothes off."

They all laughed and Anna grabbed Cara's hand. Faith was pleased she'd asked them out; she'd needed their company. "We're going to dance. Just have fun with Nate, okay? Don't worry about us. In fact, pretend like we're not even here."

"Thanks for the drinks!" Cara called over to Nate before the girls disappeared through the crowd.

Faith watched them go, quickly sipped most of her drink, and then turned back to the table. Sam had his head bent close to his girlfriend's, listening to something she was saying, and Nate was staring at Faith.

"What happened to your friends?" he asked.

"They're off dancing. Man hunting."

The look on Nate's face was priceless, the line of his mouth tightening. "Are you going to join them?"

She finished her drink and placed it down on the table. "No."

"Good." He knocked back the rest of his and slammed it down on the table. "I'll get us all another round then."

Sam got her attention as Nate disappeared again. He looked more mellow than he had before, but she guessed his girlfriend probably had to take credit for that.

"You okay?" he asked with big-brotherly concern.

"Fine. Great, in fact," she said.

"Nate sorted out your ex yet?"

Faith prickled just at the mention of Cooper. "Not that I know of." Maybe Nate had? The truth was, so long as Cooper never came near her again she didn't really care.

"I'll talk to him about it when he gets back."

Nate was back before she knew it, her drink in front of her and his hand sliding down her back again. She'd come to crave his touch, the indent of his palm against any part of her enough to make her shudder. She wasn't sure what it meant, but she liked it.

"Thank you," she said, taking a welcome gulp of alcohol.

"You're welcome."

"Stop making eyes at my sister and slide me my beer," her brother grumbled.

Faith saw the way Kelly touched his arm, smiling to herself as she gave him a look that said, *Enough*. Faith hadn't seen her brother in a serious relationship before, and she liked that it was someone else keeping him in line for once. Fingers crossed he managed to hold on to her.

They chatted about nothing in particular, and Faith leaned across the table for a bit to talk with Kelly again, but Faith was so aware of Nate that she found it almost impossible to concentrate on what she was saying. His body was warm against hers when he shuffled closer, his mouth so tempting when he spoke to her, her eyes dropping to focus on the fullness of his lips every single time. The more she tried not to think about him like that, the more she wanted him.

"I'll be back in a moment," Faith said as she stood, carefully smoothing her hands over her skirt to make sure it was in place. She collected her purse and made her way through the crowd, heading in what she hoped was the right direction for the restroom. She needed a minute to gather her thoughts, to figure out what the hell she was doing.

Once she was in there she checked her reflection in a mirror, reapplied her lip gloss instead of splashing the cold water on her face that she was craving. After spending so long on her makeup she wasn't about to ruin it. What she did do was let the cool water run over her wrists, cooling her body and calming her at the same time. Nate hadn't even done anything, yet she was all twisted in knots over just the thought of what he could do to her.

Once she'd finished in the restroom she stepped out, was about to brave the crowd and head back to their table when a hand closed over hers, taking her by surprise.

"Faith."

Her pulse ignited, first from the shock of a man grabbing her unexpectedly, then all over again when she realized it was Nate. Her heart was pounding, her initial reaction to shove his hand off and run. But he wasn't Cooper. It was Nate. Nate wasn't going to hurt her.

"I was just making my way back," she said, trying to slow her breathing.

"Your brother's up dancing. I was just coming to get you."

She stood dead still, stared up at him, heart pounding so loudly she was certain it was about to beat right out of her chest.

"Nate . . ."

He stepped closer, released her wrist, his eyes fixed on hers.

Screw it. Maybe it was the alcohol, the fact that they'd been dancing around whatever the hell it was going on between them since the moment she'd arrived at his place, or the fact that she'd harbored a secret fantasy for him since she was a teenager; whatever it was, she wasn't going to just ignore it any longer. *Couldn't*. It was Nate—she could trust him; she *needed* to trust him.

Faith pushed him back against the wall, her hands to his chest, his only protest a grunt as he let himself be moved. She stood on tiptoe and pressed a kiss to his lips, tentatively at first and then with more force, her hands on his shoulders before snaking up higher, fingers looping through his too-long hair, tugging him closer. She was no man's victim, wasn't going to let her ex ruin what she could have with another man.

Nate groaned; she heard the noise at the same time as his body tightened, his shoulders bunching like he was about to pull back, before giving in, his mouth suddenly crushing hers. His arms wrapped around her, holding her close, pulling her body forward and hard smacked into his. She relaxed, pushed any stupid thoughts away that told her to stop.

Because Faith couldn't get enough of him; the taste of him, the feel of him, the . . . she moaned as his tongue found hers, his lips moving fast one moment, then slow the next, his hands skimming her back, settling just above her butt.

"We shouldn't be doing this, Faith," he murmured, his sinful dark eyes trained on hers.

"Don't stop," she whispered back, still on tiptoe, her mouth hovering over his.

"This is every kind of bad." He plucked at her lips with his again. "So bad."

"I want you to teach me, Nate. I need you to"—she kissed him back, her knees turning to liquid and making it almost impossible to stay upright—"show me what to do." It was what she'd always wanted, Nate in her bed. And this was her chance to get what she'd been craving, to prove to herself that she was nobody's victim. And to make sure no other man could ever insult her like Cooper had.

"Sugar, you know exactly what you're doing." His kisses were like fire across her skin, the most delicious, sensuous, burning-hot fire.

"I'm not talking about kissing, Nate," she murmured, moaning as his tongue dipped into her mouth again, his lips so slow and careful one minute and rough the next.

"You . . ." He paused, his mouth hovering over hers, recognition shining in his eyes. "You want me to teach you *in the bedroom*?"

She nodded, refusing to be embarrassed, not wanting to back down now she'd finally said the words. "Yes."

Nate's groan wasn't an answer, but she couldn't mistake his desire, his arousal impossible not to notice pressed against her, his mouth no longer slow even for a moment, just rough and sexy as hell and making her want to strip her clothes off right then and there.

"Faith . . . ," he muttered, but his hands were tangled in her long hair, like his mouth couldn't stay away from hers even for a second.

"What the fuck!"

Nate's hands were still on her, but his mouth was gone, leaving her wondering what the hell had happened and who was— *Shit.* Her brother was barely a foot away from them, the disbelief on his face fast turning to all-out fury.

"You fucking asshole!" Sam roared, moving so fast

that Faith jumped back, hard against the opposite wall in the narrow space leading to the restrooms where they'd been standing.

She heard herself scream as Sam launched at Nate, his fist connecting with the side of his face, Nate's hands rising to stop him but Sam moving too fast. It was like she was at a train station, right on the tracks, a roaring noise so loud in her ears that she couldn't hear anything, could just watch on helplessly as her brother swung at Nate again. It brought everything back, the terror she'd felt the night Cooper had hit her, and she wanted it to end now, wasn't going to sit by and watch them fight.

"Sam, no!" she yelled, forcing herself to act, moving closer but not wanting to get in their way. The way they were acting right now, especially Sam, his rage was so absolute that she doubted he'd even see her if she tried to intervene.

But it looked like Nate wasn't going to take any more punches. Faith wrapped her arms around herself, felt Kelly put a hand on her shoulder, yelling at Sam, too, but the fight was over. Her brother wasn't small, but Nate was bigger. Suddenly he had his hand around Sam's wrist, not letting him swing again, dodging his other fist as it came swinging, ending up grazing past Nate's neck.

"Enough!" Nate commanded, his booming voice so loud it sent chills through her. "Enough, Sam!" Her brother had turned into a maniac, throwing his head forward and trying to head butt Nate now that he couldn't successfully use his fists.

"Sam!" Faith demanded, moving closer now that the worst of the fight was over. "Just stop. Stop!"

He looked at her, the fury in his face simmering to a

different kind of anger, one she thought looked more manageable than rage since it seemed to be filled with disappointment. She wasn't used to disappointing anyone, least of all her brother, but she was pretty sure that's what she was seeing right now.

"Don't you ever fucking touch my sister again. You hear me?" Sam spat out the words, looking at Nate like he'd kill him with his bare hands if he had to. "Don't you fucking dare."

Nate stared at Sam. He hadn't looked over at Faith, not once, but his words were for her.

"Are you okay?" he asked.

"Yes," she replied, her eyes fixed on him now instead of Sam.

"Leave her out of this, Nate. She's not yours to protect and she never will be."

Faith swallowed, hard, looking between the two men. She loved Sam; he'd been an amazing brother when they were kids and he still was. She was insanely proud of the career he'd made for himself and the man he'd become. But just because she loved him didn't mean he could decide who she was allowed to kiss, or do anything else with. If she wanted to get into Nate's bed, that was her choice, and no one, not even her brother, was going to stop her.

The two men were still staring at each other, like they could be fistfighting in a second without warning, but Nate was slowly backing away and putting some distance between them.

"She's a grown woman, Sam," Nate finally said. "And after what she's been through I don't think she needs to see us fighting."

"She's my fucking sister! My *little* sister."

They were talking like she wasn't even standing there, but from what Nate had told her this was a feud that had started when she was a teenager, something that had been simmering between them for some time. Sam had thought he'd stamped it out all those years ago, and now his worst nightmare had come true.

"Can we at least talk about this in private?" Nate asked, his voice still deep and calm as ever.

"What, you don't want everyone knowing that you're trying to get into my sister's pants?" His laugh was cruel as he turned to her. "Because that's all he wants from you, Faith. And once he's had you, he'll discard you. And who'll be there to pick up the pieces then, huh?"

Silence stretched out between them, but Faith was at least starting to catch her breath, her heart no longer hammering like it had been. Her only concern was what Nate was about to say now, because if he told Sam the truth it might end up making the entire situation even worse.

"Don't forget that Faith came to me, Sam. I never went looking for her, did I? I stayed the hell away, just like you asked me to."

"So now it's her fault? Now that she's near you it's her problem that you can't keep your tongue out of her mouth?"

Faith felt like she was about to stop breathing, all the oxygen in the room gone, waiting for his answer. He'd turned what had just happened between her and Nate into something forbidden and it wasn't.

"No. But I'd never make a woman do anything she didn't want to do, and you're still my friend, Sam. The best fucking friend I've ever had." Nate ran his fingers through his hair, glancing at her for the first time, the look in his eyes one she couldn't decipher. "I wouldn't do anything to ruin our friendship, Sam."

"Yeah?" Sam glared at Nate like he'd like to kill him. "Well, you just fucking did. We're through."

Sam spun around and marched off, leaving her standing there wondering what the hell had happened as Kelly ran after him. Nate was immobile for a moment, then launched forward, went to go after him, but Faith quickly grabbed his arm.

"Don't," she said. "Just give him some time."

Nate stopped without her needing to try to restrain him further. He turned slowly, his eyes falling to hers, his smile grim, nothing like the brightness she'd witnessed earlier when she'd been in his arms.

"We really screwed up," Nate said, reaching for her anyway and stroking his fingers down her arm. "

"No, I screwed up," Faith said, wishing she didn't crave his touch quite so much. She wasn't going to lie— Nate's skin on hers sent shoots of pleasure rippling through her, the anticipation of what could happen between them almost as sweet as each touch. And she wasn't afraid of him, had expected to be scared of him touching her, of going there so soon, but she wasn't. "This is all on me, not you."

He shook his head, one side of his mouth curving up into a smile. "I didn't exactly try to push you away," he said, cupping her face and looking deep into her eyes. "I've wanted you for a long time, Faith, which is why I never should have let you stay."

Her pulse had ignited again, the flames in her belly

stirring into a full-on fire now. "But you did," she murmured. "And you didn't seem to mind me kissing you."

"Darlin', kissing you is something I could do all night." Nate chuckled and cupped her cheek, staring at her, before letting his hand fall away. "Every damn night of the week if I had the chance."

Faith swallowed, moistened her lips with the tip of her tongue. "So just because my brother tells you I'm out-of-bounds, that's it? You're going to let him control you like that?"

"No one controls me, Faith. Make no mistake about that." Nate's voice had gone from smooth and sexy to deep and gravelly now. "But Sam and I have been buddies since pre-K. He's the only friend I've ever trusted, and I'm not going to throw that away for—"

"A night between the sheets with me?" Faith interrupted.

"*Anything*," Nate corrected. "I was going to say that I wouldn't throw away our friendship for anything."

Faith wrapped her arms around herself again, suddenly feeling a chill even though it probably wasn't even remotely cold where they were standing.

"You need to let him calm down before you go after him," she said, wishing things could be different between them but not wanting to ruin their friendship, either. "He'll need some time to himself; otherwise he'll just try to kill you again."

"I let him have that first punch," Nate muttered.

She stepped closer to him and put her hand to his chest, palm flat as she pushed him back into the light to see how bad the bruise was.

"*Damn!*" she swore softly under her breath.

"Does it look bad?" he asked, staring down at her.

"Yeah. It's gonna be a serious black eye." Faith traced gently around the skin of his eye with one soft fingertip. "Sorry."

She looked up at him, no longer focused on the purple bruise, and her breath caught in her throat at the look on his face, at the desire so evident in the way he was looking at her. He was a different kind of hurt than she'd been, but it still wasn't nice to see.

"We can't." Nate's voice was guttural and it only made her want him more.

"He already hates you right now, Nate," she said, her eyes fixed on his lips now, her breath coming in fast pants. "What harm could it do if he never finds out?"

Chapter 7

NATE groaned, the noise coming from deep within him. She might be younger than him, his friend's little sister, but she was sure as hell all grown-up just like she'd claimed to be. There was nothing about that girl left.

"That's the worst excuse I've ever heard," he muttered, but he still didn't back away.

"Sam's gone," she said, both hands to his chest now, then running up and over his shoulders. "It's just you and me."

"No." He forced himself to say the word, wanted so badly to do the right thing, but it still wasn't enough. Because he wasn't good, never had been, and the more he knew he wasn't allowed something . . .

"I wasn't lying that I needed a teacher," she whispered, on her tiptoes now, mouth so, *so* close to his.

"And I made it very clear that you don't need a goddamn teacher." His fists were balled, his fingers tightening as he tried to resist the urge to touch her. Why was she doing this to him?

"You'd rather I find another man for the job?" she teased.

But he didn't want to be teased, wasn't in the mood.

Nate used every inch of his willpower as he slowly closed the gap between them, mouth hovering over Faith's as he bent down. "You so much as mention another man . . ."

She sighed into his mouth as he closed his lips over hers, kissing her so softly it almost killed him, was almost impossible to maintain.

"I won't," she whispered when he pulled back. "I feel safe with you. It's only you I want."

Nate slipped an arm around Faith, the other hand snaking around the back of her head, fingers tangling in her long hair so he could lock her in place, kissing her rough. He wanted to do bad, bad things to her, things he'd fantasized about for years and refused to ever think could come true.

"No one can know about this," he muttered.

"About what?" she innocently replied, the rise and fall of her breasts as she caught her breath making him want to rip her dress down to expose them, to finally see what she looked like bare.

"We're going home!" he commanded. "And I'm not touching you until we're away from here, okay? If Sam sees me so much as look at you like I want you in my bed, the next time I see him he'll have a gun to my fucking head." He looked down at Faith and wished he'd kept that last part to himself. "Sorry."

"Let's just go," she said. "You can make it up to me later."

Nate grabbed her hand when they neared the crowd, needing to get past a ton of people to make the main exit. He'd only had a couple of drinks all night, so he was fine to drive, and he just wanted to get the hell out and to his car. Faith's petite hand fitted perfectly into his, her hold tight. Whatever the hell he'd just done, there was no going back. And as much as he didn't want to piss Sam off, Nate also wanted Faith. *Like he'd never, ever wanted a woman before.*

"So here we are."

Nate pushed open the front door and took a few steps inside. It was dark and he'd forgotten to turn any lights on, so he fumbled his hand along the wall until he connected with the switches. His brothers had all sorts of fancy lighting at their new places, but he didn't care that the main house was a bit ancient. It was immaculately maintained and the old girl had one hell of a history, so he wasn't exactly hankering for something brand-new. He dealt with shiny glass and chrome buildings on a daily basis, so many of their investments in New York were in the city, and he liked a bit of history at home.

He glanced back at Faith, saw her standing awkwardly near the front door still, suddenly looking a whole lot like the young Faith he'd been warned away from so many years ago and not at all like the confident young woman who'd just propositioned him in the bar.

"I was half-expecting Sam to be waiting on the porch for me."

She smiled, but her lips only just moved, hovering at

the corners. "He's had too much to drink to be able to drive, and I don't think Kelly will let him out of her sight until he sobers up."

"He wasn't drunk; that's what worried me," Nate said grimly. "It's gonna take a while to repair the damage."

"And us?" she asked, her bottom lip catching beneath her top teeth.

Nate groaned and stepped toward her, taking her hand in his and looking down into her eyes. "There is no us, Faith," he said. "It's not because I don't want there to be, but you don't need me as some sort of a rebound guy. And you sure as hell don't need a pissed-off brother on your hands."

She raised her gaze, reaching to touch Nate's face. "I don't want you to be my rebound, Nate."

He sighed and fought the urge to kiss her. "I can't be any more to you than a rebound, Faith. Any ideas you have about something more . . ."

"I don't want more," she said, her fingers strumming a gentle note across his skin, his cheek, and then his jawline. "I just want to have fun for the summer, before life becomes a whole lot more serious. And I want you to . . ."

"Teach you," he finished for her.

She moved even closer to him, her body skimming his, breasts to his chest and her head tipped back. "I don't want to be told that I don't know what I'm doing again," she whispered. "I want to . . ."

"*Stop.*" They were getting in a bad habit of interrupting each other's sentences, but he didn't want to hear any more of what she had to say. He couldn't teach her, couldn't take her to his bed, couldn't . . . *or could he?*

And what kind of jerk had been telling her that she didn't know what she was doing in the bedroom?

"Why not?" she asked. "Is it just because of Sam?"

"You make it sound like that's a stupid reason. It's not," he growled back.

"What if he never had to know? Isn't that why you just brought me back here?"

"Do you want me to lie to him?"

Her smile made Nate want to do wicked things to her mouth just to wipe the grin away, to stop her from being so goddamn cocky when usually she was a whole lot more demure. Maybe it was because he'd never seen her drinking before, but she was turning into one hell of a confident woman.

"Is it lying if we just pretend like I'm only your housekeeper? That what he walked in on was a onetime-only mistake?"

He cleared his throat, staring down at her, into the deepest-brown eyes he'd ever looked into. "Was it a mistake?"

She laughed. "You tell me."

The only mistake was letting himself near her in the first place. He should have let her in, then jumped on his jet and headed back to New York. Or maybe the mistake was not dragging her to his bed right now and getting her the hell out of his system.

"The mistake was letting you through my front door when I found you here the other day," he muttered.

"You're actually regretting it?" she asked, putting her palm to his chest and pushing back a little. "I don't believe you."

He grunted, not liking the distance she'd just put between them even though he was telling her the exact opposite. "I'm just pissed off at my sudden lack of self-control."

"Because you're always used to being the one calling the shots?" she asked.

"Exactly."

They stood, staring at each other. Faith was waiting for him to make a move, he could tell, but as much as he wanted her, he still had a shred of control left when it came to her and his friendship with Sam. She'd been ballsy at the bar, but here in Nate's home she looked a whole lot more uncertain all of a sudden.

"I think we need to call it a night," he said firmly, finally letting go of her hand.

She nodded, cheeks flushed like she was seriously embarrassed, touched with the softest hint of pink.

"I'm not saying no, Faith, and it's sure as hell not because I don't want you." He couldn't help but smile at her. "Because I do want you, Faith, with every damn fiber in my body."

Her mouth flexed into a big smile again. "Good night, Nate."

Nate stood and watched her go, refused to go after her, resisted the urge to confess to being an idiot and kiss the hell out of her again. Because he needed time to think. Because Faith was forbidden. Because, *damn it,* it just wasn't right.

Faith splashed cold water on her face and took a deep, shaky breath. She had no idea what the hell had happened tonight, but she was sure as hell grateful for having her own bathroom adjoining the guest room she was staying in. At least she wouldn't have to see Nate again until morning, and even then she'd be hiding under the covers for as long as she could. He'd never specifically mentioned her having to make him break-fast as part of her live-in-housekeeper role, and she had no intention of offering this weekend. Not when she could do a perfectly good job of keeping her head bur-ied in the sand.

What had possessed her to kiss Nate like that? It would have been fine if something more had hap-pened between them, but he'd rebuffed her as soon as he'd had time to think it through, the moment they'd arrived home. The only thought keeping her sane was how he'd responded to her when they'd touched, but that was nothing if she never got to feel his hands on her again. *Or his lips.* She'd gone from being scared of a man's touch to downright craving it.

Faith turned the faucet off and stared at herself in the mirror. She'd screwed up, read the signs wrong. And she'd never forgive herself if Sam and Nate didn't mend their relationship—they'd been friends for so long, and as much as she wanted Nate, she also didn't want to be the cause of a serious rift between them.

She ran her fingers through her hair, the curls almost completely fallen out now, and turned from the mirror. What she needed was a good night's sleep. Every-thing would seem better in the morning; it always did. That was one of the few things she remembered her mom saying, something that had always stayed with Faith even after she'd left. When she had gone when Faith was just a teenager, it had been Faith's choice to stay. But at that age, the idea of leaving her friends behind, not to mention her brother, had been almost unbearable, even though in hindsight she could see it had been the wrong decision. Instead of trying to understand, she'd turned her mom into the villain without seeing that her dad was to blame for so many of the reasons their marriage had broken down, and she doubted she'd ever be able to repair the damage even if they ever reconnected.

She undressed, put her dress on a hanger, and pulled on the tank top and boy shorts she always wore to bed, sighing as her head hit the luxurious feather-filled pillow. Everything about Nate's house was incredible—the duvet was incredibly warm but light as a single feather, with a soft cashmere blanket at the end for extra warmth if she needed it and extra goose-down pillows in the closet. The bathroom was full of oversize supersoft towels, with tiles floor to ceiling, and the bedroom carpet was plush enough to wiggle her toes deep into. As much as she loved it, she was terrified of getting used to such luxuries—another thing she had in common with her mom.

Faith pulled out her iPad, looked up one of her favorite New York galleries, a place in Brooklyn that was showing some of the best street art and graffiti artists. Maybe she should have just gone there, soaked up the atmosphere, and seen all the art she'd researched first-hand. She sighed, deciding to put her iPad away instead of scrolling through. One day she'd get there, but right now she needed to stay focused on finishing her degree and saving her money.

She shut her eyes and sighed, wishing she could just fall asleep right then and there. There was a reason she'd never let herself fall for Nate, why she only wanted to have fun with him and not let anything serious happen between them, and it wasn't because she didn't want to settle down one day. Nate might be best friends with her brother, but it didn't mean he'd ever marry her. Her mom had fallen for a man not so dissimilar to Nate, had dropped everything to be with the man she loved, until eventually he'd finished with her to please his family, then married a woman from a family more similar to his own. No one was ever going to make Faith feel like she was anything other than marriage material, which was why she'd wanted to call the shots with Nate. And after seeing the way her dad had gone on to treat her mom, she wasn't sure marriage was what it was made out to be, anyway. She didn't want to compromise, not her career, her life, her choices—nothing.

A knock echoed out on the door, just softly. If she'd been asleep she never would have heard it. Faith flicked on the bedside lamp, a soft light now illuminating the previously pitch-black room.

"Faith?"

Nate's deep whisper made her heart start to race. She'd known it was him, there was no one else in the house, but just to hear his voice and know that he was standing outside her bedroom door sent chills through her body.

The door handle turned and she quickly ran her fingers through her hair, scooping it all over one shoulder. She glanced down to check her top was in place, opening her mouth to say something, until she saw the look on Nate's face as he entered the room.

"Nate?" she murmured.

He was standing dead still, his hands balled into fists at his sides, mouth fixed in a straight line that didn't give away any of his feelings. Until he ran one set of fingers through his hair and stepped forward, the look in his eyes like she'd never seen before.

"I can't do this," he muttered.

She dug her fingers into the duvet and tugged it up a little higher. He was an imposing figure just standing there like that, filling the doorway that he was standing in front of, but she wasn't afraid of Nate. He was one of the few men in the world who could never intimidate her physically, because he was one of the only men she actually trusted. He'd protect her no matter what—and he was one of only two people in the world she could say that about.

"I don't understand," she said. As far as she understood, there was nothing happening between them. He'd made that clear less than an hour ago.

He stepped closer, his eyes pleading with her, the line of his jaw so rigid she didn't know whether he was about to give in to anger and slam his fist into a wall or launch into bed with her. Anticipation hummed through her body as she thought about the latter. She still wanted him. Nothing would make her stop wanting Nate King. *Nothing.*

"I can't sleep knowing you're down here alone," he muttered. "I can't lie in my bed without thinking about you, without wanting to . . ."

"What?" she whispered, digging her nails into the duvet she was clutching. "What is it you want, Nate?"

She wasn't going to make a move again. She'd shown him what she wanted, made it clear, and if he wanted her he was going to have to damn well take the initiative.

"I want to do wicked things to you, Faith," he

muttered as he stalked closer to her, eyes never leaving hers for a moment. "I want to throw back these covers and strip you naked. I want to taste every inch of you. I want to do anything and everything to pleasure you until you can't take a second more of it."

Faith gulped. Her entire body felt like it was on fire, her skin alight as if being stroked by flames. Just the thought of Nate touching her intimately was enough to ignite her pulse.

"So what are you waiting for?" she said, as brazenly as she could even though she was equal parts terrified about what he wanted to do with her.

"Don't tempt me, Faith," he as good as growled.

"This only has to be between you and me," she said. "If no one else knows . . ."

"I can't." He was standing only a few feet from the bed now, still in his jeans but his torso bare, giving her a glimpse of the body she was desperate to explore. Now he was closer and bathed in light, she could see his abs, every single one of them, impressive on his tanned torso. His shoulders were big and broad, balanced by biceps so large she wanted to touch them to see how hard they were. He was built like an athlete; only he was a six-foot-four hulk of a man who wore Italian suits and was perfectly at ease running a billion-dollar corporation.

"So don't," she taunted.

"*Damn it!*" he swore softly under his breath, finally releasing his hands from the tight fists he'd been sporting until now.

Faith sucked in a breath, anticipation licking over every inch of her body. She couldn't breathe, couldn't think, couldn't do anything except watch Nate as he lowered himself onto the bed and reached for her.

"We shouldn't be doing this," he muttered as he cupped her cheek in one of his hands, staring into her eyes.

"I know," she murmured back, lips parting as his mouth came closer.

Nate was done talking. His kiss went from soft, his touch gentle, to rough almost immediately. One second he was cupping her face; the next his fingers were tangled in her hair, his mouth rough on her lips and then her neck, his stubble a barely there roughness that reminded her just how damn masculine he was.

His mouth moved down her neck, his warm lips a contrast to his wet tongue that was trailing sensually across her skin. Faith moaned, she couldn't help it, as one of his hands brushed her breast. She wasn't scared of his hands—she wanted them everywhere.

"We need to slow down," he muttered against her collarbone.

Faith laughed. "You're the one racing ahead."

He grunted and stopped, lifting his head. "It's not my fault you've got such a goddamn irresistible body."

"Touché," Faith murmured, cupping the back of his skull to force him forward again, looping her other arm around his neck as she kissed him, surrendering to his mouth.

He plucked at her mouth, then deepened his kiss, exploring her body with his hand, stopping at the waistband of her boy shorts and dipping his finger under and against her skin. Faith went still, *silent,* the only noise the rasping of their breaths.

"Are you sure this is what you want?" he asked, voice so deep and husky she hardly recognized it. "Are you absolutely sure?"

"Yes," she whispered back, raising her hips, forcing her body against his. His erection was rock solid against her belly, his desire for her more than obvious. It sent sparks of pleasure through her just knowing that she could have that kind of effect on the infamous Nathaniel.

"I'm only a man, Faith, and that means there's only so long I can resist you." He said the words against her skin, his breath hot. "If you say no, I'll stop, but I can only be the good guy where you're concerned for so long."

"You *are* the good guy," she told him, moaning as his mouth dipped to a sensitive spot on her neck. "But I want you to be bad tonight, to show me how to be a good lover."

His laughter was muffled against her skin until he raised his head. "Whatever jerk told you that was lying," he told her, stroking her face, brushing the hair from her cheeks. "I don't need to teach you a thing. You know exactly what you're doing."

She'd been embarrassed, *mortified,* when Cooper had accused her of being a crap lay, but she also believed him. It wasn't like she had a lot of experience, she had only had a few boyfriends, but she never wanted to feel ashamed or incapable in the bedroom again.

"Just show me what to do, Nate," she said, staring deep into his eyes. "Please."

"Sweetheart, I'll show you anything you want," he muttered, rising so he was sitting astride her, thumbs looping into the waistband of her boy shorts, not tugging them down straightaway, leaving her to wriggle beneath him. "But just remember, if it feels good for you, it'll feel just as good for me."

Chapter 8

FAITH'S body was humming, Nate's touch driving her so close to the edge, and he wasn't even naked yet. The roughness of his jeans against her thighs was the only distraction from what he was doing to her, and even that felt great.

He had her naked from the waist down now, trailing kisses down her thighs, his fingers stroking so close to her . . . *oh my god*. His hand brushed against her most intimate parts, made her gasp, but he was only teasing her, his hands focused on ridding her of her top. He grabbed the hem and pushed it up, forcing the fabric up. She arched her back so he could get it off, raising her arms so he could lift it above her head.

And then she was naked.

"Your pants," she croaked, barely able to summon her voice as Nate stroked one finger from her collarbone to the top of her breasts, dipping between them and then circling around one.

"Your breasts," he whispered straight back.

Nate's circles across her skin became smaller, until he was almost touching her nipple. But his mouth got there before his finger, sucking so gently, licking her so softly, that she couldn't help but moan.

"Stop!" she moaned, not wanting to let him get away with being the boss. "Your jeans."

He laughed and sucked harder until she was forced to wriggle away from him.

"Nate!"

He gave her a devilish look and pushed back, shrugging as he unzipped his jeans and stepped out of them. He was already barefoot, and suddenly he was standing in front of her with only his boxers on, his physical intentions more than clear.

"Tell me you're not having second thoughts." His voice was a sexy rumble.

She swallowed, eyes tracing over every inch of him. "No second thoughts."

He dropped over her again, his big body swallowing hers up. "Good."

"You're not the wolf in sheep's clothing anymore," she muttered. "Just the wolf."

Nate winked and covered her mouth with his, his hands back to exploring her body. She kept up with his touches, didn't miss a beat, delighted in the feeling of everything he was doing to her. After so long wanting him, imagining what it would be like to be in his bed, it was every bit as good as she'd expected.

"Let me . . . ," she started, wriggling down, mouth to his skin as she tried to get lower.

"No," he said, dragging her back up and kissing her again.

"How can you teach me if you won't let me learn?" she asked, her confidence surprising her. She'd never been so brazen before, not when she was being intimate with someone, but something about Nate was spurring her on. Maybe it was just his practiced touch, the laid-back yet attentive way he was pushing all her right buttons without even going further than second base.

"I'll teach you another night." He spoke against her skin, taking her hands and putting them above her head, fingers firm around her wrists. "Tonight is all about you."

She wanted to protest, to tell him that this wasn't part of the deal, but she couldn't. The idea of Nate pleasuring her, lying back and letting him do anything and everything with her? That wasn't something she had the strength to say no to. She tried to retrieve one hand, wanted to run her fingers through his thick black hair, to grip it hard, but he wasn't relenting. She was powerless to move.

Nate's breath was hot against her skin, his kisses even hotter, searing as he made a trail across her skin.

"Whoever told you that you didn't know what you were doing?" he said, voice low as he looked up, eyes on hers. "Probably didn't have a damn idea how to pleasure a woman anyway."

She gasped when he lowered his head, wasting no time, his free hand gently pushing her thigh down so he had better access to her most intimate parts. His tongue barely touched her, but it was enough to make her moan.

"And you do?" she ground out.

"Yes." The word was barely a whisper, but she heard

it, and she didn't doubt his confidence for a moment. "I enjoy giving as much as I like taking."

Everything else drowned out when he started to pleasure her, his mouth doing the most wicked of things to her, leaving it impossible to think of anything except the building heat inside of her. His tongue was doing circles, his mouth clamped over her, and he was no longer holding her wrists captive.

"Nate!" she moaned, threading her fingers hard through his hair and holding on tight.

If it hurt him, he never said, just continued to work his magic, not letting up, her climax building hard. She wrapped her legs tight around his head as he pushed her to the edge, spasms of pleasure taking over every bit of her body.

When she released him, finally let her fingers ease off his hair and unclamped her thighs, he kissed her intimately before trailing fingers across her skin, up and down her legs. His mouth soon followed, warm kisses against her burning stomach, every part of her still feeling like it was on fire.

Nate had always been an overachiever, and he'd clearly decided to make sure he excelled in the bedroom as well as the boardroom. If she could have spoken, if her voice wasn't still a prisoner in her throat, unable to make a noise, she would have told him exactly that.

He was above her now, his mouth closing down on hers, making her eyes pop open.

"It's not over yet, sweetheart," he whispered, his deep drawl more delicious than ever.

Nate's smile was even more wicked than his words,

but instead of saying anything he slid straight inside her, going slow but not stopping until he couldn't push any further.

Faith's legs wrapped around him, she gripped hard, her body eagerly meeting his. The man was relentless, and she was just as keen as he was to keep going, to ride her way to the edge again.

"You're naughty," he muttered in her ear. "So, so naughty."

"You're the one"—she let out a sharp breath, a hiss of air, as his thrusts became harder, all gentleness long gone—"doing bad things to me."

He paused, his body still, muscles slick with sweat. "Want me to stop?"

She gripped him tighter, dug her fingernails into his shoulders, and forced him down closer, their bodies pressed tight. *"Never."*

Nate knew how much she wanted him; it would be impossible for him not to given how tight she was holding on to him, matching his every movement. But what was turning her on the most was how obviously he wanted her, how much he was enjoying it, too.

Just as she started to feel like her body was getting closer to the edge, just as she thought that she could hardly bear the intense pleasure inside of her any longer, Nate pulled out, kissing her mouth, eyes open as he looked down at her.

"Don't stop," she begged. *"Don't. Stop."*

He laughed. "Not stopping. Just trying to figure out how to make this even better for you."

Her mouth was dry, her eyes roving over every inch of him. He was built like a gladiator, his body a well-honed machine, every part of him muscled and exquisite. His skin was golden, the only smattering of hair an arrow that extended from his belly button to his . . . She looked up, caught his naughty smile.

"How do you like it?" he asked.

She didn't even know what to say, wasn't used to a lover being so direct about her needs or body parts. "I don't know."

"Yes, you do," he insisted, bending to kiss her, to tease her lips, his erection hard against her belly. "Just tell me." His words were husky, low. "Whisper in my ear."

"I want . . . ," she started, clearing her throat, annoyed with herself that he'd had to push her just to say how she wanted him, what her fantasies were. "I want you to hold me up. I want my legs around your waist and my back to the wall."

He arched an eyebrow. "You want me standing and you up in the air, in my arms?"

She nodded. "Yes."

He was on his feet in moments, scooping her up like she was weightless. Which she wasn't. He was just damn strong.

Nate kept her in his arms, positioned her so she was facing him, her legs around his torso, as he backed her against the wall. Her back hit the cool wallpaper and he pushed her higher, angling her so he could fit inside her. He thrust hard, up, her arms looped around his neck.

"Like this?" he asked, his mouth to her neck.

She moved so he was kissing her lips instead, wanting to taste him, to kiss him, while he fucked her. "Yes," she exhaled the word. *"Yes."*

Nate was relentless, didn't stop or slow down until she started moaning his name, until he knew she was close. She'd never had a lover like him, and it had been worth the wait. Nate fricking King was worthy of his reputation and then some.

His lips were hot, wet; his body was slick with sweat; and the feel of him inside of her was exactly how she'd imagined it would be. She could let him pleasure her all night . . . and then again, and again. Sex had never felt this good, not in her lifetime, anyway.

Chapter 9

NATE stretched out, smiling when he realized he wasn't alone in bed. The night before came flooding back, the memories almost as good as the real thing. He rolled a little so he was facing Faith, her long dark hair splayed out on the pillow, lips full and slightly parted. He pressed a kiss to her cheek, wanting to wake her, desperate for her to stir so he could rouse her from sleep and make her beautiful body hum again, but he didn't. She was living with him for Christ's sake, which meant unless she changed her mind about what she wanted, she'd be in his bed again before long.

He stroked a strand of her hair, a mental picture of her sitting astride him while he fisted handfuls of inky black silk around his wrists flashing through his mind. After years of imagining what it would be like to have Faith between the sheets, his curiosity had only just been piqued.

Nate rose, glancing back at Faith and wishing he could just crawl back under the covers and spend the entire day in bed with her. But he couldn't. There was something he should have done the day after she arrived and he still hadn't. He quietly opened his closet, retrieved a clean pair of jeans and a shirt, and headed for the bathroom with them. He showered quickly, pulled on his clothes, and grabbed an apple as he passed through the kitchen, his stomach growling in response. He collected his keys and headed straight out the door. Food could come later.

He pulled out of the garage slowly, checking his reversing camera the entire time, paranoid that a dog or his little niece might surprise him, then turned and drove down their long, seemingly endless driveway. Nate passed Chase as he was coming out of his house, coffee in hand still, work boots on.

"You're heading out early!" Chase called out.

"Got a job to do," Nate replied, window down and his hand hanging out the side as he smiled to his brother.

"Ranching never stops," Chase said with a laugh, winking as he walked off. "I'll see you around later on. If that little niece of ours doesn't have me tied up attending a tea party or something in between Harrison tying me to a tree playing cowboy. For some reason I'm always the bad guy in that game."

Nate drove off, chuckling at his brother as he glanced in the rearview mirror. Who would have thought that big, bad Chase would be shacked up and playing the role of doting father *and* uncle. He grinned again. *He* was just as doting, so he shouldn't be laughing—the little girl had them all wrapped around her little finger. The only difference was that he was still a bachelor and he had no intentions of settling down. Ryder and Chase could produce plenty of kids between them for the ranch and business to be passed down to; his role was to make sure there was one hell of an empire to leave them as a legacy. Nate stopped a few yards down the road, got out, and surveyed the land to his left. It wouldn't be long before the trucks and specialists would be rolling in, accessing part of the ranch from this exact part of road. He couldn't wait for the moment they found oil there, knew in his bones it was going to be incredible. He just hoped his granddad was around to see it.

He got back in the car and settled in for the drive, glancing at his phone to make sure he had the address right. His memory rarely let him down, but he still wanted to double-check what the investigator had given him. What he was about to do now wasn't something he wanted to do to the wrong person.

Nate slowed as he approached the street, making the turn, then scanning the numbers. Once he was close he dialed Sam through his voice command, listening to it ring, wishing his friend would just answer the damn phone. He ended up getting his voice mail.

"Sam, it's me. I know you're pissed with me right now, and I get it. I shouldn't have let her . . ." Nate sighed, deciding that telling Sam that his sister had been the one to kiss him probably wasn't such a great idea. "Look, I just want you to know that I deserved the black eye. For the record, it's a goddamn shiner. Anyway, I'm dealing with that other business now. By the time I'm finished with her asshole ex he'll never even think about laying his hand on another woman again."

He hung up and parked the car, jumping out and rolling up his shirtsleeves to his elbows, folding the fabric first so they were the same length and wouldn't fall down. He debated grabbing the baseball bat out of the back but decided against it. He didn't need a weapon— his grandfather had taught them all that. Weapons like guns were for cowards and criminals. A man could settle his issues with words and his fists, and Nate had chosen the latter. His granddad hadn't been opposed to violence, just the kind that didn't involve a man having to roll his sleeves up first.

He locked the truck, shoved his keys in his back pocket, and crossed the road. The houses were okay, fairly modest but tidy, and he didn't want to cause a disturbance to anyone enjoying a lazy Saturday morning. In fact, he wished he wasn't doing this at all, but then again there would be an element of satisfaction in beating the shit out of the guy who'd hurt Faith.

Nate knocked on the door, being careful not to pound too hard. He stood back, arms at his sides, not wanting to alert the guy to anything and stop him from answering the door. Nate knocked again, a little louder this time.

"Who is it?" a male voice sounded out.

"Nate King!" he called back.

The door opened a crack. "What the fuck do you want?"

Nate smiled, shoving his boot in the opening before it could be slammed on him. "You know a young woman named Faith Mendes?"

The guy's eyes widened, recognition dawning.

"And I take it you're Cooper," Nate said, forcing the door open.

"Get the fuck out of here; this is my house and you can't just—"

"What?" Nate asked, storming inside and slamming the door shut behind him, forcing Cooper to stagger backward. "You gonna say I just can't come in here un-invited?" He laughed, his fist flying as grinned, slamming it into the side of the guy's face. "That was for touching Faith," Nate muttered, "and for being an ass-hole."

Cooper fell back against the wall opposite them when Nate punched him a second time.

"You're insane!" Cooper yelled. "What the fuck are you on about?"

Nate wasn't even breathing heavy yet, adrenaline surging through every vein in his body, but he kept himself in check, wouldn't let himself lose even a shred of self-control. "You have anyone here? A woman?"

The change in Cooper's face told him the answer.

"Get dressed and get out of here!" Nate yelled out. "This is between me and this douche bag, and if you saw the bruises he left on his last girlfriend, you'd be running."

Nate waited, eyes never leaving Cooper. He folded his arms across his chest, listening to footsteps, then stepping back as a woman wearing not a lot rushed straight past them and out the front door. He waited until the door shut, then smiled again at Cooper.

"There's two things I'm here for today," he said.

Cooper wasn't moving, had stayed still slumped against the wall, but he was starting to move now, looked like he was about to swing a punch or something.

"Don't do anything stupid," Nate said.

Cooper jumped up and charged, but Nate was ready. He was doing this for Faith, could still perfectly recall the silky feel of her otherwise blemish-free skin, which meant he could still remember the ugly purple bruise across her belly.

Nate dodged the punch coming his way, grabbing Cooper and throwing him back, slamming his fist into Cooper's face.

"You bastard!" Cooper swore, cradling his face. "You broke my fucking nose."

Nate ignored him. He wasn't sadistic, didn't take pleasure from causing other beings pain, but he did believe in an eye for an eye or, in this case, ten punches for one. Man against woman wasn't a fair fight, which meant he had some catching up to do on Faith's behalf.

"I'll break every bone in your body if you ever come near Faith again," he told Cooper, staying calm, breathing heavier than usual as he fought to keep his head. "And if I ever hear you've ever touched any woman, ever again, with your fists?" Nate shook his head, lips curling up into what he was certain was an evil smile. "I'll hurt you so bad you'll end up ten feet under."

Cooper's nose was bleeding, the blood dripping down his face and onto his T-shirt as he looked at Nate.

"She fucking deserved it."

Nate stopped dead, his pulse racing. *"What did you say?"*

"You heard me," he said, spitting blood at Nate. "The bitch deserved it."

Nate made a noise that sounded more animal like than human, only just keeping a lid on his rage. He launched at Cooper and pummeled him, punching his face, kicking him, unleashing hell on the asshole. Nate was careful not to go too far, didn't want to kill the guy, and when he was done he walked away, changing his mind about getting any of Faith's things together. Whatever she needed he could buy her new.

Nate checked Cooper was still breathing, propped him up, and headed back to his vehicle. The deed was done. He left his sleeves rolled up, cursed when he noticed he had a smear of blood on his shirt, and drove the hell out of Dodge.

No one touched Faith and got away with it. *No one.*

When Nate arrived home, the house was silent. He dropped his keys and the brown paper bags he was carrying on the hallstand and kicked off his boots, calling out and receiving no response. *Damn it,* he should have left a note. She probably woke up to him gone and thought he'd just left. He wasn't used to having to think things like that through, because he never usually hung around. Or came back.

"Faith?" he called again, running up the stairs two at a time and stopping in the open doorway to his room. The sheets were rumpled, the covers discarded at the end of the bed, but she wasn't there, and he could see she wasn't in the bathroom, either.

He glanced at himself in the mirror and grimaced at the blood on his shirt, stripping it off and throwing it in the laundry basket. He got a T-shirt instead and pulled it on, then headed back down, collecting the bags again.

"Faith!" he called, louder this time, her name dying on his lips as he spotted her sitting outside. Her dark hair was pulled back up into a ponytail, straight almost-black silk hanging from high on her head, and as he got closer he could see that her legs were tucked up beneath her and she was nursing a cup of coffee as she stared out into the distance. He glanced out himself, never tired of looking at the land he'd grown up on.

"Am I interrupting?" he asked.

She glanced up, her eyes taking a moment to focus like she'd been a million miles away.

"No," she said simply.

Nate moved closer and dropped to the sofa beside her. He smiled as she looked at him, holding up the bags. "I dropped into that French bakery, the new one that's just opened up. I got a whole heap of sweet pastries, something with chocolate in it. . . ." He raised an eyebrow and looked up, saw the frown on her face.

"You snuck out on me to go to the bakery?"

"No, I left you peacefully asleep to go get a job done; then I went to the bakery to buy the most beautiful woman in the world breakfast."

She went to laugh, but he didn't let her, dropping the bags down beside her and cupping her face before she could pull away, pressing a kiss to her lips. He meant to only kiss her once, but it turned out to be impossible. Her mouth was so soft he couldn't help kissing her over and over again.

"You're a smooth talker; I'll give you that," she muttered when he finally let her free.

"No, I'm honest." He shrugged. "I've admired you from afar for years, so when I tell you that you're the most beautiful woman, believe me when I say I've had a lot of time to think about it."

She laughed and snatched a bag from him. "If you hadn't bedded half of Texas I might believe you."

"Half?" He frowned. "That might be underestimating a little."

"Nate!" She slapped him hard on the hand as he reached for her. "You're disgusting."

He shook his head. "I haven't been with half as many women as you probably think, but I'm not going to deny that I love the opposite sex."

"Do you regret what we did?" she asked, tearing at a piece of pastry as she watched him.

"No." He took a mouthful himself, gave himself time to think. "I regret Sam seeing what he did, because he's one hell of a good friend to me, but I don't regret anything we did. How could I?" Nate leaned in and kissed her again, her lips sweet from the pastry.

"And you've honestly never had a woman in your bed, here, before?" she asked, glancing up at him.

"Honestly. Except for when I was a teenager and we used to sneak girls into the house. But that was a different bed." He looked out at the view again, leaned back into the sofa, and stretched out his legs, his thigh still hard against hers. "I don't like complications, and I like to keep this place private. Life's busy these days, and coming home is my sanctuary. It has to be or I wouldn't be able to shut off from work."

"Meaning you don't want me here?" she asked, her voice lower now.

He turned back to her, tugging the tie out of her hair and making it tumble around her shoulders. He stroked it, the strands having a strange calming effect on him.

"Meaning I don't want just anyone here," he told her, meaning every word. "You're different."

"Because I'm Sam's little sister?"

"No, because you're you."

They stared at each other, her eyes locked on his. He had no idea what was happening between them, how he'd ended up betraying his closest friend by doing something he'd sworn never to do, but he had, and all he could do now was live with the consequences of his actions. He didn't want to hurt Sam, but there was no part of him that could push Faith away now she was here with him.

"I stayed away from you for so long, Faith," he said, studying her face, the angles of her cheekbones, the fullness of her sinful lips. "I was so good, but being that good just doesn't come naturally to me."

"What do you want from me, Nate?" she asked, her voice husky. "Is this just between you and me? A secret that we're never going to share?"

He groaned as her hand landed on his thigh, her fingers stroking over his jeans. "I want you. Now. Tomorrow. Yesterday."

"But that's all this is? Sex?"

Nate pulled back, forced himself to stop even though his body was begging him to change his mind. *What the hell was he doing?* The whole reason he was supposed to steer clear of her was so he couldn't hurt her, break her heart, and he hadn't even been clear with her about his intentions.

"Faith, I don't want to give you the wrong idea."

"Please don't tell me you want something more from me?" she asked. "Don't ruin what we have going on."

He raised an eyebrow, taken aback. "You don't want any more? You don't have any, ah, *expectations*?"

She smiled, just one corner of her mouth tilting up,

and stroked his face. Her touch was light, impossibly gentle, and it made him only want to be rougher with her, to take her right there on the sofa.

"I thought I made it clear last night," she said. "I want you to be my teacher, Nate, to have fun until I find somewhere else to go. No strings, no emotions. I don't want any commitment from you." She sighed. "One day I'll be valuing beautiful art and putting collections together, and maybe I'll be ready for a real relationship then, one with a picket-fence future, but not right now."

He grunted. Was she serious? "So just fun and sex?"

"Just fun and sex," she repeated. "And it can stay just between the two of us."

"Deal."

She tossed her pastry over onto the other sofa, her eyes wide as she raised both arms and looped them around his neck. "So no falling in love with me, okay?"

"Sure thing," he replied. Only trouble was, for the first time in his life, he was with a woman he could actually fall for, no matter how badly he wanted to make sure he never, ever let his guard down and let someone too close. There were things in his past that made him want to keep a part of him hidden away, closed to the world, forever, and he had to make sure that nothing, even Faith, came close to getting through.

Faith rose and sat astride him, her hair falling down and covering his face until she scooped it up and placed it over her other shoulder. She kissed his mouth, lips warm and moist, plucking at his in a way that got him hard real fast.

"What is it you want me to teach you?" he asked.

"Everything," she replied, staring down at him. "I

want to be good. . . ." She sighed. "I want to know what I'm doing."

"Sweetheart, I don't think you need any pointers. Haven't I made that clear already?"

She sighed again. "Not what I've been told."

He pulled her down closer to him, breasts crushed against his chest. He was obviously going to have to try harder to get her to believe that she had nothing to worry about. "Some guys get off on making women feel incompetent," he murmured in her ear, running his hands up and down her back. "Me? I get off on women feeling sexy and confident. Real men like to see a woman enjoy sex as much as they do, okay? So if it's feeling great for you, it'll be feeling damn good for me."

"You're sure?"

"I'm not into lying, especially in bed. If I say something it's the truth; you can trust me," he said with a chuckle. "How about we get started and I can tell you just how amazing you are?"

She laughed. "Nate, be serious."

"Oh, I'm serious." He flipped her so she was beneath him, pinning her arms above her head. "But how about I get things started? Then you can take the lead?"

She willingly gave in to him, eyes popping open when he stroked her cheek. Nate had been fantasizing about her for so long, pleasuring himself and imagining her naked, and the reality was even better.

"You're so damn beautiful," he muttered, taking her nipple into his mouth and sucking just hard enough, making her moan. "And I want to do so many wicked things to you."

She fought for her hands and ran them down the firm

muscles of Nate's back. "So start now!" she demanded, forcing his head up and planting her lips on his.

Now it was Nate groaning. "You're trouble."

Faith giggled and dug her nails into his butt. "I know."

"So tell me," Faith said, stretching out alongside Nate and smiling up at him. They were still outside—he'd sworn there was no chance of anyone being able to sneak up on them, which she seriously doubted, but she'd decided to give him the benefit of the doubt. "What kind of woman would make the infamous Nate King settle down once and for all?"

He chuckled, stroking her arm, his touch light. "A woman like you."

His words were as soft as his hands, but they still took her by surprise. "Like me?" she managed.

"I'm happy being a bachelor," he said, "but if I was ever crazy enough to settle down, then yeah, it would be a woman like you. Beautiful, caring, determined . . . hell, I don't know. You're just you; I can't describe it. And I've been warned away from you for so many years that I haven't let myself think about how incredible you are, until now."

It was as far from the answer she'd expected as possible, had shocked her into silence. "But you don't want to, settle down, I mean?"

He dropped a kiss to her lips, his gaze hooded, propped up on one arm looking down at her. "No." He frowned. "I thought we'd discussed all this just before."

"We had, only I still don't know why you're so determined to stay a bachelor, especially now that your brothers are both happily settled down."

"If I was the only son to the King fortune, hell, I'd be making sure I had heirs to take over the land and businesses one day, but that's not something I have to worry about thanks to Ryder and Chase."

"So you just think about it all as some kind of business arrangement?" she asked, perplexed. She didn't want to get married or serious yet, but to *never* want to? She just didn't want to put her dreams second to anyone else's, but that didn't mean she wanted to end up a lonely old spinster. She'd presumed Nate was the same— too busy for marriage now, but it was something he'd want in the future.

"Not for my brothers it's not; I mean, I don't think that. Hell no. But me? I don't know. I've got too much to do, too much to achieve. And I just don't . . ."

"What?" she asked, snuggling closer to him, not wanting him to just stop talking when he'd been so close to letting her in. She might not understand him, but she wanted to hear what he had to say.

"Look, I have my reasons. Can we just go back to not being so damn serious?"

Faith reached up and kissed Nate, wished she hadn't pushed him so far. It was none of her business; they were having fun and that was that. But she'd known him way too long not to care about him.

He rose and reached for her clothes first, passing them to her before pulling his own on. "Sorry, I didn't mean to bite your head off like that."

"No apology necessary." She pulled her top over her head and ran her fingers through her hair. She'd brushed it out when she'd risen from bed, but now it was all tangled again, thanks to Nate loving to rough it up when they were intimate.

"I might not want anything more than fun right now, but I do give a damn about you, Nate. Always have, always will."

He smiled and reached for her hand, linking their fingers before standing and pulling her up, too. "I know you do. And the feeling's mutual." A look crossed his face, pulled his eyebrows together as he looked back up at her. "You know, I could ask the same about you. Why the hell are you so determined not to be in a relationship?"

"Maybe I'm just all kinds of fucked up after the excellent example my parents set of marriage."

"Swearing doesn't suit you," he said with a frown. "I'm a goddamn cursing machine, but every time you say the *f* word it makes me . . ."

"What? Want to tell me off because you still think of me as the kid sister?" she interrupted, trying to be serious but unable to hold back her chuckle.

"I think it's fairly obvious I don't think of you as anyone's kid sister after what we've been doing." He squeezed her hand. "But back to my question."

"How about we save that conversation for another day?" she said.

"You don't want to talk, that's fine by me. I just didn't pick you for a no-strings-attached kind of affair. Then again, you're on the rebound."

"How about you stop asking questions and make me a coffee with that fancy machine of yours? Then we can eat the rest of your even fancier bakery goodies instead of talking?"

He slipped his hands around her waist, hands on her ass as he shoved her forward against him, his mouth rough on her now where before it had been soft. She loved the change in him, how he could go from gentle lover one minute to rough and wicked the next.

"I'd eat you up if I could," he murmured against her lips. "And I don't give a damn if you don't want to talk."

"Once again," she whispered, "the feeling is most definitely mutual."

She squealed when Nate slapped her hard on the backside, escaping and running inside ahead of him, her feet bare and her hair loose. She felt good. Better than good, she felt amazing, like her old self, like there was nothing in the world she couldn't accomplish if she set her mind to it. She'd always had big dreams, to have an art gallery of her own one day, to become one of the most respected women in the art industry once she'd finished her post-grad, and she just needed to find her feet again and make it happen. Nate was fun in the bedroom, but he was also one hell of a businessman, which meant there was more than one thing she could learn from him.

He caught up with her, grabbing her from behind and planting a wet, delicious kiss to her neck. Although right now she was happy with him just teaching her all the bad things he knew. They could talk business another day.

Chapter 10

"STOP!" she called out, so exhausted her legs felt like they were about to collapse beneath her.

Nate spun around, jogging backward as he watched her. "We're almost there."

She groaned. "Has anyone told you what a cruel taskmaster you are?" Faith dropped to the ground, head between her legs. She actually felt like she was about to be sick, which was the last thing she wanted to do with Nate watching her. She could have blamed it on the alcohol in her system, but she'd hardly had a lot to drink, and it was hours ago. Almost twenty hours ago to be exact.

He jogged back toward her then, she could feel the vibrations through the grass, and he blocked out all the sun as he stood towering above her.

"I thought you liked running?"

"Yeah," she scoffed, "for a few miles at a decent pace."

Nate laughed and she snapped her head back up to

glare at him. "Sorry. How about we walk the rest of the way back?"

"You run. I'll walk," she told him, wishing she'd just taken the opportunity to stay at the house and lie in the sun or flick through a magazine. Hell, she'd probably have preferred cleaning the kitchen to keeping up such an insane pace alongside Nate for so damn long.

"I'm used to running with Chase," Nate confessed, holding out a hand to haul her up. She took it, grudgingly, but she still appreciated the hand up. "We're pretty hard on each other, but we've been training together a while."

"Yeah, and I'm the featherweight in comparison. I shouldn't have tried to impress you."

"Darlin', you've already impressed me today. The fact that you kept up for that long like it wasn't killing you?" He dropped a kiss to her forehead and she winced. "What, you don't want me to kiss you anymore?"

She frowned. "No, I don't want you to kiss me when I'm all sweaty and gross."

"Maybe I like the taste of your sweat," he teased, wrapping his arms around her and pushing his pelvis against her. "*Maybe* it turns me on."

"I'm starting to think everything turns you on," she grumbled, but it was hard to stay annoyed with him when he was looking at her like he was about to eat her. The wicked look in his eye almost made her forget all about her burning calves. "Maybe I shouldn't have chosen such a sex maniac as my teacher."

His laugh was almost as wicked as his smile, and his wink made her knees go weak again. She really needed to get a grip on the effect he was having on her.

"What fun would a sex teacher be if he *wasn't*?"

She made a noncommittal sound in her throat and pushed back from him. "Come on; let's get this run over with and then you can make me something to drink. Something cold and alcoholic that'll start to numb me before the pain hits."

"Deal." He held up his hand for a high five, but she just stared at him. "Or not. Come on; let's go slow."

She forced her body into a slow jog beside him and winced. She shouldn't have stopped. Taking the break had only made her body seize up, and she was ready to collapse for the rest of the day. If not the entire month.

Nate was lying on the sofa, stretched out in just a pair of jeans, his hair still wet from showering and a bottle of beer in his hand. He was waiting for Faith to join him, although he was starting to wonder if she'd gotten out of the shower and just fallen straight into bed.

He was about to haul himself up when she appeared, wet hair loose around her shoulders, wearing boxer shorts and a little blue tank. Nate cleared his throat and took another sip of beer, trying not to stare at the fact that she had no bra on and her nipples were hard enough to make them visible. Just the idea of her naked made him hard, a fact he was pleased hadn't been the case until she'd landed on his doorstep. If Sam even knew the thoughts Nate was having about his sister, let alone what he'd done with her . . . He pushed those thoughts from his mind. Right now he was operating on a what-Sam-doesn't-know-won't-kill-him basis, which was only applicable given the fact that Faith had wanted to keep what was happening between them secret, just like he did.

"You still want to murder me?" he asked.

"Do you have another cold beer for me?" she asked back instead of answering him.

"Yep." He motioned to the fridge. "Grab a bottle and come crash with me."

She groaned and did as he'd suggested. "I want to kill you less now that I have beer."

He grinned. "Says the girl who never drinks beer."

"Yeah, I know. But I'm so hot still. And sore." She stretched in front of him, arms reaching for the ceiling and her top riding up high, showing off her flat, tanned stomach.

"Come here," he grumbled, sick of looking without touching.

"I'm not having sex with you," she muttered, lying half on top of him, half on the sofa. "I'm dying here."

"I like you for more than just sex, if you really want to know," he said, stroking her lazily. She might be feeling annoyed-exhausted, but he loved the way working out made him feel. If his body wasn't aching then he hadn't run hard enough, and the fact that he was tired from sex *and* running was enough to keep a smile on his face. Besides, it didn't take him long to recharge. Nate flexed his hand, wincing. The only thing that annoyed him was the fact that his hand hurt like hell when he moved it a certain way after having to deal with Faith's ex. If it wasn't pain-free by morning he'd be taking a trip past his doctor's office to get it checked, but for now Nate was choosing to ignore it.

"Do you like me enough to talk business?" Faith asked.

He shifted his weight so he could look at her properly.

"Are you secretly here to unearth secrets about me? Because I don't give interviews, I don't like journalists, and I sure as hell don't like undercover anyones."

"Nate, I . . ."

He laughed. "Sweetheart, I'm just kidding. Well, I'm not actually, all that was true, but I trust you."

"I just, well, I want to be successful," she admitted. "I want to make something of myself."

"Well, you're talking to the right person."

She scoffed. "Either you're making fun of me or your ego is stupidly big."

Nate leaned closer so he could plant a kiss on her mouth. "Neither. What I meant is that I take success very seriously. Plenty of the businesspeople I deal with might call me an asshole because I'm tough when it comes to the deals I put together, but you'll never hear me telling someone they can't reach the goddamn sky if they make it their goal."

She sighed. "So you wouldn't laugh at me if I said I want to be the most successful female art consultant and trader in Texas?" Her voice was softer than usual, uncertainty clear in her tone.

"Faith, I don't think you're aiming high enough," he said honestly, taking a sip of his beer and watching her do the same.

"Really?"

"There's no reason you can't be better than the best man, for starters, and don't just limit yourself to Texas. Dream big, baby, and don't let anyone stand in your way."

That made her crack up. "Like Cooper-type douche bags, you mean?"

"Hey, he's not going to be bothering you again anytime soon." Nate smiled to himself, pleased that he'd dealt with the situation personally. He'd done what he had to do without going too American Psycho on the guy, and Nate genuinely doubted Faith would ever hear from him again. "Let's just say that if he saw either of us again, he'd cross the street to avoid a confrontation."

She smirked. "Can I ask what you did to him, or do I not want to know?"

Nate shrugged. "I didn't kill him, but I did teach him a lesson." He held up his bottle and clinked it against hers. "To your successful career."

"One day," she muttered. "Right now it's just a dream."

"Quit working at places like Joe's and find a gallery to start out in," Nate suggested. "Offer to work for free if they don't have an opening; learn the ropes from the bottom up. I'm not knocking your degree, because you sure as hell need it and it's incredible how hard you've studied, but if you want to impress people you need to show you have the practical skills, too."

"There's that little issue of money, Nate," she said, moving away from him a little so she could lean against the back of the sofa and tuck her knees up. "I can't work for free, finish off my post-grad, and work somewhere for money to pay my bills, too."

"So stay living here for a while," he said, like it was the most obvious answer in the world. He sipped his beer and kept his eyes on her at the same time, wondering why the hell he'd just said that. Two days ago, hell, *one* day ago he was cursing the fact that he'd let her stay at all, and now he was suggesting she stay longer? *Indefinitely?*

Then again, one day ago they hadn't been sleeping

together, and having her around was a whole lot nicer than he'd expected. His house had always been so strictly off-limits to anyone other than family, which meant his fun with women had been confined to the apartment or hotel rooms. Seeing Faith curled up on his sofa and knowing she'd be crawling into his bed later on was kind of a turn-on.

"You mean that?" she finally asked.

"Yeah. Why the hell not?" Nate kicked his feet up and stretched out. "You keep the house tidy and cook a few meals for us, and in exchange you can live here for as long as you need."

"But—"

"No buts," he insisted. He'd made the decision and he was going to have to live with the consequences of dealing with Sam and any other shit that came his way. "Stay or don't stay, the choice is yours. But if you want a shot at the career you're dreaming about, take the opportunity and don't look a gift horse in the mouth when he's staring straight at you."

"Thank you," she whispered, setting her bottle down and pushing up on her knees so she could shuffle forward.

Nate put his bottle on the floor, less interested in drinking than the beautiful woman approaching him. Her hair was still damp and falling over her shoulders, which had had the enticing effect of wetting the thin material of her cotton tank. Faith's mouth was slightly parted, her eyes on his as she moved even closer.

"I thought we weren't having sex?" he joked, sitting up slightly and reaching for the hem of her top so he could lift it up and over her head.

Faith obliged. "It seems only fair that I thank you for your generous offer."

He chuckled, hands covering her breasts, loving the fullness in his palms.

"So you're going to be my mistress?" he asked, giving up her breasts so he could put his hands around her back and force her forward and back on top of him again.

"Yes," she muttered. "Your mistress that still needs to be taught what she's doing. There's no point being successful if I'm still crap in bed."

His laugh was muffled as her hair fell over his face. "Would you give up on the crap in bed business? You're fucking incredible, and the only reason I'm putting up with you telling me I have to teach you is because I'm too damn selfish to say no."

"What do you propose then?" she whispered, her lips moving against the side of his mouth as she talked.

"I propose," he said, hands on her butt to lock her down hard against him, so she could feel just how interested he was, "that I show you how a man is supposed to look after a woman in bed. Then you'll always have a good benchmark to measure other men against."

She laughed, but he cursed the words he'd just said. He might not want to commit to anything long-term, but the idea of Faith ever being in another man's bed made his head pound so hard it felt like it could explode.

"I'm scared of you even looking at me again," Faith murmured, standing behind Nate as he sat on a chrome and leather stool at the kitchen counter. She dropped a kiss to his neck and wrapped her arms around him.

"Scared of what?" he quipped, closing the lid on his laptop and spinning around in his chair to face her.

"Your appetite," she groaned

Nate kissed her, his lips soft against hers, but it was a slow, sensual kiss rather than the hot, hard lip crushes they'd shared less than an hour ago.

"Want to order in?" he asked.

"Who delivers all the way out here?" she asked, perching on his knee as he held her close with both of his arms around her.

"Plenty of places. I tip well to make it worth their while."

"I'd rather stay in than go out," she admitted.

"Me too. I thought it'd be nice to hang at home for a couple of days. It's been a long few months for me."

"You sure you're not just staying home to avoid seeing my brother?" she asked, only half-teasing. "I like getting my own way, but I hate seeing the two of you fight like that."

"Sam and I will be fine." His voice sounded convincing, but she didn't believe him, not for a second, that he was that confident. "Anyway, I was catching up on some work then, and I recalled a couple of contacts I have in the art world. Granddad has quite a collection, not my taste but incredibly valuable now, but we'd been talking to a few different gallery owners in recent years."

Faith's pulse picked up, her heart beating that little bit too fast. She'd been so unsure about telling Nate in case he didn't think she was capable of fulfilling what she'd dreamed of for so long, but it was starting to seem like the best decision she'd ever made.

"Anyway, to cut a long story short, I've called in a few favors," he said, dropping a kiss into her hair. "I've e-mailed two contacts, mentioned how capable and driven you are, and I've told them to reach out if they hear of anything or if they might need some assistance."

"I don't know what to say." Aside from Sam, no one in her life had ever truly given a damn enough to want to help her out, and she'd sure as hell never had any handouts. So to know that Nate had dropped everything and tried to help her only hours after she'd confessed her career plans to him was amazing.

"Just say thank you," he said. "And agree to Thai takeout."

"I'd agree to eat fried worms right now."

He laughed, a throaty, deep rumble that for some reason reminded her of the noise his Ferrari made. "Well, that would just be stupid. You have to realize that telling people what you want from life is the first way to make them take you seriously. And if people take you seriously, they're more likely to recommend you."

She hugged him again, hardly able to believe that not only was she shacked up in Nate's house, but also she'd already had sex with him more times than she could count in twenty-four hours and now he was giving her business advice. It was a win-win situation if ever she'd been in one.

"You know, I think I'll call in and collect dinner. You mind if I head in to see Granddad for a bit, check he's okay? I'll be back with dinner in less than ninety minutes; I promise."

"Go for it," she said, extracting herself from his lap

and getting a glass so she could pour herself some water. "I've got a few phone calls to catch up on, might even have a quick chat with Sam."

"Yeah, you break the ice before I have to jump into the water with him," Nate muttered.

He stood, his plain grey T-shirt hugging his frame, faded jeans making him casual and sexy as hell. His worn boots were on but not laced up, he had more than a day's worth of dark stubble, and his hair was messy, not to mention the dark shadow around his eye where Sam had punched him. Nate was so damn hot she didn't even know what part of him to admire first.

He kissed her, stubble grazing her chin slightly as he pulled away. "See you soon, gorgeous."

Faith watched him pull on a leather jacket that had been slung over a chair, collecting his keys on the way past. She was under no illusions about what they had—she knew that this was a fun part of her life that she'd never forget in a million years, but it was just fun. Nate was sexy and successful and everything she'd ever admire in a man, but he was also ruthless, and she doubted he'd ever be happy with a woman who wasn't a perfect Stepford wife, at home and popping out his babies. If he ever admitted wanting someone permanent in his life.

Or maybe not. Maybe he'd like the idea of having a permanent girlfriend one day who didn't expect a lot from him. Either way, it wasn't going to be her. She was young now and fun was fine, especially after the relationship she'd just come out of. She'd thought Cooper was a nice guy—he managed the bar; he owned his own home; he'd had a plan. But in the end he'd just shown her why she needed to rely on herself and make her own plans. Nate was different, because she could trust him and she respected him. They might be having sex, but he'd agreed to help her before he knew that anything was going to be happening between them.

Faith reached for her iPhone and checked through her missed calls and texts, leaning against the cool marble of the counter. She'd neglected her girlfriends with everything going on and she owed them phone calls, plus she had to deal with Sam. But first she called her friend Rachel, who'd worked part-time at Joe's with her.

"Hey, gorgeous," Rachel answered after a few rings.

"Hey," Faith replied, dropping onto the sofa and making herself comfortable. "Sorry I've been MIA."

"Rumor has it that Cooper's black eyes and broken nose have something to do with you."

Faith sat back up, pulling a cushion closer and hugging it against her. "You've seen him?"

"Um, yeah, we've seen him. He stormed in here about an hour ago, all pissed off and yelling orders, and said he wasn't going to be back in for a while. He put Fran in charge."

"Hmmm," she mused out loud.

"'Hmmm'? That's all you've got to say? How about doing some explaining?" Rachel demanded. "You guys get in a row, you call it off and disappear, and then he turns up all beaten up. There's definitely a juicy story there."

Faith cleared her throat. "He hit me, Rach. He turned out to be an asshole, so I packed up and left. I don't know what happened to him, but he sure as hell had it coming."

She managed to steer Rachel onto a different topic,

chatted for a bit, then said good-bye. When she looked down, her hands were shaking and she had to sit on them to stop it. Faith knew she shouldn't have cared about Cooper being beaten up, hell, Nate had made it clear that he'd done something, but to know the man she was shacked up with could be so kind and gentle with her and so ruthless with another human being was kind of scary.

Her phone vibrated then and she glanced down to where she'd discarded it and saw it was Sam. She sighed, trying to decide whether to answer or not and deciding she'd be a bitch if she didn't.

"Hi, Sam," she answered.

"Hey. How are you?"

"Good. You?" He sounded way too normal, not anywhere near as angry as she'd expected.

"I just wanted to say that I'm sorry for flipping out last night," he said. "I was out of line, and I shouldn't have—"

"Your girlfriend made you call me, didn't she?" Faith asked, stifling her laugh. "What did she threaten you with?"

"Moving out," he muttered.

"So you actually still want to kill Nate and you're pissed with me, but you can't say anything right now because she's listening?"

He didn't say anything for a long moment. "Yep, pretty much."

At this Faith laughed out loud. "Look, Sam, when I came to Nate, he was the perfect gentleman. Anything that has or hasn't happened between us is because of me, because I've initiated it, so give him a break, okay?"

"I just don't want you to get hurt. I've seen it all before, over and over. Why won't you listen to me?"

"I'm a big girl now, Sam. I'm gonna be fine." She paused. "And from the rumors I'm hearing, someone dealt with my ex. I'm guessing it was Nate, so don't be too hard on him."

"I'll give him that. Someone hurts someone he cares about, he takes matters into his own hands, does his own dirty work."

Faith reached for the TV remote. "I'm going now. Talk soon."

Sam grumbled and said good-bye, and she curled up to flick through channels. She could catch up on all the other gossip from her friends tomorrow. Right now, she was tired and all she wanted to do was shut her eyes. She only hoped Nate would wake her when he got home, because she was still starving hungry and it was all his doing.

Nate had been surfing channels for a while and he'd ended up watching a documentary about wolves. Hardly his usual viewing, but he didn't often just kick back with his feet up, so he wasn't complaining.

"How long have I been out for?" Faith stretched and repositioned herself, curling into him like a cat.

"I arrived home an hour ago. So a while, I guess." He smiled down at her, an unusual sensation running through his body. He wasn't used to feeling content like this with a woman, and it equal parts scared the shit out of him and pleased him. "I couldn't wait, but I've left something of everything for you to try."

Faith's stomach made a noise and they both laughed. "I think I need it."

Nate got up and headed for the table, opening containers. "I got a few different dishes. It's damn good Thai."

Faith smiled as she sat down and he joined her. "How was your granddad?"

"Sometimes, like tonight, he seems like his usual self and all I want to do is get him the hell out of Dodge and back home." Nate shrugged. "Then he loses his breath or the pain comes on so strong and he needs morphine and I realize I'm only kidding myself thinking he'll ever get back here."

Faith reached over and touched Nate's hand. "So this is it for him?"

"That's why he's there now." Nate's voice cracked and he cleared his throat, reaching for a spare pair of chopsticks that had come in the paper bags. "We waited until we couldn't keep him home any longer, and he didn't want to be a burden on us, but I'm starting to think we should just have kitted the ground floor of this place out as a private hospital for him."

"From what Sam's told me, he was like a dad to you." Her voice was soft, as if she wasn't sure whether she should be asking or not.

Nate didn't mind; it wasn't like she was prying. They'd covered a lot of ground since she'd moved in, and he was surprised how much he liked talking to her. Getting information out of him was usually like extracting blood from a stone, but opening up to her wasn't half-bad.

"As far as I'm concerned, he was my father. *Is* my father," Nate said, poking around at some noodles even though he'd already eaten. Faith was using the chopsticks like a pro and watching her eat was making him hungry all over again. "My own dad was an asshole as far as I'm concerned. I mean, who treats their kids like shit after their mom dies, then walks out when his father-in-law offers him money to leave?"

"Your granddad . . ." Faith had stopped chewing.

"Yeah, he saw how our dad was treating us on a daily basis and offered him money in exchange for signing over custody to him," Nate told her. "From what I gather, he didn't need time to think about it."

Faith's mouth had turned down and Nate immediately leaned over to kiss her, smiling at the hotness of her lips when they connected, fresh chili making his mouth tingle as it transferred between them.

"Don't look so sad, sweetheart. I'm long over what happened. There's no me lying on a psychiatrist's couch lamenting over what could have or should have been."

"But you never blamed your granddad?" she asked. "I mean, don't you hate what he did?"

Now it was Nate frowning. "Why would I hate him for it? It's like that adultery Web site for married people. They tried to put the blame on the guy who started it, but he wasn't forcing anyone to participate. He was providing the platform, not coercing anyone. My granddad didn't make my father the way he was, but he did make sure he wasn't around to screw us up, gave him the choice to man up or ship out."

Faith set down her chopsticks, folding her arms and sitting back in her chair. "For starters, I freaking *hate* that Web site and what it did to so many couples, so don't even get me started, but—"

"Like it or hate it, it's not the Web site making people cheat. They were going to cheat anyway; the site just makes it easier and a whole lot more honest," Nate interrupted. "My point is that my dad was an asshole every way you looked at the situation. Offering him an out when he wanted exactly that was the best thing my granddad could have done. He and Grams raised us, and we had this amazing stable family home. The only sad thing that happened was Grams dying, and our realizing our dad really didn't give a crap, because he never once reached out to contact us. He didn't even bother to come to her funeral, and if he comes to Granddad's I'll escort him off the property with my shotgun."

Faith had picked up her chopsticks again, but she was picking now rather than eating with the gusto she had been earlier.

"Do you still remember your mom?"

"Yes," Nate answered immediately. "I remember the smell of her shampoo and the way she used to turn and look at me. I loved her hair, curling up with her before bed, and listening to her read. I was the oldest, so those moments meant everything to me. I had her for longer than the others did, so I remember a lot more."

Faith's expression was hard to read, but the fact that she had tears in her eyes wasn't escaping him. She'd lost her mom, too; he knew all about that because Sam had shared everything with him. He knew how badly she'd hurt, that it had affected her worse than it had Sam, and maybe it was one of the reasons he was telling her what he was. Only his mom had been his world, would never have left them if there was anything she could have done about it.

"I think there's a reason we understand each other so well. We've both lost a lot."

Her smile was sad. "Yeah, except your mom sounds like an angel and she probably would have traded anything in the world to have more time with you boys." Faith shrugged and speared a prawn with one chopstick. "Mine couldn't leave fast enough once she'd gotten us through to what she called an *independent* age."

"You were only thirteen. I remember," he said, wishing he hadn't even opened up to Faith, because then they wouldn't both be dredging up painful memories.

"So am I guessing correctly that the reason you're so happy being no strings attached is because you're scared of being hurt by a woman again?"

Nate chuckled. "What is this? Therapy? I thought I told you I didn't need that shit."

"No, just putting the pieces together. You loved her, it broke your heart, and you don't ever want to feel pain like that again. Am I right?"

"Maybe," he said with a shrug, not about to tell her that she'd just given him the best, and only, therapy session of his life and that she was bang on the money with her diagnosis. "Except for the fact that the pain I'm feeling over losing my granddad is pretty close to what I felt as a boy losing my mom. The pain is just as real, only I should know how to process it better."

She laughed, but it was a quiet, pained laugh. "You know, we're not so different, you and I. My mother leaving the way she did taught me to never let anyone tell me what I want, to never let anyone walk all over me or make me feel like second best. I might not have stayed entirely true to that, given my most recent bad choice in men, but it's only made my resolve stronger."

Nate reached out to touch her arm, trailing his fingers across her skin absentmindedly. "But you will, one day, meet someone you let yourself fall in love with. You'll have children, be happy, all those things."

Faith smiled. "Maybe. Maybe not." She smiled at him before showing interest in the takeout again. "It's not what I'm going to let define me, Nate. I want to be my own person, not compromise on what I need and want. But yeah, I like the idea of finding a man who'll let me be me, being a mom if that's what I want someday, but not because it's expected of me."

"And you'll find that man, darlin'; you will."

Her smile was infectious. "But right now, you'll do," she said with a laugh, climbing into his lap. "Fun, fun, and more . . . *fun.*"

Nate kissed her lips, his mouth pressed to hers in a lip-lock that she hoped wouldn't end for hours. He wanted her, so badly that he almost wanted to promise her more. But that would be a promise he couldn't keep. And Nate King never made a promise he couldn't keep.

"I've got to admit that you've kind of surprised me," Faith mused, pulling back a little so she could look into his eyes, her hand cupping his cheek. "It makes me wonder whether you let anyone else see this side of you."

Nate looked back at her, into beautiful brown eyes that seemed to see straight into his soul. "The truth? No. I don't." He stroked her hair. "There's something about you, Faith, and I don't know what the hell it is, but I like it."

She let him draw her closer again. "You're nowhere

near as tough and scary as you look on the outside sometimes."

"Ha," he grunted, "you just haven't been on my bad side yet."

And he doubted she ever would be.

Chapter 11

"HONEY, I'm home!" Nate called out, cracking himself up. He was so far from the kind of guy who'd ever imagined saying that when he got home from work at the end of the day that it never failed to make him laugh that he said it every day now. "Faith?" he called out when she didn't reply.

"In the bedroom!" she called out.

Nate took the stairs two at a time, following her voice. "What're you doing up here?" He half-expected her to be lying on the bed waiting for him to join her, which made him hard just thinking about it. "I hope you haven't been waiting for me too long. I had a late meeting and—"

He stopped in the open doorway to find his bed littered with clothes and Faith standing in her underwear. She threw her hands in the air when she saw him. "He called me. The guy you reached out to told a colleague of his, and they want me to come in tomorrow."

Nate smiled and held out his arms, frowning when

she completely ignored him. She had her hands on her
hips, staring at the strewn clothes, her breasts way too
good to ignore all pushed up in a black lace bra. And
the panties that matched made him want to throw her
back on the bed just so he could slowly strip them off
her, sliding them down her tanned, toned legs.

He decided not to wait for her and crossed the distance
between them, reaching out to touch the smooth, delicate skin of her torso, fingertips light on her stomach.
"How about we discuss this further. In bed."

She sighed. "Nate, this is serious."

"So am I, baby," he whispered in her ear, pushing his
pelvis into her backside and wrapping his arms around
her from behind. "Deadly."

"Nate! Your belt buckle," she complained, wriggling
away from him.

He only let her go enough to unbuckle his belt, using
one hand to tug it from the loops and drop it to the floor.
"You're so sexy when you get all flustered."

She groaned and fought to get out of his arms,
squirming around so that she ended up facing him,
palms to his chest. Her hair was pulled up into a messy
ponytail and it took every inch of his willpower not to
reach up and yank the tie out so her hair was tumbling
down his shoulders just how he liked it.

"Nate, I have to figure out what to wear. This could
be my one and only chance to impress them."

"They'll be impressed," he said, not ready to give up
just yet. He kissed her, slowly, gently, just how she
usually liked it. "How could anyone not be impressed
with you?" he asked when he finally pulled his lips away.

"Can you just sit down over there and take a look at

what I'm thinking of wearing?" she pleaded, stepping back and reaching for his hands to tug him over to the chair.

"I was thinking we should celebrate," he suggested, winking at her, then laughing when he got absolutely no reaction. It was a first; she was usually just as up for it as he was, which was saying something.

"Just sit and watch," she said, pushing him back so he fell down into the chair.

It made him laugh and he decided to just do as he was told. "Fine. Show me all the outfits, do a twirl in each one, and I'll tell you what to wear."

Faith bent over the bed, her G-string-clad butt enough to make him groan. Why did she do things like that to him?

"So this one is kind of my nerdy but sexy look. I just don't want to look slutty and . . ."

All he heard was the word "slutty," the rest of what she was saying drowning out as he watched her zip herself into the black pencil skirt and then slip the cute black top over her head. The neckline wasn't particularly low, but her breasts were so high that he still got a pretty good view of her cleavage.

"So?" she demanded, slipping on a pair of plain black heels. "What do you think?"

"I think it'd look better off," he admitted.

"Nate!"

"Sorry." He held his hands up in the air. "I'm just finding it hard seeing you get dressed when I'm usually up here getting you *undressed*. It's not the natural order of the world."

Faith threw her hands up in the air. "I just don't want

to screw this opportunity up, Nate. It's the first step on turning my dream into a reality."

"Come here," he said, opening his arms and not breaking eye contact with her. "Come here," he repeated. "Promise I'll be good."

She finally did, dropping into his lap and slipping her arms around his neck. Her head fell against his chest as he leaned back, content in his arms. Nate dropped a kiss into her hair.

"You'll look beautiful in whatever you wear, sweetheart. And they'll love you. How could they not?"

"I don't have the same confidence in myself that you do. I wasn't the one born with . . ." Her voice trailed off.

Nate hugged her tighter, not about to push her away because of what he'd known she was about to say. He'd heard it all before and it wasn't like she was trying to offend him.

"A silver spoon in his mouth?" he offered.

"Something like that," she mumbled against his shirt. "Sorry. I didn't mean it to be cruel."

"I've heard it all before; don't sweat it." Nate ran his hand up and down her back. "But I'll tell you, just like I've always told everybody else, that I might have been born into money, but it was never my right. I've worked hard for everything, and I will continue to have to work hard to keep our businesses profitable. Nothing in this life comes easy; it's just that some of us have more opportunities to seize than others, and some of us start with a leg up."

She snuggled closer, her legs tucked up so that he was completely cradling her. "The last thing I meant to do was offend you after you've been so good to me."

Nate chuckled. "I'm made from tough stuff, sugar. It'll take more than one offhand comment to piss me off. Now how about you get all this stuff back in the closet and I'll go down and pour us a drink, make us some dinner."

That got her attention. "You're going to make dinner? Like in the kitchen?"

"You don't need to sound so shocked. I've been a bachelor a long time."

"A bachelor with a Mrs. T to look after you and keep the freezer stocked with delicious food for you to heat."

He pushed her, making her laugh but catching her before she actually fell. "I'll have you know I can grill a mean steak, and Chloe said she dropped some around and popped them in the fridge earlier today."

Faith flicked him on the shoulder with her forefinger and stood over the bed looking down at her clothes. "So just steak and nothing else then?" she teased.

"Well, I season it pretty well." He jumped up and undid a couple of buttons of his shirt, slapping her bare butt cheeks as he passed on his way to the bathroom.

"What happened to getting the steak on the grill and my wine poured?"

"Geez, woman, this is why I don't usually open my house up to the ladies. Enough with the questions!"

He walked into his closet and undressed, pulling on a pair of jeans and T-shirt. He hung up his trousers and took off his Rolex, putting it with the rest of his collection in his top drawer. When he sauntered back out he stopped and watched Faith. She was beautiful. Jaw-droppingly, goddamn beautiful, but it was like she still had no idea the effect she had on him. She'd taken her hair out now, the band around her wrist instead of her hair, and it fell forward over both shoulders. He watched as she reached for it, twisting it and pushing it away, top teeth pushed into her lower lip as she studied a jacket that she'd reached for.

He was in seriously dangerous territory with her. On the other hand, he was damn worried that she'd change her mind and end up like virtually every other woman he'd dated, telling him when things came to an end that she'd expected more, that she thought she'd be the one to change him, and probably hating him for it. And he did care for Faith, cared about her more than he'd ever cared about a woman who'd been in his bed before, but he wasn't going to let himself love her. He couldn't.

No matter how he felt for her, how selfishly he wanted her all to himself, he wasn't going to pretend like he could offer her what she needed from a man. Faith needed to be loved and cared for unconditionally, needed a man who wasn't so damaged that he had made it his life's mission never to be vulnerable again or let anyone hurt him. He didn't trust easily and he sure as hell didn't want to be anyone's husband, and Faith deserved her cake and all the trimmings.

"Dollar for your thoughts?" Faith's soft, kind voice jolted him back to reality.

"I was just thinking how gorgeous you look in your underwear." It wasn't a lie—up until that moment it was all he'd been thinking about.

"How about I promise to show it to you again later if you get that steak on the grill?"

"I love the way you think," he replied, grinning and waiting for her to pull a sweatshirt over her head and slip into her jeans, before hooking his arm around her neck and kissing her cheek. "I'll help you put all that away later. Right now, I need to unwind over a cold drink with you."

"Hard to believe I've been your concubine for over a week now," she said, arm slipped around his waist as they went sideways through the door, then stayed stuck together like glue as they descended the stairs.

"Sure is."

And no matter what he wanted to tell himself, what he wanted to pretend, he'd miss her like hell once she was gone. But he wasn't interested in clipping the wings of any bird, let alone one who was just coming into her own like Faith was.

"Sam came by to see you today."

Nate groaned. "Now I really need that drink."

"He knows you've been avoiding him." Faith leaned against the counter as he took out a beer and popped the top, taking a long gulp before setting it down and taking out the wine she liked. "He said it was time the two of you had a talk, man-to-man."

"I'm not avoiding him," Nate insisted.

"Yes, you are."

He poured her wine, slid her the glass, then downed at least half of his beer. "I just don't know what to say to him. I mean, 'I'm fucking your sister, but she likes it' probably isn't what he wants to hear right now."

Faith burst out laughing, wiping away tears from her cheeks she was laughing so hard. "Nate, just let him be pissed off with you for a bit. Listen to him rant and rave, then tell him what he needs to hear."

"And what is that, exactly?" he asked.

"That you won't hurt me. That I'm the one far more likely to hurt your poor heart than vice versa."

"Oh really?"

She laughed. "Look, we both know what this is, and we both want to spare Sam from being hurt. So what does it matter what we say so long as it keeps us all happy?"

"Let me get this right," Nate grumbled. "I thought we were keeping the two of us under wraps? Now you want me to confess my sins after I told him I'd stay away from you?"

Her smile was contagious as she grinned at him. "We are. I just don't think we can completely pull the wool over Sam's eyes. He's going to know something is going on. Will already, in fact."

"Fine." Nate pulled open the fridge and took out the steaks, wrapped in brown paper and with a smiley face drawn on the front from his sister-in-law. It made him smile, which only reminded him just how much he was starting to enjoy having so many women permanently in his life. It wasn't a shock to him that he loved female company, just a shock that he'd opened himself up so readily to his brothers' wives, and now Faith.

"How about I make a salad to go with that," Faith suggested, trailing her fingers across his back as she passed.

Nate took out some utensils and headed for the grill, just outside the side door. "I was hoping you'd say that."

He walked outside to the sound of Faith's laughter, shaking his head at how easily she'd managed to rub off on him. After he spent so long putting up walls around himself, it had been damn easy for a few particular women to find an opening and just wander on in.

Faith ran her hands down her skirt, not used to having sweaty palms. She was seated in the office, waiting, having been shown in by an older woman with a wide smile. It had settled Faith for a moment, until she'd been left alone.

"You must be the amazing young woman Nate told me about."

Faith blew out a breath and rose, game face on. "Faith Mendes. Thank you so much for taking the time to meet me."

The owner of the gallery was probably fifty, maybe older, but his head of thick silver hair made it hard for her to pick. She liked that he held her eye contact, and she calmed down as she sat.

"I took the time to look through the gallery first. I love some of your contemporary pieces."

He raised his eyebrows. "Which ones caught your eye?"

She recognized the challenge, knew he wanted to catch her out in case she was bluffing. "I'm a huge fan of Eddie Martinez, so naturally his piece caught my eye. The colors he's used in his recent collection are stunning."

"Any other favorites?"

"Contemporary painters?" She smiled. "That's tough, I could rattle off names all day, but Katherine Bernhardt from Canada and Zeng Fanzhi would be two who always surprise me with their forms and textures."

"You know your art." He chuckled. "I didn't think Nate would personally recommend just anybody, but now I know for sure."

Faith maintained her smile, felt like it was going well.

"So what are your plans after you graduate? Where to next?"

She watched as he settled back in his chair. "I'm not going to deny that I want to live and work in New York, at least for a time, but I want to learn everything I can and I would really like the opportunity to do that here first." She paused, not wanting to sound desperate, wanting to portray confidence. "I'm a hard worker and I'm not afraid to put the hours in, and I'm impressed with the art you have here."

Faith dug her nails into her palm, still smiling, waiting for his response.

"Sometimes things happen for a reason. It just so happens I was about to start advertising for an intern, but now that I've met you I'm not sure that I need to."

She couldn't stop the grin that spread across her face. "Really?"

"Look, you clearly know what you're talking about, you have genuine passion, and you seem like a capable, driven young woman. Not to mention the fact that your knowing the King family might help me in making some sales to Nate or the old man!"

"So do I have the job?"

He stood and held out his hand. "Yes, Faith. You have the job."

Nate was walking alongside Sam, dressed down in jeans and boots. He'd decided to work from home for the day,

getting his assistant to reschedule a few things and e-
mail through everything he needed, and he'd decided
that Faith had been right about him catching up with her
brother. He was on the ranch working horses with Ryder
all day, and Nate had headed down to the round pens to
talk to Sam before he started. Before this they'd never
gone more than a week without chatting, and when Nate
was home he was always making sure to spend a few
minutes catching up with his friend.

"Are you booked to do some handling with the
yearlings?" Nate asked, stopping when Sam did to lean
on the railings and look down to where the younger
horses were grazing.

"Yeah, I'll go over the basics again with them soon,"
Sam said, hand raised to shield his eyes from the already
bright sunshine. "One of the colts is a bit of a handful,
but the others are fairly quiet this year."

Nate nodded, scuffing his boot back and forth into the
wood. He propped his elbows against the rail. "I appreciate the fact that you haven't tried to give me a black
eye yet again."

Sam looked sideways, his expression suddenly fierce.
"Don't bring up my sister, Nate. Just don't."

"So you'd rather pretend like nothing was going on?"
Nate asked, grimacing when Sam balled his fists.

"Whatever the hell is going on between the two of
you, I don't want to know about it. I've warned her away
from you until I'm blue in the fucking face, I've told you
not to go near her, and look where it's gotten me." Sam
groaned and leaned deeper into the fence, head down
like he was trying to catch his breath after a run. "I
just . . ." He pushed up and looked at Nate, eyes burning

into him. "She's my sister, Nate, and I've been the only one looking out for her for so goddamn long that it kills me to think I don't have any control over protecting her right now. That I can't tell her what to do."

Nate nodded and held out his hand. "Sam, you know I never break a promise, and I'm telling you now that I will never, ever, hurt your sister. You've seen me be bad, so I get why me being with her scares the shit out of you, but it ain't going to happen here. Aside from the fact that she's got bigger aspirations that don't involve her staying here with me, I'd never hurt her."

Sam hesitated, then clasped his hands together like he was trying to stop them from smacking into Nate. "I don't approve, okay? But I can't exactly slam my fist into your head every time I see you, and I doubt Faith would like me to keep her on a leash and tell her what she can and can't do."

"So we're good?" Nate asked. "Or as good as we can be given the circumstances?"

"Just don't talk about her to me. I don't even want to hear you say her name," Sam muttered. "Ever."

"Deal." Nate slapped his friend on the shoulder and received a grimace in reply.

"Too soon, Nate. Way too soon."

He backed off and held up his hands. "How about we stick to talking horses? And ranching?" Nate joked.

His phone rang and he pulled it from his pocket, pushing it straight back in when he saw the caller ID. When he glanced at Sam he knew he didn't stand a chance of lying and saying it was just someone he couldn't be bothered talking to.

"It was Faith, wasn't it?"

Nate nodded. "Yes."

"You suddenly think it's okay to send my sister to voice mail?"

Fuck. "Sam, man, I . . ." He was about to laugh, thinking it was a joke, when he saw the look on Sam's face and wasn't so sure he could read his friend after all.

"You know what, just give me a sec," Nate muttered, wondering how the hell he could go from thinking of Sam like a brother and knowing exactly what he was thinking most of the time to feeling like he was treading water around the guy. "Hey, Faith," Nate said when she picked up after a couple of rings. "I'm just hanging out with Sam."

"I got the job," she said, far too calmly and then screaming down the line so loudly he had to pull it away from his ear. "Nate, he hired me on the spot and he offered me a paid type of intern position. Just part-time, but I'm so excited."

"Baby, I'm so proud of you," Nate said, genuinely pleased for her. Then he saw the grimace Sam shot him and he wished he hadn't called her that. He cleared his throat. "I knew they were going to love you. What time are you home?"

She nattered away for a bit, telling him blow by blow how she'd excelled when he'd asked her about specific paintings he had on display as they'd walked around after the formal interview, until Nate finally managed to say good-bye to her and turn his attention back to Sam.

"What was she so excited about?"

Nate grinned. "Her new job. I put the word out and

she got an interview at a gallery about forty minutes from here."

Sam groaned. "You helped her get the job she wanted?" he asked.

"Yeeesss," Nate replied, saying the word slowly so that it dragged on. "Is that a bad thing?" He honestly didn't know what was going to piss Sam off right now.

"No, I just didn't want her to owe you anything."

"She doesn't owe me anything, Sam. I would have helped her out without having—"

"You mention sleeping with her and you'll have more than a broken nose to worry about," Sam threatened, interrupting him.

Nate nodded. "How about we just head down and I watch you work the horses for a bit, huh?"

Sam grunted again. "Fine."

They walked in silence for a bit, the only noise the sound of birdsong and the odd whinny of a horse. The grass was yellow and parched underfoot, already drying out despite the hottest of summer yet to hit.

"Mornin'!"

Nate looked up at the sound of Ryder's call. He waved back to his brother. "Thought I'd come down and say hi."

Ryder walked over and fell into step beside them at the same time as Sam took a few steps sideways and launched himself over the rails of the round pen. He'd been quiet ever since the phone call, just a curt nod and hello to Ryder.

"He still upset that you're playing house with his little sister?" Ryder asked.

"Yeah, you could say that."

"So what're you really doing working from home today? You hardly ever work from home anymore." Ryder had a piece of straw sticking out the side of his mouth, flicking it back and forth with his teeth as he watched Sam halter one of the horses.

"Faith wanted me to talk to Sam, so I can check that off my to-do list," Nate said, stretching out. "And we're looking like it's all go with the oil drilling, too. Granddad was right, it's just where he told them to start, and I'm going on-site to go through everything shortly."

Ryder hooked his boot on the rail. "Smart old bastard. When are we going to learn that he's always right?"

They both laughed, before the conversation turned more somber. Nate preferred to keep his head buried in the sand over Granddad, but talking to Faith about him had made the whole situation even more real. Made Nate realize that he needed to open up instead of keeping everything inside when it wasn't going to help him any.

"I think it's almost time, Ryder."

His brother turned to face him, mouth pulled down at the corners now. "Yeah, I know."

They stood in silence for a while before Nate finally figured out what the hell to say. "You told him everything you need to?" he asked. "I mean, I just don't want any of us to have any regrets. We need to talk this shit through."

"I've told him what I need to tell him," Ryder replied.

"Me too. I'm gonna miss him like hell." Nate slapped Ryder on the back and took a step backward. "Better get back to the office. I've got a ton of work to catch up on before the oil guys show up later."

"Want me to head over when they arrive?" Ryder asked.

"Yeah, good idea. Then we can catch up for a beer later and talk through some things."

Ryder laughed. "Sounds serious."

"I just want to make sure we're all on the same page," he said. "I don't want any feuds over the years, no bullshit that could come between us. If we're drilling, I want to make it as un-intrusive as possible, make sure it's not going to disrupt anything either you or Chase are already doing. We need to figure out the logistics since it's all coming together faster than any of us expected."

"Sounds good, Brother," Ryder said, holding up his hand as Nate walked a few more steps backward. "Oh, and before I forget, Chase wants to know why you haven't been running with him. Thinks you're too scared that he's gonna beat your ass."

Nate chuckled. "I've been working out, don't you worry, just not with Chase."

Ryder shook his head and Nate waved out to Sam. "See you around, Sam!" he called out.

His friend raised his hand but didn't look up from what he was doing, his concentration on the horse he was working absolute. And that's why he was the best damn horseman around, because when he picked up the lead rope and started work for the day nothing broke his concentration. Not even thoughts of his friend banging his sister.

Faith was still on cloud nine. She'd been working at the gallery for a week, and even though she was exhausted, she was loving it. Her only worry was how she was going to keep up working with finishing her final papers, but she was just going to have to make it happen. If she had to go without sleep for a week or a month, so be it.

"Hey, gorgeous."

She sighed and leaned back into Nate as his arms circled her from behind. "Hey to you, too."

He kissed her neck, his lips warm and way too tempting against her skin. Just as it always did, a few kisses and his hard body against hers started to make her hum, and she turned in his arms, taking the opportunity to scoop her hands around his neck and pull him down for a kiss full on the mouth.

"I'm getting used to this," he muttered as they touched foreheads, staring into each other's eyes. "And you know what?"

She kissed him again, muttering against his lips, "What?

"It scares the hell out of me." He wrapped his arms around her. "This wasn't supposed to feel like this."

Faith hugged him tight, too. "I know. We've kind of fallen into a happy little routine."

"Yeah, and I'm advertising for another housekeeper already."

Faith pushed back. "You what? But that wasn't part of the—"

"Relax," he said, chuckling as he dragged her by the hand into his office on the ground floor near the front door. "You're too busy to worry about the house, and to be honest, I wasn't really comfortable with you feeling like you had to do it. This way you can focus on the work you care about."

Heat started to rise in her body and her hands trembled. She tucked them into fists so tight that her fingernails dug into her palms. "But Nate, that's part of our deal. That I'm supposed to do the housework in exchange for living here. I don't want to freeload."

He frowned and let go of her hand when they reached the leather sofa in his office. She dropped into it and he crossed the room and poured himself a whiskey, raising an eyebrow at her. Faith shook her head.

"What does it matter? I can afford a housekeeper, Faith, and it means it's something you don't have to worry about."

He took a sip from the heavy crystal glass he was holding and suddenly she was wishing she'd said yes to one. This was not how things were meant to be happening. They'd had a deal. She wasn't supposed to be freeloading off Nate; she was supposed to be keeping the house tidy and making their meals in exchange for her staying there.

"That deal we had is bullshit anyway," he continued. "We're way past sex with benefits, aren't we?"

"Are we?" she asked, her voice shaking. "I know I like you, Nate, and we're having fun, but this . . ."

His expression hardened, the steely glint of his eyes reminding her of the man she'd seen him be in front of others. The ruthless businessman, formidable, the way most other people saw him.

"You're right, Faith. This is just a temporary thing. *Fun.*" The word was cold as ice when he said it. "But you don't need to worry about cleaning the house. Surely what we do in the bedroom more than makes up for the rent you don't pay."

Faith felt as if he'd just slapped her across the face. Her voice caught in her throat, but she forced herself to reply, wasn't going to let him get away with being an asshole to her. "Is that how you think of me, Nate? As if I'm a prostitute?" Where the hell had this come from? She'd arrived home happy and carefree, only to walk into an argument she hadn't seen coming.

His lips had been drawn in a tight line, cold and unforgiving, but the moment the words left her mouth he frowned and immediately put down his drink. "No." He slammed his hand into his desk, cursing as he did so. "Fuck, Faith. No." Nate shook his head and came toward her. "I'm sorry. I'm so sorry; I should never have said that."

She raised her chin, defiant. "You damn well should be sorry." She knew what mean men were like, how cruel a man could be when he didn't get his own way, and she wasn't going to let Nate get away with it.

"I didn't mean it, Faith. You know I don't think of you that way." He dropped into the sofa beside her and reached to cup her cheek, but she turned away. "I just meant that the money wasn't a big deal to me and I don't expect you on your hands and knees scrubbing the floor when you've got so much else going on. Is it so wrong that I want to look after you?"

"We said we'd do this while it was fun, Nate, and not a moment longer." Her anger was still there, silently simmering from what he'd said.

He grabbed her hand when he couldn't touch her face, smoothing his fingers over her skin, then lifting her hand and pressing a kiss to her palm and then the delicate part of her wrist that he knew was so sensitive for her.

"You've done something to me, Faith," he admitted. "The idea of not having you here pisses me off so much that I want to smack something." He frowned when she raised her brows. "As in my desk again. Not you," he assured her.

"What happened to not wanting to get close to anyone?" she asked, bracing herself for his answer, not wanting to have this conversation with him even though she knew they had to have it.

"I'm not asking you to marry me, Faith. I'm just saying that what we have has been . . ."

"Fun," she said for him, repeating the word, needing to believe it. "We've been having fun. We've lived in a little bubble of fun and sex and food and no commitment. That's why this feels so good. *That's* why it's worked."

He reached for her face again and she let him. "Whatever the hell we might have had hasn't finished yet," he told her, stroking her face so gently it almost erased all the thoughts rushing through her mind, all the worries. "Is it so bad that I want you in my bed?"

She let him kiss her, her body stirring as it always did when his lips melted against hers. "I can't fall in love with you, Nate," she whispered when they finally separated.

He smiled, all of the coolness she'd seen reflected in his eyes before replaced with the kindest, warmest gaze she'd ever felt trained on her. "I know. And I can't fall for you, either. I love having you here, but I can't offer you what you deserve."

Her heart started to pound, a roaring sound in her ears so loud it was like being at the beach and listening

to the fiercest of waves crashing down. Maybe she
wanted him to love her; maybe she'd tried to hold back,
push him away, because she'd wanted him to take her
into his arms and tell her that he had fallen for her hard.
She sucked it back, told herself not to be so stupid. She'd
given up on fairy tales being true years ago, had seen
the realities of relationships that weren't meant to be,
and if she admitted to wanting more from Nate then she
was as stupid as her mother had been.

"You sound so sure about what I deserve, Nate, but
what about you?"

His smile was sad. "All I know is that I don't deserve a woman like you, Faith. Because there'll always
be a part of me that I have to hold back, to protect
myself."

"Hurting is better than never loving, isn't it?" she
asked, wondering why the hell she was asking him these
questions when she should have been happy that he still
only wanted to have fun. That it was no more than . . .
fun.

"If you've hurt the way I have, felt pain the way I
have," Nate started, standing up and pacing over to his
desk again and downing the rest of his whiskey. "Hell,
I don't know, Faith. When it comes to getting close to
someone, I'm damaged goods and I always will be." He
stared at her. "Why are we even having this fucking conversation?"

She stood and followed him, taking the glass that he'd
offered before and pouring herself a generous whiskey.
Faith wasn't one for drinking straight spirits, but she did
it anyway, closing her eyes as they watered from the
burn.

"I've loved being with you, Nate."

He grimaced. "Why does this sound like good-bye all of a sudden?"

She smiled and finished her drink, throat on fire as she walked around his desk, discarding her glass and slipping her arms around him. "It's not good-bye; it's just us reminding ourselves that this is a finite thing," she said, tipping back to look up at him. "How about we stop talking about how screwed up we both are about commitment and just keep having fun a bit longer?"

He grunted as she nipped his jawline, playfully biting him. "Be careful, little wolf."

Faith laughed. "Said the big bad one?"

Nate's mouth closed over hers, his kisses just what she needed. They didn't need to ruin things by talking about what they couldn't have, and she didn't need to admit to herself that the past month had been one of the happiest of her life. This was Nate. Her brother's best friend, the guy who never settled down, the man she'd lusted after for so long and had just wanted to have filthy dirty sex with. She'd never meant to fall in love with him. She'd never meant to think about a future with him.

Nate's kisses became more insistent, his mouth hot and heavy as his hands ran up and down her body, fingers suddenly working on the zip at the back of her skirt, pushing her back onto his desk.

"Nate!" she moaned.

"Fancy being my naughty secretary?" he asked, eyes shining with heat as he stared down at her.

"Nate, you in here?"

Faith jumped at the sound of a female voice in the

house, way too close for comfort. She wriggled off the desk, struggling as Nate tried to manhandle her *back* onto it.

"Nate!"

"It's just Hope," Nate whispered in her ear.

Faith glared at him. "I don't need your sister-in-law seeing you molest me!" she muttered.

She quickly righted herself, kicking Nate's leg with the point of her stiletto on her way back off the desk.

"In here!" Nate called out, winking at Faith and making a grab for her again.

"Oh, sorry, am I interrupting?" Hope asked, eyes wide as she saw Nate standing with his hands spread, palm down on the desk, and Faith trying to tuck her blouse back into her skirt.

"Yes," Nate drawled.

"No!" Faith shot daggers at him. "No, you're not interrupting anything."

Hope smiled, glancing between the two of them as if she knew exactly what they'd been up to. "It was you I was looking for anyway," she said, ignoring Nate. "Chloe and I are going out for a few drinks. The boys are having a meeting at our place, so we've told them they can put the kids to bed and have a few quiet beers while we go out and have some fun for once. Wanna come?"

Faith glanced at Nate and he shot her a smile. "I was about to tell you that I was heading over to have a beer with the guys, before you went and distracted me."

She blushed, the heat rising into her cheeks. "I'd love to join you. Do I have time to freshen up?"

"You sure do." Hope grinned. "And it's about time

we all had some fun together, instead of Nate keeping you tucked away all to himself."

"So half an hour? An hour?" Faith asked, refusing to look over at Nate again for fear of seeing the familiar glint in his eye that told her exactly what he wanted to do to her.

"No rush. We have to get the kids dinner and I'll take Harrison over to Chloe's. He can go down there. Then I want to get ready." Hope grinned. "Between being a mom and a vet, I don't exactly get the chance to get all dolled up very often."

"I'll come over with Nate, then?" Faith asked.

"Perfect, see you soon."

Hope left and Faith turned back to Nate, backing away when he stalked toward her. "No," she insisted, shaking her head.

Nate pounced, launching forward and grabbing for her. Faith spun around and tried to run, but he had her, throwing her down on the sofa and slamming his hard body down on top of hers.

"You're not going anywhere yet," he mumbled against her lips.

"I have to go get ready," she protested, trying to wiggle away from him and not even moving an inch.

"Just let me get to second base then," he whispered. "We don't need to go all the way."

She laughed at his old-fashioned terminology, deciding to just give in to him, because resisting him was futile when he was so strong and determined, especially when her body was betraying her by wanting to grind into him. She could pretend all she liked, but she didn't really ever want to turn him down. "I don't even know what second base is these days."

"Then just lie back and let me show you."

Faith should have said no, pushed him away. She loved that Nate was big and strong, that his body was heavy over hers, that he could lift her as if she were no more than a featherweight. He might be holding her down, but if she told him to let go he would do so immediately. But what were a few minutes of play before she headed upstairs to change? If they were only on limited time together, she needed to make the most of every second.

"I can't believe we're the ones at home looking after the kids and they're out on the town," Ryder grumbled.

Nate laughed. "Missing the single life?"

Ryder shot him a filthy look. "Let me think. Do I wish I was still partying all the time instead of coming home every day to the most beautiful goddamn woman in the world? Not to mention a kid who melts my heart every time I look at her? Ah, that would be a definite 'no.' "

"Yet you want to moan about being the one to stay home tonight?" Nate said dryly.

"He's just scared shitless that Chloe's out on the town without him and other guys could be hitting on her," Chase said. "They all looked smokin' hot tonight."

Ryder downed his beer and stood up. "That's it; I'm going. They shouldn't be out on their own."

"They're grown women, Ryder, not little girls in need of a big bad guy to protect them," Nate said, flipping the top on his beer and sitting down at the table across from

Chase. "Besides, it's nice to just hang out, the three of us. Like old times."

"You've got no idea, Nate," Ryder growled out. "One day when you finally get rid of the rocks in your head and actually let someone crack open that rock-solid heart of yours, you'll get it."

"What, so suddenly because I'm not married means I don't know how to protect a woman or want to care for her?"

"Well, do you?" Ryder asked. "Because you've got a pretty awesome fricking woman living under your roof, right now and you're still giving us that bullshit about not wanting to commit."

"Easy," Nate warned, leaning deeper into the chair and trying to keep his cool. He'd thought coming here would mean some time not thinking about Faith.

"What, I can't bring up Faith? She's been living on the ranch for the better part of a month now, Nate, and she's out with our wives tonight." Ryder shrugged. "Seems pretty stupid that we have to act like she doesn't exist."

"I said back off, Ryder," Nate growled.

"Knock it off, you two," Chase interrupted, standing up and giving them a sharp stare. "You okay, sweetie?"

All the anger Nate had been feeling toward Ryder disappeared the moment he turned around and saw Harrison standing there with his worn rabbit hanging from his hand.

"Daddy, can you come cuddle me?"

Chase was already around the table and bending to scoop his boy up. It still amazed Nate that his brother had taken to parenting so readily. He hadn't even known he had a son until almost a year ago, and now he was married and in full-on daddy mode. They'd bonded immediately and Chase loved hanging out with his son, spending as much time as he could showing his son the ropes around the ranch, how to ride, just enjoying being a father.

"You guys kiss and make up. No fists flying while I'm gone," Chase warned, carrying Harrison back to bed. He had his legs and arms looped around Chase, eyes already shut now, his head against his dad's chest. Harrison looked almost too big to be cuddled like that, but for his sake Nate hoped he didn't realize it for a long time yet.

"Sorry," Ryder said, holding his beer up to clink against Nate's.

"Yeah, me too," Nate said, touching bottles. "I can't help it."

"I get it," his brother said. "How about we just let you simmer about Faith and agree not to talk about the girls tonight?"

"Sounds good to me."

Ryder jumped up and grabbed a bag of potato chips, ripping them open and pouring them into a bowl before heading back to the table.

"Fancy." Nate chuckled. "Don't think I've ever seen you use a dish before. You were always more of an eat from the bag and guzzle milk from a carton kind of guy PC."

"What?" Ryder asked, mouth full of chips.

"Pre-Chloe."

He laughed. "First of all, I thought we weren't talking about the girls. And second." He got up and grabbed the still half-full bag of potato chips. "She's fucking whipped me, hasn't she?"

They both laughed and Ryder kept munching from the bag just to make his point that he hadn't been pussy whipped.

"Like you said, she's worth it. What you have is worth being told that you need to not behave like a sloth," Nate said.

"Damn right. Now tell me about this oil business. You gonna make us all even richer now they've struck the black gold?"

Nate grinned. "Hell yes. I just wish I could get confirmation before Granddad . . ."

Ryder nodded a few times. "You can say it. Before he kicks the bucket. There's no way to lessen the blow, so we may as well just talk about it."

"I want him to know he was right, that it was there just like he said and that we're gonna make millions from it."

"What did I miss?" Chase asked as he walked back in. He picked up his beer, took a swig, and made a face. "You guys want a cold one?"

They both nodded. "The oil. We're looking like it's all go."

"Good. That what you wanted to talk about tonight?"

"Yeah," Nate said. "I just wanted to get a handle on what you both want long-term, make sure we're still all on the same page. If we're all gonna live here on the one ranch, I don't want any shit getting between us and ruining what we have."

They might each own a third of what had once been a single ranch, but they ranched it like it was still one piece of land. And they all treated King Ranch as if nothing had changed, except for the fact that each had his own home now.

"I just wanna be a rancher," Chase said, reaching for the chips. "The organic beef is starting to do well, we're making a name for ourselves now we have the new branding, and the PR we've had recently means we've got a waiting list longer than we'll ever be able to fill. Despite all that shit with the insemination, it all turned out for the best. We're fielding plenty of calls about our young bulls now, too."

Nate nodded. "Last time I was in New York I got one hell of a kick seeing our name on the menu beside the beef fillet. You've done well, Chase. Granddad's damn proud that you've been able to keep the cattle ranching profitable by diversifying when so many others are struggling."

Chase smiled, but it was a sad kind of smile. They all felt it, the weight of knowing that the man they had looked up to all their lives was so close to passing.

"And those bulls are coming along well, Nate," Chase said, talking about Ryder's new endeavor. They'd covered it the other night, but Nate wanted them both to know that he actually gave a damn about what they were doing on the ground. "Ryder's done a damn fine job of making a heck of a lot of money from a small amount of space on the ranch."

Nate grinned. "Now that we've all learned to stay clear of Bruce, right?"

Chase glared at Nate, but Ryder burst out laughing, tears streaming down his cheeks as they reminisced about the time Chase had been attacked.

"I still don't get how that fucking bull could let me stand there talking to him one minute, and then charge me down like I had a goddamn red flag attached to me the next."

Nate laughed so hard his cheeks ached, unable to look at Ryder without cracking up again.

"He could have killed me, Nate. You hear me?" Chase was furious, slamming his hand down on the table, then shoving Nate hard.

He fell sideways, landing on the floor alongside his chair. "Come on; seeing you fly through the air when he hooked you was pretty funny."

"Oh yeah, funny, ha-ha," Chase grumbled. "My ass hurt so bad I couldn't sit for a week, and I broke my bloody arm."

They settled down and Nate reached for his beer. "Heads up on the oil, just so you know. The whole area's going to be permanently reserved now, looks like it's finally all go."

"No problem," Chase said. "You handle the signage and fencing to keep it safe?"

"Sure will." Nate settled back into his chair. "Now that that's all settled, wanna play poker?"

"While the cat's away the mice will play," said Ryder with a mischievous grin.

"Oh yeah, we're so bad these days," Chase groaned.

Nate laughed, pleased that his brothers were happy. Compared to the havoc they used to wreak as a trio out on the town, they'd virtually turned into a bunch of old men. But Nate didn't mind. When he hung out with his brothers now it was as family men, on the ranch or out for a few quiet beers, and it suited him just fine. When he traveled he partied, dined at the best restaurants, flew on their private jet. He had the best of both worlds. Just because he'd settled into something comfortable with Faith didn't mean he wanted what his brothers had. He never had and nothing had changed.

Except Faith. Faith had changed him. He was lying if he tried to pretend that he didn't care for her. But he couldn't let her get closer to him, couldn't crave the kind of home life that his brothers had, because that would be admitting that he could fall for her. And he wasn't going to fall in love with anyone, couldn't go through losing a woman he loved.

He gritted his teeth. Because what if he did and they had children and then he lost her? What if he turned into the same man his father had when he'd lost his wife? To hell with the fact that Nate didn't think he was anything like him, because they were blood and he could end up repeating the same pattern that he'd suffered through himself. That wasn't going to happen, which meant he had to keep Faith at arm's length. Stop pretending like what they had could just keep on going like they were.

"Nate?"

He looked up, realized he'd shredded the label off his beer bottle. "Sorry, I was a million miles away."

Chase chuckled. "Come on; stop thinking about the femme fatale living with you and get your head into the card game."

Nate went to say something smart back, then shut his mouth. His brothers were only having fun with him; the last thing they needed was for him to snap their heads off just because he was all fucked up over Faith. Instead he downed his beer and reached for the cards he'd been dealt.

"I think we should switch to whiskey," he said.

Chase shrugged. "You guys do what you like. I'm just having a few beers in case the kids need us. One of us needs to stay sober."

Ryder nodded and Nate rose to find the Jack Daniel's. "Nice to have a night just the three of us without Chloe here to kick our butts at poker."

"I'd tell you off for talking smack about my wife, except for the fact you're abso-fucking-lutely right."

They all settled down around the table to play.

"Let's go, boys," Nate muttered. "Fast game's a good game." And it was also the only way he was going to be able to keep his mind off Faith.

Chapter 12

"THIS is amazing," Chloe said, dropping into the booth seat and grinning. "I can't believe we're actually doing something without children attached to us. Or the guys for that matter."

Faith smiled at Chloe's enthusiasm, taking a sip of her vodka, lemon, and lime. "Sorry we couldn't go to Joe's."

"Ugh, Joe's isn't that great," Chloe said. "Seriously, I worked there long enough not to need to go back for a very long time."

"You mentioned the other day that you met Ryder there. Was it love at first sight?"

"Ha-ha, yes and no." Chloe sipped her drink. "I was working there to save up for my college tuition and I ended up making a bet with Ryder. Funnily enough, it was one bet I've never regretted."

They all laughed.

"Once you've fallen for a King you never go back," Hope added, grinning.

"So this ex of yours, I never said anything before, but he took over as manager just before I left," Chloe said. "He was fine to me, but I never liked the guy."

"Funnily enough, my friend said the same thing," Faith admitted. "I'm starting to wonder if he just laid on the charm when I was around, did it to impress me, and I just never saw the true him until it was too late."

Chloe patted her hand. "It's all right; you have Nate now."

"Yeah, and he's smitten," Hope chimed in. "I still remember that time when we saw you at Joe's and he just froze. We gave him so much shit."

Faith had frozen, looking between the two woman seated across from her. "You're kidding, right?" That was almost the same thing Chloe had told her that first time they'd met at Nate's house.

"Honey, he's definitely smitten," Chloe told her. "I've only known him a couple of years, but I've never seen him like his. Surely you've known him long enough to know he's not usually like this."

"With one woman, she means," interrupted Hope. "According to Chase, he's never been in a relationship longer than, well, never, I don't think."

"We're just having fun," Faith managed to say, holding her glass to stop her hand from shaking. "I wouldn't exactly call it a relationship."

"You might be having fun, but he's definitely in love with you." Chloe sighed. "A million and one girls have tried to hook that big fish, and none have even come close. Then you come along and bam, he's caught the bait and not even trying to get away. I say just enjoy it."

Chloe and Hope giggled, but Faith was still in shock.

Was he actually in love with her? She took a long, slow sip of her vodka. That was being stupid. There was no chance he was in love with her. He'd told her as much tonight, that they were still just having fun, that he loved having her around but that they were still on the same page about where their relationship was going.

"I . . ."

"There's nothing to be embarrassed about, if that's what's worrying you," Chloe assured her. "And if you want us to shut up, just say so. We're not easily offended."

Faith took a deep breath and smiled. "It's fine. I just think you've both got the wrong idea about what's going on with us."

The other two exchanged glances like she was the crazy one.

"We've kept it quiet because we decided before anything happened that we just wanted to have fun for a while," she continued. "Neither of us wanted something serious, so we're definitely on the same page there."

"Except for the fact that Nate has gone kind of gaga over you." Chloe giggled. "He hasn't worked from home all year as far as I know, and he's usually traveling all the time, but miraculously now that you're here he's hardly left the ranch."

Hope nodded and Faith just sighed. "Please stop."

"Because you're embarrassed or because you feel bad that he feels differently than you?" Hope asked.

Faith picked up her drink and tipped it back until she'd drunk every last drop. She dropped it with a bang on the table and groaned. "I've lusted after Nate since I was a horny teenager looking at him like he was a sex god," she admitted. "All I wanted was for him to make me feel good, to have fun for a bit until I was back on my feet again. And now it's turned into something a whole lot more serious than it was supposed to and I don't know how it even happened."

Hope reached over and squeezed her hand. "We shouldn't have said anything. I guess we both just presumed that you and Nate were, um, serious."

"I've got to admit that we were eyeing you up as the perfect sister-in-law," Chloe teased, still grinning. "But look, so long as you and Nate know what's going on and what you both want, that's between the two of you. We'd hate to see him get hurt, that's all."

Now Faith was the one laughing. "Me hurt Nate?" She shook her head. "No possible way. He'd just shrug it off and move on to the next woman."

"Whatever you say," Chloe said. "But I don't think he'll ever be getting over you in a hurry. You might just be the first one to break his heart."

"Don't listen to us," Hope interrupted. "Yes, he obviously cares for you and his brothers think it's hilarious seeing him like this, but it's none of our business. Let's just get another round of drinks and have some fun."

"This might be my last chance to let my hair down for a while. Ryder's getting all clucky and talking about having another baby, so I'll probably be knocked up before I know it. Then I'll be back sipping ginger ale or sparkling water."

"Chase is the same," Hope admitted, smiling as she toyed with her straw. "I think they get all primitive and like the idea of us being at home barefoot and pregnant, as much as they claim to like our independence."

Faith was pleased to change the subject, even if it did reinforce the fact that she was doing the right thing by emotionally distancing herself from Nate. If the women were right about the way he was starting to feel about her, then she needed to end things now before they got any deeper into something she knew neither of them really wanted. Being with Nate was amazing, she could never deny that, but what would happen if she stayed? Either they'd end up married and he'd want children, she'd have to sacrifice what she wanted and end up being someone she didn't want to be, or he'd tire of her or decide she wasn't the right kind of girl to marry and she'd end up heartbroken and scarred by the one man she'd put all her love and trust into.

She stared down into her empty glass. Either way she'd be repeating the mistakes of her mother, except that Faith would never leave her children like her mom had, and what was the point of vowing not to repeat the mistakes she'd witnessed if she just changed her mind and gave in because she had a hunch Nate might be different?

"I think someone definitely needs another drink," Chloe suggested, holding out her hand to her.

Faith looked up, completely lost to her thoughts. "Sorry, what was that?" she asked.

"Drinks," Chloe repeated. "We all need something else to drink, and then we're dancing. No more talking about Nate or any of the boys, okay?"

Faith nodded. "Okay. Sounds good."

She got up, grabbed her purse, and forced Nate from her mind. She knew how stupid her jumbled-up thoughts would sound to anyone else, so she wasn't even going to try to explain to Chloe and Hope, or to any of her friends, either. Walking away from Nate would be hard, but staying would only end up being harder.

She held tight to Chloe's hand as they walked through the crowd back toward the bar. They had abandoned their table, which meant it was time to knock back another drink, then dance, and if there was one thing that would take her mind off anything it was letting the beat take over her body and just having fun moving to music.

They stopped at the bar, Chloe pushing past a few guys and Hope following. They were both great to hang out with, and she'd definitely miss them. Hope was busy during the week working as a specialist artificial insemination vet, which was how she'd ended up crossing paths with Chase again, so it was Chloe she'd seen the most of on the ranch, although she liked them both.

"Hey, gorgeous, can I buy you a drink?"

A rough hand landed on Faith's arm and she froze, wincing as the hold tightened. Arrows of fear shot through her. *Nate.* She wished he was right here beside her, keeping her safe. But he wasn't.

"I said—"

"No," she said, voice frosty. She went to pull her arm away, but he kept hold. "Let go."

"Sweetheart, I was just having fun."

She yanked her arm back, glaring at him before moving closer to Chloe and Hope. When Nate called her sweetheart it was one thing, but not some random stranger.

"Uptight bitch," the guy muttered in a loud voice.

"Excuse me?" She should have ignored him, but she

couldn't. All that talk about Nate and getting all pissed off with her own thoughts, and now this?

Hope slipped an arm around her waist and whispered in her ear, taking her focus off the scumbag smirking at her, egged on by the guys standing with him. "He's not worth it. Let's go."

Faith doubted Hope had even seen what was going on, but she'd quickly come to her aid. The music was starting to get louder and Chloe was turning around with their drinks. It wasn't in Faith's nature to back down and take it on the nose, but they were right. If Nate had been here she'd have welcomed his fist flying in the direction of the asshole's face, but it was time to act like the single, capable woman she kept saying she was.

"Dickhead!" she called over her shoulder just to make herself feel better as she walked in the opposite direction. "What is it with guys thinking they have the right to buy us drinks or chat us up even when we're not remotely interested?" Faith asked the other two, heads bent together as they sipped their vodkas through tiny black straws.

"Beats me," Chloe muttered. "Although I have to admit I had a hell of a lot of fun playing hard to get with my man."

They all laughed and carried their drinks with them toward the dance floor. About a third of the place had been cleared to make space for dancing, and there were already a heap of people up making the most of it.

"To dive bars and good friends," Hope toasted.

Faith held up her glass. Tonight was fun, but it was

also sad. Because in the morning she was going to have to make some tough decisions.

Nate heard the front door open, then shut. He'd been lying in bed for over an hour trying to get to sleep, but all he'd done was toss and turn and get the sheets in one hell of a tangle. He stayed still and listened, heard the tap of heels on the wooden floor, the pipes groan as the water in the kitchen was turned on, then silence.

He stayed on his side, quiet as he waited for some noise to alert him to where she was. It had taken every shred of his willpower not to phone her or get in his car and race off to see if she was okay, but his brothers had talked sense into him, just like he'd talked sense into Ryder earlier in the evening. Not to mention the fact that after a beer and a few whiskeys Nate had had too much to drive anyway. And besides, the overprotective, overbearing boyfriend type wasn't really him, even if he was scared out of his wits that something might have happened to her.

And then he heard her. She'd been quiet as a mouse walking through the house, no doubt padding across the carpet on bare feet. But still he stayed silent, the only noise coming from him the shallow inhale and exhale of his breath.

He listened to her undress, the swoosh of fabric as it hit the ground. Nate shut his eyes, imagined seeing her body bathed in the moonlight that was filtering into the room through the open drapes. She'd be almost bare now, standing in her panties and bra, her long hair tumbling down her back or over her chest, skimming past her bra. He wanted to turn, to acknowledge her and watch her, to pull her down onto the bed and ask her where the hell she'd been when he wanted her right here by his side, but he didn't. He stayed silent. He didn't move. Because she was being as whisper quiet as a leopard on a hunt, which meant she didn't want to wake him, or didn't want him to know she was home.

Faith discarded some jewelry, placing it with a soft clink on the bedside table before pulling the covers back, the fall of her body on the bed making it move ever so slightly. Then her body was closer to his, the coolness of her skin like ice against his. She wriggled until he could feel every inch of her nakedness, her breasts pushed to his back, legs tangled against his. Faith either wanted to warm up her cold body or she . . .

Hell. Her hand slid down his thigh, nails scraping every so slightly against him, moving down to the front and . . . *fuck.* Her fingers closed around his cock, just the lightest of touches, but he wasn't staying silent any longer. He groaned and pushed back farther into Faith, his hand grabbing at her butt, locking her into him.

"I thought you were asleep," she whispered in his ear, biting at his lobe.

"I was," he ground out, teeth locked together when she started to rub him harder.

"You weren't," she murmured.

"You're right," he muttered back. "I wasn't. I was listening to you and trying to figure out how I was going to get you naked."

"So you weren't expecting this?" Faith whispered, sucking harder on his lobe as she pumped, getting him so hard there was no chance he was going to be lying on his side much longer. The primitive need to turn around, flip her, and pin her beneath him was almost too much for him to resist.

"Damn you, Faith. I've been worried about you."

She laughed. Nate growled in response. "I'm here now. Do you want me to go?"

"Go?" He turned around and tangled the sheets some more, kicking his legs to free them of the damn covers. "Don't you fucking dare."

Faith stretched as he pushed her hand away, not about to let her get him so damn excited that he had to hurry things. There was something different about her tonight, more confident, determined maybe, but he wasn't going to ask questions when she was clearly in the mood.

"Any admirers tonight?" he asked, hating that he was jealous, an emotion he'd never experienced before. It was clawing at him, had been all night, the fact that he wasn't there by her side with her looking so beautiful. He didn't mind the thought of other men admiring her, but the idea that she could tell a guy to go jump and he might not take the hint made Nate insane.

"A few," she said, running her fingers through his hair and tugging him closer. "But none that even came close to you."

"You've ruined me for any other woman, Faith. I can't get you out of my head even when I'm not with you."

She went silent then, reaching for his face, cupping his cheeks, and leaning in to kiss him. After the way they'd started out he'd expected fast and rough, but she took her time, kissing him so carefully, so softly. Nate took her into his arms, held her close as he kissed her back. Their lips were brushing, so tender, her tongue touching his, exploring, tasting him like it was the first time they'd been together. The spark between them had never dulled, the electricity like a current that just continued to burn.

"I've been wanting to do this all night," she told him, one hand still to his face, her legs tangling around him as he slid his body over hers so he could look down at her.

"I've been wanting you beside me all night," he whispered back, lips back on hers before she could say anything else.

Their kisses were endless, unhurried. Nate had no idea whether minutes had passed or an hour, but for once his impatience didn't get the better of him when it came to Faith. He reached behind her, took his weight off her completely so she could arch her back and let him unclip her bra. It was lacy, like all her underwear seemed to be, and he slowly took it off her, savoring her body like a Christmas present he got to slowly unwrap and discover.

Nate reluctantly stopped kissing her, moved away from her lips and down her body, trailing kisses across her breasts instead. He cupped one, loved that it fitted perfectly in his hand. He licked and sucked her nipple, smiling to himself when her toes clenched against his leg, her moans only spurring him on more. Faith's fingers were in his hair, tugging, trying to encourage him back up, but he was on his way down her body and he wasn't planning on stopping.

"Nate," she murmured, fingers loosening their hold as he ran his mouth over her belly. Her skin was so soft, her flat stomach taut as he rained kisses over it.

"Slow," he muttered, "tonight we're gonna take it slow."

There had been something about the way she'd first kissed him tonight, the way she'd moved, that felt different, but he wanted to savor every minute of being with her. He wanted to pleasure her and make love to her, to enjoy every moment like it was their last together.

"Nate . . ." This time she hissed out his name on her breath at the same time as he grabbed her panties between his teeth, tugging them down, fingers hooked to the sides of them helping him to slide them down inch by inch. She raised her pelvis, let him take them off completely, kicking them past his head when they got to her ankles. And then she stopped moving, knees bent, her body quivering beneath his touch as he ran his fingers up her thigh, stopping when he reached the top of her leg and trailing the rest of the way with his tongue instead. He touched her so delicately he doubted she'd even feel it, but her body still bucked, jumping away from him before resting down again, sensitive as hell.

Nate smiled and tasted her again, carefully, slowly, wanting her to enjoy every sensation. Faith's moan only made him more determined to take his time, to push her to the brink and guide her to climax.

"Nate, stop," she begged quietly.

He ignored her completely, her groans of pleasure telling him that she was only being silly, legs locking around his head like stopping was the last thing she wanted him to do. She was so determined to be the one pleasuring him all the time, and that wasn't the kind of sex he liked. Pleasure him? Sure. But only if the woman he was with was getting as much enjoyment out of sex as he was.

Nate reached up and cupped Faith's breasts, loving the hard pebble of her nipple, trying not to laugh as she almost choked him when her legs tightened around him. She'd had them around his head before, but they'd slid down as she'd wriggled.

And then her body arched and he cupped her butt, caressed her with his tongue until she climaxed, her legs stiff around him one moment, then soft and supple the next.

He kissed her thigh and then her belly, trailing his way back up her body and then staying poised above her, holding his weight with his elbows to either side of her, knees in between hers.

"You're wicked, Nate." Her eyes were still shut, lips moving and tempting him to kiss her.

His willpower was in tatters and he did exactly that, covering her mouth with his and dropping his pelvis, showing her just how much he wanted her. He was still hard and he was ready to pleasure her all over again in an entirely different way.

Nate nudged at her entrance, groaned at how slick she was, then leaned over her to reach in his bedside drawer for protection. He ripped open the packet and sat up to roll the condom on, before settling straight back between her legs again. Faith still had her eyes shut, but a smile played across her lips when he dropped more of his weight onto her; then suddenly her eyes were locked on his when he slowly slid all the way inside of her.

Faith's nails dug into his back as she pushed her body

up, meeting his thrusts with her own. She was making it hard for him to take it slow, but he did, determined to enjoy every single minute without rushing any part of making love to her.

"I thought we were taking this slow, beautiful?" he whispered in her ear, kissing her neck as he kept sliding back and forth into her.

"Faster, Nate," she begged, "*please.*"

He ignored her wishes, wanting it to last, but eventually she wriggled so hard that he did start to move faster, slowing only when she forced him to.

"Stop," she said, voice firm.

Nate stopped immediately, looking down at her with concern. Only he was met with a smug grin as she moved from underneath him and pushed at his shoulders, palms flat as she forced him to his back.

"I think I need to practice what you've been teaching me," she murmured, moving to sit astride him and leaning forward, her hair covering his face until she shook it away and kissed him on the mouth.

"What's that?" he asked, happy to be part of any performance she wanted. For all the talk about him being her teacher, there hadn't exactly been so much teaching as just plain old fun happening between them.

"To do whatever feels good for me."

He chuckled, then groaned as she moved up, lowering herself over him and starting to rock back and forth. Her head was tipped back, long hair touching his thighs as she moved, brushing against him, teasing him. Faith moved slowly at first, and he raised his hands to cup her breasts, loving the fullness of them above him, holding them as she rode him. Faith's eyes were shut, but he didn't shut his for a second, wanting to watch every move she made, keep his eyes locked on the breasts that drove him crazy.

Then she started to ride him faster, her body locked to his, and he cupped her ass instead, held on to her hips, and rocked hard inside her. Just when he started to lose control, knew there was no way in hell that he could hold back, Faith slowed, her body more gentle, the intensity of her actions gone at the same time as he gave in to his own climax. Nate kept hold of her, not letting go of her butt until his body relaxed, then scooping his arms around her so she could collapse on top of him.

Nate inhaled the sweet smell of her hair, hated that it was mixed with the faint aroma of cigarettes from her night out but liked that it was covering his face nonetheless. He kissed her neck, held her tight, their bodies still fused together as they lay in silence.

"You're amazing," he told her, surprised by how gruff his voice sounded. "Best sex of my life."

She let out a low laugh. "How can one man make me feel like utter crap and then you come along and make me feel like a goddess?"

He held on to her tight, wishing she knew how amazing she was without him having to tell her. But then if she knew that already, he probably wouldn't have fallen for her so hard. The fact that she seemed to have no idea how goddamn beautiful she was or that she was incredible whatever she was doing was all part of the reason he liked her so much.

"I'll tell you now and I'll tell you again, Faith," he said, smiling up at her as she looked down at him. "You are the most amazing creature I've ever met. I only wished you could see in the mirror what I see whenever I look at you."

"Thank you, Nate," she whispered, looking shy as he stared at her.

"For what?"

She dropped back down on top of him, mouth just close to his ear. "For everything. What you've done for me will change my life forever."

Faith fought the tears that were burning—stinging—her eyes. Just saying the words to Nate made a choke form in her throat, the finality of what she'd done weighing on her so heavy she could hardly stand it. When she'd come home tonight, she'd told herself that this was it. Her last night with Nate. They couldn't keep going on like this, couldn't live in this delicious bubble any longer without one of them getting hurt. And so she'd decided to give herself one more night with him. One more night to enjoy him, to let her body feel pleasure like it might never feel again. To lie with the man who'd changed the way she looked at the world.

She wasn't lying when she'd told Nate that he'd changed her life. He'd helped her find the job she had, which had put her on the first step of the ladder in the art world. He'd explained to her how to make a success of herself, been so genuine in his appreciation for her, made her feel worthy and beautiful, like nothing or no one would ever be able to stand in her way again.

Which was why leaving him was so heartbreaking. She'd told herself repeatedly to leave before she fell in love, but the reality was that she'd already fallen.

"You okay?" he asked.

Faith nodded and held him tighter. "Yes."

They lay a bit longer together, neither one of them wanting to move. Their bodies were warm, her mouth was against his skin, and Nate's hands were stroking her back in big, slow circles.

"Are you going running in the morning?" she asked.

Nate cleared his throat. "Yeah. I'm heading out at daybreak with Chase."

She excused herself to go to the bathroom, kissing Nate before she pulled away from his embrace.

"Why? You want to come?" he asked with a chuckle.

"No!" she called out, the door to the bathroom still open.

Faith washed the makeup from her face and brushed her teeth before joining him back in bed, still naked, and tucking up beside him. Nate lay on his back and she dropped her head to his chest, making herself comfortable.

"Good night, gorgeous," he said.

" 'Night."

She listened to the steady beat of his heart, heard his breathing change as he fell asleep almost immediately. Faith stroked his chest, squeezed her eyes shut to block the tears again, then eventually moved and reached into her purse that she'd left beside the bed to pull out her phone. She texted her brother, hoping Sam would have his phone with him. He always rose early, which meant he should at least get it first thing if he didn't receive it now.

Need you to pick me up from King Ranch just before 7 am. Don't be late. I need you. F xo

Faith switched her phone to silent and curled up beside Nate again. She'd miss his big, muscled body against hers for a very long time, but she was doing the right thing. Or maybe it wasn't the right thing, but it was the only thing that made sense to her right now.

Chapter 13

FAITH'S hands were shaking as she zipped up her bag. Nate had risen early, had bent over to kiss her cheek before he'd left, and she'd just stayed still and listened to him go. The second the door had closed she'd jumped up, hurriedly dressed, and grabbed her two bags, stuffing in as much as she could.

She glanced at her phone, left discarded on the bed while she got ready to flee. The screen was lit up, so she grabbed it and scanned the message. It was Sam.

Tried to call u before. Driving. Be there in 15. Hope u ok.

Faith pulled another tissue from her purse and wiped her nose, blinking the tears away as they started to fall. She just needed to hold it together a bit longer, not completely fall apart just yet. She'd check into a cheap motel for a few nights until she found somewhere to rent; now that she had a job she could afford to cover her own expenses, and she already had enough money saved to finish her post-grad to get through that. It was going to be tight, but she was in charge of her own destiny and doing it on her own started now, even if she had called her brother to come get her.

She put her coat on and pushed her phone into her pocket, taking one last look around the bedroom. It was the last time she was going to see it, going to be in Nate's room, part of his life. It would have been so easy to throw everything back in the closet, undress and hop into bed, wait for him to get back from his run, and join him in the shower. Lather him up, both slick from the water, and let him have his wicked way with her.

But she couldn't. It was time to go, and she needed to leave now while she had the chance to go in private. Faith stopped in the kitchen, tears still streaming down her cheeks, and reached for the notepad she'd put on the counter earlier in the month to jot groceries down on. She picked up the pen and leaned forward, taking a deep breath before writing. She had no idea what to say, especially after the night they'd had, but she couldn't go without saying something.

Nate. This seems irrational and stupid after the night we just shared, but I have to go. Thank you for making me feel beautiful, for the weeks of fun & telling me so genuinely to follow my dreams. I will never forget the time we spent together, & I will never, ever forget you. Faith.

Her tears fell onto the paper, soaked through the notepad as she dropped the pen and backed away. She'd been planning what to write all morning, trying to figure out how to tell him how she felt, but all the practicing in the world didn't make it any easier.

A noise outside made her look up and she grabbed her bags and walked toward the door. Sam's pickup truck was outside and she moved quickly to the front door, opening and closing it and hurrying toward him. Her brother was already out and walking toward her, his face turning from surprised to angry when he came closer.

"What the hell did he do to you, Faith?" Sam demanded.

She started to sob then, unable to keep it together any longer. She thrust her bags at him.

"Nothing," she managed. "We need to go. Now."

Sam stared at her, then started toward the house. "He in here? I'll fucking kill him!"

"Sam!" she cried. "Please. Just get in the truck and go."

He turned and looked back at her, eyes wild with anger.

"Please," she begged. "Just get me out of here before he comes back."

Sam glanced at the house again and then to her, grabbing her bags and walking past her to throw them in the bed of the truck. She got in quickly and clicked her seat belt, leaning her head deep back into the seat and staring out the window at the homestead. The wisteria growing along the porch was so stunning, the house the type of home that she'd always dreamed about living in as a little girl, all part of her childhood dreams of an idyllic life. There had been so many times she'd wished to live in a house just like this, to have a family like Nate's. Only as a child she hadn't realized that her brother's best friend had experienced pain like she had with his own parents, that the family she saw was, in fact, his grandparents caring for the three boys as if they were their own.

Sam started driving, and she kept staring, hoping they didn't end up seeing Nate. He was usually gone an hour, which meant they were cutting it fine.

"I told you he was going to hurt you, Faith. I told you he was going to break your heart and I was going to have to pick up the pieces, and look what I'm doing," he seethed. "I warned him what I'd do and I wasn't damn well kidding."

Faith let him rant, knowing he had to get it all off his chest before she interrupted. "Nate hasn't done anything wrong," she managed, finally back in control and no longer sobbing. She wiped a few stray tears away, brushing them aside, and dabbed at her nose with a tissue she found in her pocket.

"You're my sister, Faith; I know when someone's hurt you," Sam said. "Tell me what he fucking did and I'll—"

"Sam, listen to me," she quietly demanded. "Nate hasn't hurt me. I'm the one who's doing the hurting here, and he's going to hate me for leaving like this. Which is why we have to get out of here now before he tries to stop me."

"But why are you leaving?" Sam asked, taking his eyes off the drive as they neared the road. "What did he do to make you leave?"

"Nothing," she admitted. "Nate did absolutely nothing wrong, and that's why I have to go." Faith didn't expect him to understand, hell, she didn't truly understand why she was so scared of being hurt or falling in love herself, but what she did know was that she'd had to do it.

"You're sure?" Sam asked, slowing before turning out onto the road.

Faith breathed a sigh of relief as they left King Ranch. It had been her home for over a month, and it might just have been the best month of her life. But it wasn't real; it was just a moment in time of them both having fun and wanting the same thing at the same time. The bubble would have burst one day; it was just a matter of when.

"Where am I taking you?"

"A motel. Somewhere cheap where I can wallow for a few days before finding a place to rent."

"No way." Sam took a hand off of the steering wheel and reached for her. "You can come stay with us."

"I appreciate the offer, but I need some time to myself." She didn't want to be staying with her brother while she was heartbroken over Nate, was craving just being alone for a while.

"I'm not leaving you alone," Sam insisted.

She squeezed his hand back. "Well, you're going to have to," she said. "This is just something I need to do, Sam."

He grumbled but didn't say anything else, and she leaned across and pressed her forehead against the cool glass of the window. She was going to make the most of the next few days. She was going to cry and wallow, but she was also going to make goals and plans. She was going to take charge of her future and make sure nothing and no one stopped her from getting what she wanted from life.

Nate had been fun. Nate had been delicious. Nate had been exactly what she'd needed at a time when she'd been low. He'd made her feel amazing and worthy and confident. Which was why he'd always hold a place in her heart that she doubted any other man would ever be able to fill.

"You sure about the motel?" Sam asked, his tone more gentle now. "Because Kelly would never mind you coming to stay for a bit."

"Yeah, I'm sure," she said.

And so Sam drove and she stared, wondering if she'd perhaps just made the biggest mistake of her life or whether she'd done exactly what needed to be done. Either way, she'd done it, and there was no going back.

Nate was still breathing heavy when he walked into the house, laughing with Chase as they headed for the kitchen.

"You're all fired up today," Chase joked. "I thought I had you at the bend, but you smoked me."

Nate hauled the fridge door open and passed his brother a bottle of water. They both unscrewed their bottles and guzzled.

"I had a good night. Maybe that helped."

Chase groaned and leaned forward, grimacing as the cool of the stone hit his bare skin. "Lucky you. We had Harrison in bed with us all night. I'm craving the night he starts to sleep through. Morning sex is a thing of the past."

"Morning sex is overrated," Nate said with a laugh, seeing a notepad and pen discarded at the other end of the counter. "Just go to bed earlier and get it on. Then you don't have to worry about morning breath. Or rushing to work."

"Hey, I only have to roll out of bed and I'm at work. When I say I miss morning sex I mean it. Hope's hot in the morning, all rumpled and warm from sleep."

Nate laughed and reached for the notepad. He set his water bottle down when he realized it was a note from Faith.

"Faith!" he called out, walking fast through the kitchen to the bottom of the stairs. "Faith!" he called louder.

Nate paused when he didn't hear anything, read the softly scrawled words on the paper he was holding. He read it once, then again, before dropping it and taking the stairs two at a time. He stopped outside his room, looked at the empty bed still rumpled from the night before, threw the closet door open, and saw the empty space where her things had been hanging. *Fuck.*

She was gone. Faith had gone like a ghost that had never been there in the first place in the short space of time that he'd been out running.

"Fuck!" he bellowed.

Chase appeared behind him, still bare chested and holding his water bottle, top tucked into the waistband of his running shorts.

"What's happened?" he asked.

"She's fucking left me," Nate muttered.

Chase didn't say anything, just took a step forward and gave him a firm pat on the shoulder, his hand lingering. "She'll be back. You guys were great together."

"No, she fucking won't." Nate stormed into his bathroom and turned the faucet on, stripping off and stepping under the water. "She's gone," he called out to Chase from the shower, "and this is exactly why I never should have let her move in in the first place!"

Damn Faith Mendes. She'd played him like a pro, seduced him and wiggled her way into his life until he'd wanted her there for good. Last night they'd made love like it was their last night together, and now he realized that it had been exactly that. Faith had known she was leaving in the morning; it was why she'd asked about his run. So she'd fucked him and tricked him.

He rubbed shampoo furiously into his hair, fingertips dragging against his scalp. Faith was gone and he had to forget she'd ever been part of his life. So what if he'd been falling for her, if he'd started having irrational thoughts about what it would be like to have her in his life long-term?

They'd only ever meant to have fun. It had only meant to be short-term. He grunted as he stood under the water and let the hot blast his face.

At least now he'd had a taste of his own medicine. All the women he'd been with, all the women he'd told he was just wanting a good time with and had ended up breaking their hearts. Now he knew how they felt.

He fucking loved her. He'd never admit it to another soul, but he had fallen for Faith, he'd fallen hard, and getting over her wasn't going to be easy. He wanted her in his bed, in his life, in his future, no matter how much he told himself he didn't. He'd spent so much of his life scared of letting anyone close, terrified of being in love with a woman he might lose one day. And now he realized how stupid that had been.

He wasn't his father and he never would be. Faith had

gone and it hurt like hell, as if someone had tried to crush his chest with a load of steel. Instead of telling her how he really felt, he'd let her walk out of his life, and his pride would never let him chase her when she'd made it clear that they were over.

Which meant he had to suck it up and get on with life. With drilling for oil. Looking after his family. Focusing on the ranch.

It was all he knew and it was exactly what would keep him going when all he really wanted to do was smash the hell out of something until his knuckles bled.

Nate got out, got dressed, and collected his keys as he walked out the door. He ran a hand through his wet hair before jumping behind the wheel and heading down the road, not stopping until he got to the field where the drilling was prepped to go ahead. He took a deep breath as he got out and crossed the grass, pleased to see there were already two guys on-site. He was paying them a lot to get work under way immediately.

"Mornin'!" he called out.

The two guys looked up, both raising their hands before going back to whatever it was they were doing. Work. Work was what he needed to focus on. Oil was his future, not Faith.

"The machines are rolling in soon. You ready to become a very rich man?"

Nate laughed. "Now that's what I want to hear!"

The field was all marked out and he walked around, surveyed the site, and listened to the conversation between the two men. And then he heard a rumble, looked up, and held up a hand to shield his eyes from the bright morning sun.

"Here comes the cavalry," Nate muttered. At least one thing was going right about his day. Soon the field would be a hive of activity, covered in machines. And he couldn't wait.

Chapter 14

"HOW are you?"

Faith smiled and tucked the phone under her ear. "I'm fine, Sam. You don't have to keep checking up on me."

Her brother chuckled. "If not me, then who?"

"Seriously, I'm great," she said. It wasn't that she wasn't happy—on the surface of it she had everything, and she wasn't complaining. She could smile even though it didn't warm her heart, and she could laugh even though it didn't make her belly tingle like when she'd been with Nate. But she was getting there. Slowly but surely she was getting there. One step at a time.

"How's the job going? You're still loving it?"

"Yeah," she said, not needing to lie or fudge the truth when it came to work. "I'm learning so much and they've offered me a full-time position as soon as I can start."

"Sometimes I wonder if you're the only person in the world who doesn't realize how amazing you are," Sam said.

It was on the tip of her tongue to say that he sounded

just like someone else she knew, but she didn't. That last night flashed through her mind, between the sheets with Nate, lying in his arms, listening to him tell her things that had only made her want him more.

"I'm your sister, Sam," she said instead. "You have to say things like that to me."

They both laughed, even though she knew he meant what he'd said. Sam didn't bother saying things for no reason, even when it was her.

"I texted you my new address the other day. Don't be a stranger if you want to come by."

"Yeah, I got it," Sam grunted. "Still wish you were here."

"Oh yeah, just what you need, your baby sister being the spare wheel and ruining your little honeymoon period with your girlfriend." She laughed, lowering her voice as someone entered the gallery. "Kelly seems really nice, so I'd rather not be responsible for screwing it up. Anyway, I have to go; I have a client. Talk soon."

Sam said good-bye and she flicked her phone to silent before slipping it into her pocket. She took a deep breath, reminded herself that she was in charge for the afternoon, that she was a capable, confident art consultant, and fixed a smile.

"May I help you, sir?" she asked, crossing the tiled floor.

"I'm interested in your upcoming auction," the man said, returning her smile. She noticed his Louis Vuitton wallet and the Rolex glinting from his wrist. If there was one thing she'd learned fast it was identifying potential new clients, and she intended to make sure she developed a list of loyal clients that one day would make her an asset to the most prestigious galleries in the country.

"Is there a specific piece that caught your eye, or would you like me to talk you through the catalogue?" she asked.

"How about we start by you telling me which pieces I should be making sure I don't miss out on," he said with a chuckle.

She smiled and touched her hand to his forearm for the barest second, careful to make him feel important without sending mixed messages. "It would be my pleasure. How about you start by telling me about the pieces you already own, and I'll make sure you continue to build your collection in the most profitable fashion."

"I'm in this for the long term, but I like traditional pieces. Brushstrokes of scenes that suit my library, nothing too modern."

"Some pieces we buy to appreciate every day until we need to sell them; others we buy simply to store in a safe place in the knowledge that one day we'll make a small fortune on them," she said.

"How about we consider both then?" he asked, chuckling. "Just don't dupe this old man into buying a lemon, okay?"

Faith got a kick out of knowing more about art than most people she met, and she'd fast learned that she loved nothing better than making a sale, either. Maybe it was Nate's business acumen rubbing off on her, or maybe it was just the fact that she was enjoying working in the gallery. Either way, she was happy doing what she was doing, being part of the art world, and she couldn't wait for the day that she worked with some of the best collections and pieces in the world. She was reaching for the sky now, and nothing was going to stop her, not even her broken heart.

Nate finally pulled the phone from his ear and took a moment to catch his breath. He was exhausted. What he wanted to do was get back to the ranch and just roll up his sleeves and get his hands dirty. Do the kind of work that took his mind off everything and reminded him of who he was and what he'd come from. Instead he'd been working at a frantic pace for the past three weeks, and if he didn't slow down he was going to drop.

He turned to check he'd locked his car and headed inside to the hospital. He'd just gotten off a plane from California, a trip long overdue to personally check on a number of their real estate investments there and secure a new property, as well as do a surprise visit to their property managers. Nate liked to turn up unannounced to gauge just how well things were running and whether he was being bullshitted just because he lived in a different state. There was no pulling the wool over his eyes, not now and not ever.

Nate stopped at a coffee machine and made himself one in a cheap polystyrene cup. He could have gotten a decent coffee if he'd wanted to wait, but he just needed a quick shot of caffeine and he was here to see his grand-dad, not sit around sipping lattes.

Nate went to down it, burned his mouth, and cursed. *Damn coffee.* Everything pissed him off these days, and a stupid fucking coffee that scalded his mouth was one of those things, even if he should have known better.

Nate continued to walk, knew the way so well he could have made it with his eyes closed. He paused as he always did outside his granddad's door, said a prayer like he only ever did when he was about to see the man he knew was slipping away from him, then entered.

And saw he was sleeping. Nate checked he was covered, made sure he looked comfortable, then sat in the chair beside the bed. He sipped slowly at the rest of the coffee even though the roof of his mouth was scalded, settled back until he finished it, and reached for one of the spare blankets, tucking it around himself. Seeing his granddad sleep was only reminding him how tired he was himself—it was about time he just shut his eyes for a bit and turned his brain off.

Nate did exactly that, letting himself relax for once. Until he thought about Faith. His jaw hardened and he went back to thinking about the ranch, to the oil they'd found. *This* was why he'd turned into even more of a workaholic than usual. Trying to keep his goddamn mind off the woman who'd gotten under his skin.

"I was starting to think you were never going to wake up."

Nate blinked and rubbed at his eyes, realizing where he was and why his neck hurt like hell. His back was stiff and even stretching didn't give him any relief.

"How long have I been out?" he asked.

"It's light outside, if that's what you mean," his granddad said with a chuckle.

"Oh hell," Nate muttered, glancing at his watch and seeing that it was almost 7:00 am. He'd slept the night.

"I came by to check in on you and then I was supposed to meet up with Chase."

"He'll think you had a good night out with a beautiful woman. I doubt he's reported you missing yet."

Nate grimaced. "Not likely."

"The woman or the missing persons report?"

"The woman."

"We never forget the first one," his granddad said, leaning back deeper into his pillows. Nate jumped up to help him adjust his position, pouring him a fresh glass of water and holding the straw to his lips so he could sip. "There's something about enjoying every woman that so much as looks in your direction, then finding the one."

Nate laughed. "First of all, she's not the one. If she was I wouldn't be pissed off at the world; I'd be with her." He grinned at his granddad. "And secondly, tell me who she was, this first one who got to you?"

"Your grandma, you fool." He started to cough and Nate held the water for him again, ready to call for help if they needed it.

"Of course it was Grandma. Who the hell else could have tamed you? Or put up with you for that matter."

He reached for his granddad's hand and held it until his breathing was less raspy and the coughing had passed.

"She made me work for it, but damn, was she worth it."

They sat in silence, Nate smiling as he thought about his grandparents. When his grandma had died, they'd all been hit hard. She'd been the true matriarch of the family, the glue that held everything together and made everything good with the world. She'd been elegant yet at the same time able to sit down with the ranch hands and throw back a glass of whiskey with the best of them; and she'd been the one to tuck the boys into bed after their dad had left and make them feel as loved as they had felt when their mom had been alive and holding them in her arms.

Nate had known too much loss in his lifetime, of those closest to him, and it was only about to get worse.

"Don't be a fool if she's the one, son. But if she isn't, then forget her. Simple as that."

Nate only wished it *was* that simple, because one part of him told him not to stop until he had her back in his arms and the other told him that everything had turned out for the best. Nothing had changed, nothing that could make things work between them long-term, so it was best to let sleeping dogs lie.

"Now tell me about that oil."

Now that was something he was happy to talk about. "It's better than we ever thought. I just wish you could be there to see that black gold spewing from the ground."

Nate looked up when a nurse entered, let her go about her business and check the charts and dispense medication. He nodded when he was offered a spare plate of breakfast and coffee, offering his thanks, then turned back to his granddad.

"There's something about oil that makes my pulse race," he admitted, sitting back and grinning at the old man smiling straight back at him.

"It's because you love the chase as much as I do, Nate. Being the one to make something big happen always gave me a kick."

The chase. It was the one thing Nate wasn't used to

doing when it came to women, beyond a point, and it was what made him uneasy about what had happened with Faith. Maybe he'd given up too easily. Maybe he needed to chase her, kick himself up the ass and just do it, to hell with being shit scared about having a future with her.

Or maybe he just needed to screw everything wearing a skirt to help himself forget.

Chapter 15

NATE was miserable. So fucking miserable that the only thing he could think to do was drown himself in alcohol. He went to Joe's, something he wouldn't have done if Faith's asshole ex was still working here. It made one corner of his mouth turn up into a smile thinking how quick her ex had left town, something his investigator had advised Nate after a couple weeks of not being able to find the guy locally, but then it only reminded him of Faith again and he was back to scowling. His theory of fucking everything with a pulse that was wearing a skirt wasn't even remotely appealing right now—what he wanted was to get good and drunk, then head to his apartment to sleep for at least ten hours straight. He was so jet-lagged he was ready to be comatose. He'd promised himself after his last trip that he was going to slow down, but it was easier to just keep going, stay so busy that he didn't have time to think about how angry he was with the world.

"Turn that frown upside down, gorgeous."

The overly sexy drawl made him look up and into a pair of heavy black lashes. Nate glanced down her body, liking her equally oversize breasts. Why the hell was he pretending to be a monk just because he couldn't have Faith?

"Hey." He pushed out his chair a bit, rocked back on the rear legs, then quit when he realized how unsteady he was. He needed to either slow down on the whiskey or switch back to beer.

"What's your name?" she asked, dropping into the chair across from him and waving to someone else. He looked over his shoulder, saw another woman hurrying across to his table. He'd scowled so much all night that he'd as good as had a *Fuck off* sign on his chair, but these two weren't so easily put off.

"Nate," he finally said. He should have asked them theirs, but he didn't really give a damn.

"I'm Sally and this is Essie," she announced, leaning in closer to him, her perfume surrounding him. "You having a good time?"

Do I look like I'm having a good time? He might be drunk, but he wasn't a complete asshole, so he just smiled. "Yeah, sure."

The woman she'd introduced as Essie reached for his hand, stroking hot-pink nails across his palm when she turned it over. "Feel like getting out of here and having double the fun?"

Nate's head snapped back. They might be kinda trashy in a faked-tan, too-much-tits-on-display way, but they weren't exactly hard on the eye. Both blond, Essie was tall and leggy, whereas her friend had a ton of curves. He retrieved his hand, grabbed his whiskey glass, and knocked the rest of it back.

"You wanna drink first or get out of here now?"

They looked at each other and giggled. "Let's go, Mr. King."

He grimaced. So they'd known exactly who he was. He'd had too much to drink, but he knew he hadn't told them his last name. He never did announce it unless it was business or a different kind of company.

"Nate?" Sally purred, sidling up against him. "What's wrong?"

Nate shook his head. "Nothing, sweetheart. Let's go."

He slid an arm around each girl, wondering why the hell he'd hadn't just picked up a beautiful woman earlier.

"You gonna take us back to your ranch, sugar?" one of the women asked.

He dropped a kiss into blond hair that smelled like cigarettes and cheap perfume. He clamped his jaw, ground his teeth at the memory of Faith's sweet, fresh-smelling shampoo.

"How about we go to yours?" he replied, not wanting to ruin the moment by thinking about what he didn't have. And there was no way in hell these two or any other damn woman were going to be coming back to his ranch with him.

The woman pouted, but he wasn't going to change his mind. He had rules for a reason, and look where breaking them had gotten him.

"I'm thinking a hotel room and champagne," he said, laughing when his ass got grabbed. He slid his own hand down and caressed a perky butt.

"Nate?"

The soft, surprised voice made him stop dead. *What the hell?*

"Hey," he managed, staring at the woman he hadn't been able to get out of his head since the day she'd left his house. He went to extract his arms, but one of the women giggled and slid closer, trailing wet kisses along his jawline, then nipping at his ear.

"You look like you're having fun," Faith said.

He groaned. The woman he'd found so appealing earlier took it as a sign he liked what she was doing and amped up her tongue exploration of his earlobe. Nate pushed her back. How the hell had he ended up bumping into Faith now, of all times?

"You working here again?" he asked.

"No." When she shook her head it made the light catch her hair, dark tresses shining and silky. He remembered exactly what it was like having those strands wrapped around his fist, the softness of her hair as it shimmered down her back when she was sitting astride him, the tips brushing his hands as he held on to her hips. "The gallery is going great; I love working there. I'm just, ah, having a few drinks with friends tonight."

Nate hadn't even noticed who she was standing with, but he glanced sideways and realized her friends were hovering slightly behind her. He smiled and said hello, suddenly a whole lot more sober than he'd been earlier. Part of him wanted to flaunt the two women standing beside him, almost purring, they were so damn desperate to get him into bed, but the sensible side of his brain was telling him not to be an asshole and to fight harder for the one woman he wanted. Because he wanted her—

if there was one thing he'd realized over the past month, it was that he wanted her more than anything he'd ever wanted before. He was just too damn proud to go chasing her when he still couldn't figure out how he could have her without giving her what she needed.

"How about we get a drink?" he suggested, sucking back the stupid stuff he could easily have said to ruin everything that was left between them. "Just the two of us," he said in a quieter voice, pleased that he hadn't bumped into her on a date, because seeing a guy with her would have tipped him over the edge.

"Nate, I don't know. . . ." Faith wrapped her arms around herself and it took every inch of his willpower not to grab her and wrap them around him, to just force her out of the door with him and back to his place.

"Nate!" Essie and Sally protested at the same time.

He ignored them, only focused on the beautifully intoxicating woman standing before him. Her full lips were slightly parted, all glossy and kissable.

"Come on, Faith." Nate chuckled as he reached for her hand, but his smile died when she moved back just enough so he couldn't reach her, like she was repulsed by him. "What are you scared of?"

Her eyes were swimming when she looked up at him. "You," she said simply. "But it looks like you're having plenty of fun without me. It's better this way, Nate; we both know that."

Nate stared at Faith. He'd never had a woman speak to him like that, her honesty as brutal as a knife to his skin. She was telling him to go, and goddamn it, but he wasn't about to beg. His jaw hardened, body like stone as he gave her a cool stare.

"Have a great night, Faith. I'll see you around."

He slipped his arms around the women again, not feeling like doing anything with them any longer but childish enough to want to hurt Faith, to piss her off and show her that he was fine without her. Which he sure as hell hadn't been.

"Where're we going?"

Nate kept his hands planted on the women's asses as they left, nodding to the doorman as they passed and exited the bar. Once they were outside, he turned to first his left, then his right, giving each of the women a kiss on the lips before pulling out his wallet. He'd made his point, but he'd lost all interest in screwing them.

"Here's enough money for a taxi fare," he said, putting some bills into each of their hands. "Sorry, ladies, but tonight's not the night. Maybe next time."

He should have just taken them to bed, had the night of his life with two women at the same time, but all he wanted now was more damn whiskey. Then his head smashed into a feather-filled pillow for the better part of a day. And if he even thought about Faith again, he was going to smash his fist into something, anything to get the visual of her beautiful dark-brown eyes staring at him like he was the one who'd gone and broken her goddamn heart, not the other way around.

He walked to his vehicle, checked it was locked, then waved to a taxi driver. He was a fool, but dammit, he was in love with her. For the first time in his life, he'd let down the shield he'd so stringently maintained. When his mom had died, he'd loved his grandma dearly, but not the same kind of fierce love he'd had for his mom, and he'd vowed as a boy never to let himself hurt like that ever again. It was why he'd never had serious relationships, why he was so determined to never have children of his own, because he didn't want to hurt like that again. He'd been the oldest brother, the one who'd had to be strong and keep it all together. And now he'd gone and let Faith get too close, and for the first time he wanted a woman he couldn't have.

He settled into the backseat of the cab, gave the driver instructions, and shut his eyes as he pushed his head back into the leather headrest. Faith fucking Mendes had screwed with his head, but he was in love with her, goddamn it, and as far as he could tell she had no damn idea.

"How are you feeling?"

Faith shrugged and planted her straw between her teeth, sucking hard. They were drinking vodka, lemon, and lime, and the cold drink was at least giving her a brain freeze. Although nothing could numb her enough into not thinking about Nate.

"I just can't stop thinking about him being with . . ." She let her voice trail off, not sure what she was actually going to say. The idea of him having sex with either one of those women made her feel physically sick, but two of them at once? It shouldn't have surprised her, but it did. "Anyway, I was the one who left, right? That means he can be with whoever he likes, because it's none of my business."

Her friends smiled and nodded, but she knew they weren't sure what to say. One minute she was telling them she was happy being single, and the next she could hardly breathe, having come face-to-face with the man

who'd scared the hell out of her by making her feel
things she'd always sworn she wouldn't. She wanted
him, but she couldn't let herself, couldn't give that part
of herself away. And with Nate there was no other way;
she'd seen that firsthand. The way she felt around him
meant it was all or nothing.

Cara and Saskia both kept sipping, and she did the
same. Then the music started to thump and she knocked
back the rest of her drink and pushed it across the bar.
The one thing she could do was drink until she was just
numb enough to forget and dance the hell out of the
night.

"Let's dance," she announced, running her fingers
through her hair.

Her friends laughed and shrugged, finishing theirs
and joining her, hips swaying as they started dancing
with her. A clean-cut blond came up to her, grabbed her
around the waist, but she smiled politely and pushed
him away, nodding toward Cara. She was the one who'd
like to be picked up—Faith, on the one hand, had no
intentions of even flirting with another guy tonight.
What she wanted was to be on her own with friends,
have fun without needing a man. Cara, on the other
hand, launched straight into some raunchy dancing,
which had Faith in hysterics.

The music kept thumping and she danced liked she'd
never danced before. *And still the image of Nate with
his arms around the blondes blasted her eyeballs.*

Chapter 16

"WHAT the hell's wrong with you?" Ryder asked as he caught up with Nate, his little girl riding on his shoulders and hanging on to him by his hair.

Nate wasn't in the mood for talking, but he checked his attitude when Rose smiled down at him. When he glanced at Ryder he made a face.

"Shit. Your eyes look like all the blood from your head spilled into them."

"Language around the little lady," Nate growled, reaching out and linking fingers with Rose. She squeezed back before going back to holding on to her dad.

"So what happened last night?" Ryder asked.

"I just went to Joe's for a few drinks."

"And came home instead of going to the apartment with any . . ."—Ryder grinned and his eyebrows shot up—"*company*?"

Nate glowered at him. He wasn't in the mood to talk shit. "I saw Faith."

"Ah," Ryder said, as if that was all the answer he needed. "Hence the bear with the thorn attitude."

"You're lucky you've got Rose with you," Nate grumbled.

"Why? What the hell did I do?" Ryder asked, chuckling. "Faith's the one who broke your heart."

"She did not break my hurt, douche bag."

"Hey, Nate, no swear-wing," Rose said, one hand on her hip.

She at least made him laugh with her cute little lisp. "It's not swearing to call your dad a douche bag, because he is one."

Ryder punched him in the arm and he was only saved by the little person on his shoulders; otherwise Nate would have loved to smack him straight back and blow off some steam.

"The reason I can tease you is because I felt the same way with Chloe," Ryder continued, hands on his daughter's legs to hold her in place on his shoulders as he walked beside Nate. "When I thought I'd lost her, it was a pretty dark place."

"How much do you remember about Mom?" Nate asked, voice gruff. "I mean, do you still remember how bad it hurt losing her, or were you too young?"

The smile fell from Ryder's face like Nate had flicked a switch. "You think you're the only one who doesn't want to hurt like that again?"

Nate stopped walking, leaned on the fence they were passing, and stared out into the distance. "You honestly felt like that? I mean, before Chloe?"

"Man, I still feel like it," Ryder admitted, taking Rose down and setting her on the wooden fence so she could be in between them. "I was damn scared of opening up to Chloe, and then when she told me she was pregnant? Hell, that was rough. I might have been younger than you, but I remember Mom and every emotion that came with losing her."

"I can't believe I'm getting love advice from my little brother."

Ryder chuckled. "Yeah, but it's the only advice you'll ever need from me. You've always been the one there for us, from the day Mom died until now. You probably don't have a clue how much we appreciate you, Nate, but you're one hell of a big brother."

He smiled, slinging his arm around little Rose and giving her a hug. "So what do you reckon I should do?" He hated being so honest about how he felt, but Ryder was his brother. If he couldn't talk to him, who the hell could he talk to, and keeping it to himself was driving him crazy.

"Do you love her?" Ryder asked.

Nate hung his head, shut his eyes, and immediately saw Faith in his mind. He'd be lying if he didn't say yes; every part of him screamed yes, except that little part of him that didn't want to admit to any sign of weakness.

"Maybe," he muttered.

"Don't give me that crap; it's a simple yes or no question."

"Yes, goddamn it!" Nate cursed, turning to stare at his brother. "I love her. Is that what you wanted to hear?"

Ryder smiled, but his grin was genuine. He wasn't kidding around. "Then we need to figure out what you're going to do about that."

"*We?*" Nate asked, eyebrows shooting up.

"Hey, I'm not leaving you alone to f–"—he paused, checked himself and grinned—"stuff this up."

"When do I ever stuff up?" Nate demanded, already sick of being the one getting advice.

"Never," Ryder told him, pushing his boot on top of the wooden rail and leaning farther forward. "Which is why I'm looking forward to actually being able to help you for once."

Nate mimicked his brother's stance, staring into the distance again. "I think I need to let her go. She's young, she wants to travel and make a career for herself, and . . ."—he swallowed, hard—"she's Sam's sister, which means I shouldn't have gone there in the first place. Besides, she walked out on me. I can't exactly chase her when she's made it clear that she's done with me."

Ryder made a grunting sound. "All excuses. You can travel with her, you can give her all the freedom she needs because you like having your own space anyway, and screw Sam. If you love her, you're gonna treat her right, and what the hell more could someone want for his sister?" He sighed. "And let's not forget that my gorgeous yet infuriating wife walked out on me, too. When she left I thought I'd never see her again, let alone get her back in my bed."

Nate nodded. "You really think Sam would forgive me? Hell, I've avoided him like the plague since the day she left."

"He just wants her to be happy, to know she's gonna be looked after and protected even if he's not around. That's all."

"Says the guy who has no idea what it's like to have a sister."

"Hey, I've got a daughter," Ryder countered, moving closer to Rose. She slung her arm around his shoulders, cute as a button. "And anyway, you could always propose. Look at how well it worked out for me."

"I'm not asking Faith to marry me." Nate thought about it, about how he could do it, what she'd say. It wasn't that he definitely didn't want to marry her, she was the only woman he'd ever been with he could say that about, but he doubted it was what she wanted. If it was, though . . . He cleared his throat. "Nope, no way am I going to ask the woman who walked out on me to marry me. If I ever decide to be crazy enough to propose, I'd have to be damn sure that she was going to say yes."

Rose clapped her hands together, giggling. "I wanna pretty dress for the wedding!"

Nate and Ryder both laughed, Rose managing to soothe Nate when for the first time in his life he didn't know what the hell he was doing, what his plan was.

"I need to do something big, though, don't I? I mean, if I can't suck it up and forget she ever existed, I have to do something to get her attention. Show her that she was crazy to walk away from what we had, right?"

"Yeah, you do," Ryder replied, lifting Rose down from the top rail of the wooden fence and placing her back on his shoulders. "If I were you, I'd take her somewhere in the plane."

"I don't want to impress her with money," Nate disagreed, rolling his shoulders in a futile attempt to ease the tension in his neck. "It's not the kind of thing she'd be won over with. You know how it is. I bet Chloe was the same."

"Then impress her with *where* you take her. Make it special. Take her where only you would think to take her."

Nate went to answer, then clamped his mouth shut.

"You know where, don't you?" Ryder asked.

Nate slapped his brother on the back. "You're a genius," he told him, "a goddamn genius."

"Here to help," Ryder said with a laugh.

Nate grinned and blew Rose a kiss before calling out good-bye and leaving them. He was going to do it. There was no way he was going to let Faith be the one to walk away from him without at least showing her that he gave a damn about her and telling her how he felt. Ryder was right, he did love her, and it was the first time he'd ever felt like that about a woman. For him, it was usually all about the chase, but with Faith it was different. Once he'd had her in his bed, his house, *his life,* he wanted her to himself all the time. Hell, he didn't even have any desire to be with other women, and that was saying a hell of a lot.

But he knew what to do, to show her that he'd listened when she'd been talking about her dreams, to prove to her that he was the right man for her, that he wasn't going to hurt her or lose interest in her. And if he stood any chance of winning her back, he needed to do it now.

Nate had walked fast and now that he was closer to the house he checked the reception on his phone, seeing two bars now instead of one or none. He dialed his assistant, pleased when she picked up on the first ring.

"It's me; I need you to—"

"Nathaniel, where have you been? I've been trying to call you for the last hour."

His back bristled at his being asked where he'd been when it was no damn business of hers; then he realized that he needed to ease the hell up a bit. If he was going to ask Faith to be part of his life, he had to get used to being accountable to someone other than himself.

"Where the hell I've been is—" he started before he was interrupted.

"It's your grandfather," she said in a low voice. "The doctor wants you all there now, which is why I've been trying to get hold of you."

Nate swallowed, his heart pounding, blood running so fast through his body that he felt like he was about to keel straight over if he tried to walk. But he needed to run, to get Ryder and then make the fastest trip of their lives into the hospital.

"Did they say . . ." He couldn't even get the words out.

"He had a massive stroke: they don't expect him to hold on much longer."

The blood that had been running through him so damn hot turned cold as ice. Nate took a deep breath, then started to walk fast back in the direction he'd come. "Call the doctor back; tell them I'll be there. Tell them to do anything they can to keep him alive until then. And call Chase."

As soon as he hung up, Nate's fast walk turned into an all-out sprint, his legs pumping, covering the ground as fast as he did when he ran in the mornings, trying to jog away his demons.

"Ryder!" he called. "Ryder!"

It didn't take long for him to find them, Ryder wandering along without a care in the world and Rose still riding on his shoulders.

"Hey, don't tell me you need more brotherly advice already?" Ryder joked.

The smile died on his brother's face faster than it had appeared and Nate took a few deep breaths, blowing hard, before breaking the news to him.

"It's Granddad. I think it's the end." Nate reached for Rose, taking her down from Ryder's shoulders and folding her in his arms instead. He needed to hold her and there was no way Ryder could run with her up there, and every part of him was screaming out that they needed to hurry; hell, they might already be too late. "We need to go now."

They both jogged back toward the house, pacing themselves, not saying a word. *Fuck.* Nate wasn't ready to say good-bye to the man who'd raised them and taught them almost everything they knew, and he doubted either of his brothers was, either. His granddad meant the world to him, and once he was gone Nate would be running the King empire without guidance. It shouldn't have and he'd never admit it to another soul, but the idea scared the shit out of him.

When they finally stopped, both heaving, Nate set a wide-eyed Rose to her feet and let Ryder take her hand. Nate stared at Ryder.

"This is the end, isn't it?" Ryder said in a quiet voice. "It's time to say good-bye."

Nate nodded. "Take her back to Chloe and I'll bring the car around."

They went separate ways. Nate broke into a run again,

but it was like he wasn't in control of his body. When he stopped, his hands were shaking as he hunted for his keys, the back of his throat burning. For a guy used to shielding himself from emotion, the pain was so bad it took all his willpower not to double over and vomit from the waves of terror draining every inch of strength from his body.

His phone rang again and he picked up before getting into the vehicle.

"Yes!" he demanded, thinking it was going to be more news, *worse news.*

"Nate, it's Chuck!" the man yelled down the line. "We've hit oil! The bloody stuff is spurting up like crazy!"

Nate's eyes stung, an unfamiliar burn prickling hard. He cleared his throat. "Great. Thanks for the call."

He hung up, stopped for a moment, needing to catch his breath. Nausea rocked him, the bile in his throat choking him as he bent over beside the car.

"Damn you!" he yelled.

The one thing he'd wanted was his granddad to see the oil, to be there and watch it, to see it happen. And Nate knew in his heart that his grandfather was already gone.

"Nate?"

Nate looked up. He was exhausted, every bone in his body weary as he finally walked away from his granddad's room. Nate was grateful to have had the last few hours alone with his brothers, so they could say their good-byes, but it had taken everything from him.

"Hey, Sam," he managed, locking eyes on his friend

as he stood from a seat in the small waiting area. The brothers had requested not to be disturbed, just the three of them wanting to spend time alone, but Nate noticed that Chloe and Hope had both been waiting, too, their arms around Ryder and Chase now that they'd walked out behind him.

"Nate, I'm sorry, man," Sam said, opening his arms and pulling Nate in for a hug, slapping his back and holding him tight.

Nate took a deep breath. He'd prepared for this, he'd known this was coming, but all the prep in the world wasn't helping right now.

"Thanks for coming," he managed.

"All this bullshit with Faith, I'm sorry. Let's just forget about it."

Nate nodded when Sam stood back. He wasn't going to talk about Faith right now, didn't want to discuss the one person in the world he wished was by his side. Sam was right, they could forget what had happened, because when it happened again it was going to be different. No more sneaking around, no more stolen kisses, just Nate telling the whole world that Faith was his. If she'd have him.

"You going to have the service at home?" Sam asked, passing Nate his coffee that had been resting beside the chair he'd risen from.

Nate smiled his thanks and took the paper cup. Sam had obviously only just made it, it was full to the top, and they both drank it the same. Strong and sweet. "We're going to bring him home as soon as we can, get him back to the ranch where he belongs, and we'll have the service within a few days."

Sam's expression was sad, his eyes damp like he was ready to shed his tears for the man who'd always welcomed him onto the ranch when he and Nate were kids.

"Clay was a goddamn legend, Nate," Sam finally said, folding his arms across his chest and shaking his head. "He made me feel like one of you boys when I was staying over, gave me my first paying job." Sam rubbed his knuckles into his eyes before continuing. "I came to see him a few days ago, just to see how he was. I used to call most weeks. And you know what hit me?"

Nate raised an eyebrow, draining the coffee as he watched Sam. He hadn't even known how often his friend had been to visit.

"How damn similar the two of you are. Were." He laughed. "You're a chip off the old block, Nate. He was so proud of you, and it's because you're the spitting image of him."

Sam's words hit Nate hard, made the bite of emotion snap at his throat again, almost took control of him, but he squared his shoulders and forced it back down.

"Thanks, Sam, it means a lot. He was always telling everyone that he knew the finest horseman in Texas, so don't forget how much he thought of you, too."

They both stood a bit longer, Nate feeling so tired his eyeballs seemed to be aching.

"Hey, you ready to go?"

Ryder's hand on his shoulder jolted him back to the present, his voice deeper than usual, more raspy.

"Yeah, I'm ready."

Sam took the cup from him and threw it in the trash. "I'll see you at the service."

Chloe pushed between Nate and Ryder, looping a

hand through his arm and then her husband's, keeping them both close.

"You guys remember how impressed he was with me that I could beat the pants off all of you at poker?"

That made Nate laugh. "Yeah. I don't know if he was disgusted by us, in complete awe of you, or both."

"Definitely in awe of me," she said with a giggle before resting her head against Nate for a moment as they walked. "You want to come stay with us? I hate the idea of you being alone in the big house."

He chuckled, glancing down at her. As far as sisters-in-law went, he'd hit the jackpot with his two. "We need to stop calling it the big house. It's not like you two have small digs."

"What's so funny?"

Nate smiled at Chase as he joined them with Hope, one arm wrapped tight around her man.

"Nothing. Come on; let's get out of here."

Nate walked with them out into the lot, the outside temperature cooler than it had been when they'd arrived. It was cold now, the sky almost black.

"I'm gonna miss him," Nate said, to himself but to his brothers, too. "There's not a day that'll go by that I won't miss him."

Ryder and Chase both nodded, standing nearby.

"Now let's head home and crack a bottle of his favorite whiskey," Nate announced. "Gone but not forgotten, right?"

"Yep, here's to Wild Turkey, straight up over ice," Ryder agreed.

Chase smiled. "Hey, we might not have Granddad, but we have you, Nate. One look into your eyes, or the way you hold yourself when you're doing business, and it's like he's with us anyway."

Nate cleared his throat, wishing to hell everyone wasn't suddenly telling him how like his grandfather he was. Maybe he was; maybe he wasn't—either way, he just wanted to get home and drink enough to dull the pain a little. If that was even possible.

Chapter 17

FAITH ran her hands over the fabric of her skirt, more used to being in jeans than pencil skirts that hugged her body tight and made it impossible to take more than a small step. She'd gone out and bought a new outfit to wear to Clay King's funeral. It only seemed right to make an effort for a man that had been as good as a legend for longer than she could remember, but it was Nate she was all sweaty palmed over seeing. In all honesty, she'd come for him, but the suffocating feeling of waiting for the moment that he came near was almost unbearable.

"You okay?"

She nodded and smiled as Sam squeezed her hand, leaning in close to her. "Fine, thanks. I'm just hot." It was the truth. She had a silk cami on underneath her jacket, and the fact that they were outside in the sun with her wearing all black wasn't exactly sensible.

"We can go on over and take a seat if you want," Sam suggested, gesturing to the rows of white chairs beneath a huge tent with no sides.

She shook her head, more content to swelter in her suit than risk running into Nate or his brothers. She wanted them to know she'd been here, but the idea of seeing Nate again, being up close and personal with him for even a moment, wasn't something she'd ever be prepared for. Faith sighed. She might have been the one to walk away from him, but it didn't mean she didn't miss him like crazy still.

"Hey, Faith."

Faith hadn't realized she'd been holding her breath until she let it go. She turned and came face-to-face with Chloe.

"Hey," she replied. "How are you holding up?"

Chloe blinked away visible tears. "Okay. It's just hard seeing the guys so cut up."

Neither of them had said Nate's name, but it was hanging between them, and Faith decided she'd rather be the one to bring it up than wait for Chloe.

"And Nate?" Faith asked, wishing her brother wasn't standing right beside her, listening to the entire conversation. "How's he been?"

"Not bad, considering!" The deep, commanding voice that rang out behind her made every tiny hair on her body stand on end, her skin covered in goose pimples. She swallowed, took a deep breath, and slowly turned.

"I'm sorry for your loss, Nate," she managed, meeting his gaze head-on and suddenly wishing she hadn't come at all. His dark eyes were stormy, slightly bloodshot, his black hair pushed completely off his face. It was longer than it had been when she'd been with him, slightly unruly now even though he was obviously trying his best to tame it today.

"Thanks for coming," he said, eyes never leaving hers as he spoke, his voice powerful even though he was in pain. "You too, Sam," he continued, turning to her brother and holding out his hand. "And thanks for coming by the other day. It was good to see a friendly face after the afternoon I'd had."

Sam shook his hand, patted him on the back, and said a few words. Faith could have listened, was standing right beside them, but all she could think about was Nate. About the fact that he was standing so close, that this big, incredible man was less than two feet from her, a man she'd voluntarily walked away from because she was so damn scared of falling for him, when what she should have done was hold him close and try to never let him go.

"Faith?"

Her head snapped up, suddenly tuning in to the conversation when she heard her name.

"I'm sorry?"

"Nate wants a word with you." Sam looked between them. "In private."

Damn it! Why hadn't she stayed tuned in to what they were saying? "How about you, ah, go get us a couple of seats and I'll join you in a second."

Sam stared at her long and hard before nodding and walking away. Chloe had disappeared without her even realizing it, and suddenly it was just the two of them. She could only watch Sam walk away for so long before she had to change the angle of her body and face him.

"Nate . . ."

"Faith . . ."

They both laughed at the same time, only instead of

keeping his distance like she had been, Nate reached for her hand.

"You go first," he muttered, staring into her eyes and rubbing his thumb across her palm, making her go all kinds of crazy at the direct skin-to-skin contact.

Faith's mouth was dry, all thoughts gone from her head. She hardly even remembered exactly what she'd wanted to say, except for the fact that . . . what? That she shouldn't have left him? That she was in love with him? That she couldn't be with him even if she wanted to be?

When she didn't say anything, he smiled. "How about I go first, then?"

Faith nodded, wishing he wasn't touching her.

"I want to take you somewhere."

She was confused. "Right now?"

"No, on Friday. I need you to take the day off, and I'll come and get you first thing."

She frowned the moment he mentioned her taking time off. "Nate, I can't. This job means too much to me."

His smile was too smug, his gaze too intense. "I'm sure your boss won't mind you spending the day with your biggest client."

"Biggest client?" she asked, confused.

"I'm intending on making a significant purchase tomorrow. I don't care what so long as my art consultant can assure me that it's a good investment. Then I plan on telling your boss that I'd like to spend the day showing you my private collection and discussing future"—he grinned—"*acquisitions*."

Heat traveled through Faith's body, the blush hitting her cheeks before she could try to stop it. "Nate, I don't think that's a good idea."

"It's a damn fine idea," he as good as growled. "I have a funeral to deal with and my granddad to lay to rest, and aside from running King Enterprises I only care about one thing."

Her hand was shaking as she retrieved it, not wanting Nate to keep hold of her. "Nate, no. It's not the right thing to do."

"Neither was you leaving me."

"Touché."

They both stayed silent, paused.

"There are so many reasons why we shouldn't be together, Nate," she murmured. "Which means that we're better not tempting fate."

"I'm not like any other man you've known before, Faith."

She paused, body dead still. "Is that a threat?"

He was stone-faced for a moment before leaning in close to her, the scent of his cologne filling her nostrils, his body blocking out everything else.

"No," he said, stroking a hand down her arm, slowly. "But I'm going to prove to you exactly why we should be together, and when I'm finished . . ."

She gulped. Waiting. "What?"

"Let's just say that I'm not good at taking no for an answer, and I don't *ever* intend on letting you walk out of my life that easily ever again."

Faith had hardly moved an inch since she'd sat down. From where they were sitting, a few rows back from the front, she could see the back of Nate's dark hair. Her fingers were betraying her by fidgeting, remembering what it was like to be lazy and content in bed with him, how it felt to run her fingertips through his thick hair.

The minister stopped talking then, leading them all in prayer, which at least forced her to dip her head for a moment and concentrate on what he was saying. And then he was announcing Clay's eldest grandson to say a few words. Faith gulped. Instead of remembering the man she was here to pay respects to, she couldn't stop thinking about the times she'd had on the property with Nate. Times they'd done their best to keep secret, which had made it all the more fun.

She straightened, noticed the way her brother shifted when Nate strode to the microphone and smiled at everyone seated before him. Sam loved Nate, they'd been best friends since Little League days, but she knew her brother was still uncomfortable with what he thought had happened between her and Nate. What *had* happened between them.

"Clay King was a man like no other," Nate began, his deep, commanding voice so like his grandfather's. "I'm proud to call him my granddad, or dad really, as he brought us up with Grams as if they were our true parents after my mom died."

Faith noticed that he hadn't mentioned his father, and she doubted he would. Nate wasn't exactly the forgiving type, and he'd made it clear that he had no love for the man who'd abandoned them.

"My granddad taught the three of us a lot of things, too many things to share today, but the one that always stands out is that we had to find what we were passionate about." Nate's voice turned husky, cracking slightly until he cleared his throat. "I think you all know that I was gunning to follow in his footsteps since I was a kid, and we've all found our own way, but he also told us that once we found out what we wanted, never to take no for an answer." Nate's eyes suddenly found hers, his gaze strong and unwavering, leaving her struggling to breathe. "I'm fortunate to have told Granddad how much I loved him, and I fought to prove myself to him every damn day while he was alive, and Granddad, if you can hear me up there, nothing's gonna change. Chase and Ryder made him beyond proud when they met their gorgeous wives and finally brought some permanent female company to the ranch, and I'm only sorry that the old fella didn't get to meet my future wife, too."

Wife? If she'd been breathless before then she was completely out of air now. Nate had always said that he'd never marry, that he had zero interest in settling down, and now he was talking to an entire crowd of people—friends, acquaintances, business contacts, and his family—about Clay missing out on meeting his future wife?

"I'd like to thank you all for coming, and invite you to stay on and celebrate Clay's life with us. We will be attending a private burial immediately after the service concludes, and then Granddad's favorite whiskey will be flowing like water until dark."

Faith gulped, watching Nate cross back to his seat, so confident in everything he did. Even emotional over losing his grandfather, he'd still managed to address a couple hundred people and talk to them as if he knew every single one of them personally. But personally, she was still stuck on the "wife" comment.

They'd already heard from Chase about Clay's life, how he inherited King Ranch and turned an already successful business into an empire like no other in Texas, and after a few more words from the minister, along with a final prayer, the service was concluded.

The three brothers walked past them slowly, with a few other men, carrying Clay's coffin down the center of the chairs. Nate's jaw looked like it was carved from stone, tears glistening in his eyes as he passed her. No one made a sound as the men escorted one of the greatest men in Texas into the long black car, the crowd folding in behind them as they all walked back out into the bright southern sunshine.

"I'm going to head off now," Faith told Sam, leaning in close to him.

"You're not going to stay for a drink? Pay your respects?" Sam asked, frowning.

"It's complicated," she said, squeezing his hand. "I just don't feel like I should be here right now."

"Because of Nate?" Sam asked, looking irritated.

"Yes," she told him, not wanting to lie. "But it's not what you think."

"I was thinking that he'd damn well broken your heart," Sam muttered. "Just like I warned you would happen. But now I'm not so sure."

She tried to act like discussing her love life with Sam was the most natural thing in the world. "He didn't break my heart. We just . . ."

"He's in love with you, isn't he? That speech about his future wife . . ."

"Just leave it, Sam. I need to go."

He didn't try to stop her and she didn't waste time.

Thank god she'd brought her own car. Faith moved silently through the crowd, smiling and nodding as she passed people she knew, until a hand closed over her wrist and stopped her from moving another step.

"You're leaving already?"

She tried to snatch her hand back, but it didn't work. Instead Nate slowly released his grip, so slowly that she had to remain almost immobile the entire time.

"Nate, I need to go."

"Is there anything I can do to change your mind?" he asked, moving closer, his body making hers ache for all kinds of things that it couldn't have.

She stared at his lips, at the gentle curve of his mouth as he smiled. His eyes were still damp, unshed tears ready to be blinked away if they weren't going to fall.

"You shouldn't hold them back," she said, because it was the only thing she could think of to say. "Your tears," Faith clarified when he looked puzzled.

"I'm not afraid to cry," Nate told her, reaching out and touching her hair, his thumb and forefinger gently caressing a strand before he let go.

But I'm afraid of you. They were the words she wanted to say, *needed* to say, but they wouldn't come out. Instead she just walked a step closer to him, stood on tiptoe, and pressed a kiss to his cheek, her lips betraying her and staying against his skin a little too long.

"Good-bye, Nate."

His smile was a confusing combination of sad and warm. "I'll be by at nine am to collect you on Friday."

She folded her arms across her chest. "You don't even know where I live."

"Yes, I do," he said, winking and sending a wave of

desire through every inch of her body. "You can run from me, darlin', but you sure as hell can't hide."

It should have sounded like a threat, but it didn't. Because if she put her foot down and told him to back the hell off, he would. Only she wasn't ready to say good-bye to him forever, not without seeing what he had planned first. She could have all the willpower and good intentions in the world, but walking away from him completely was never going to be easy. Not in a million years.

"I think we have a problem."

Nate knocked back the last of his whiskey and set down his glass. Sam was still nursing his, eyes trained on Nate as they stood in Clay's former library. Nate had taken the place over once his granddad had officially asked him to start running their businesses, but nothing about the décor or even the books themselves had changed. The dark timber panels and textured Ralph Lauren wallpaper made it feel like it could have been the early 1900s still, like something straight from the days of *Boardwalk Empire*, Clay's favorite TV show. And it was just the way Nate liked it. Different from the rest of the house, an escape where he could focus on work and drink some whiskey, read a book if he wanted to with no distractions, lamps lit instead of overhead lights. He'd come in here with Chase and Ryder to privately toast their granddad now that he'd been lowered into the ground in the private King cemetery on the land, and Sam had wandered in to talk to Nate, away from the large crowd gathered throughout the rest of the ground floor of the house.

"Nate?"

"Yeah, I heard you," he said, reaching for the decanter and pouring more whiskey into his glass. "And I take it we're talking about your sister?"

Sam dropped into the worn brown leather sofa, taking another sip of his drink. "I don't want to be an asshole bringing this up today, Nate. You know I love you, I'd do anything for you, but this stuff with Faith is fucking with my head."

Nate sighed and sat in the sofa opposite, kicking one of his legs up to rest on the other, boot to his knee. "I fucked up," he admitted. "I made you a promise that I'd stay away from her, which I damn well did for years, and then when she arrived on my doorstep that day it didn't take long before I—"

Sam made a face and held up his hand. "Stop. I don't want to hear the details."

Nate studied his friend, pleased that they were at least discussing Faith in a civilized manner instead of fighting. "I didn't ever want to hurt her, Sam. I still don't."

Sam finished his drink and stood up to pour another. "You love her, don't you?" he asked, without turning, his back still to Nate.

Nate blew out a breath. "You want the truth?"

Sam sat down again, his face hard to read. "Yeah, I want the truth. No bullshit. Tell me like it is."

"Yeah, I fucking love her, Sam. I love your sister and there's not a damn thing I can do about it."

Sam looked like he was in pain, just talking about his little sister romantically was killing him. "So why the hell aren't you together, and why is she so damn miserable? She saw you today and she fell apart."

"It's complicated."

"That's what she told me. But I've known you long enough to know that women are pretty black-and-white where you're concerned."

Nate laughed. "What the hell is that supposed to mean?"

Sam pulled a face. "Don't act all Mr. Innocent with me. You sleep with a woman until you're bored, or you think she's starting to get clingy. You make it clear from the start that you're not looking for serious, but every woman thinks she's going to be the one to change you; then you break their hearts even though you told them all along that you had nothing more than a good time to give them."

"You done?" Nate asked, pissed off but not about to deny the truth.

"No, I'm nowhere near done. Because somehow you ended up in bed with my sister. Somehow you ended up having something more with her than I'm guessing you've ever had with any other woman before, and now you're acting all weird and she's all upset."

"Which leads you to your theory about me being in love with her?" Nate asked, trying not to laugh. He should have been pissed with Sam for being so damn nosey, but at least he wasn't trying to actually break Nate's nose this time.

"Am I right?" Sam asked, knocking back a shot of whiskey.

"Yeah," Nate said. "You are. I let the little minx get

under my skin, and now I'm doing everything I can to win her back."

"You fucking hurt her . . . ," Sam warned, pointing at Nate.

"You fucking kill me; I get it." He rose, moved toward the window, and stared out. "But what you don't get is that your little sister hurt me, Sam. Not the other way around."

"And if she means it? If she doesn't want you?" he asked. "You know that saying about letting something go if you love it?"

"She tells me to leave her the hell alone, I will. But I ain't giving her up without a fight." Nate hadn't thought about the fact that she could tell him to fuck off entirely, focused only on what he was doing and what he wanted her to say. But he would let her go; if he had to he wasn't going to make a fool of himself by begging. *No damn way.*

"You give me your word that you'll respect her wishes, and I'll repress the urge to smash your face in every time I think about the two of you together."

"Deal," Nate agreed. "And I promise I won't come crying to you if she becomes the first woman to break my heart not once but twice."

They both laughed. Nate poured them each an extra shot and held his glass up.

"Who'd have ever thought my little sister would be the one to tame you, without even trying."

Nate chuckled. "Not me, that's for fucking sure."

Chapter 18

IT wasn't often that Faith was genuinely nervous. Although if she was honest with herself, she hadn't been much better at Clay's funeral. Her palms were sweaty, her hair was clinging to the back of her neck, and she was pacing. She never paced! Faith took a deep breath, shut her eyes for a moment to calm herself down, and decided to pour herself a glass of water.

The problem was that she had no idea where they were going or what they were doing. After Nate had phoned in and confirmed on a six-figure Mark Bradford painting the day before, her boss had virtually begged her to spend the day with him and see what else he might like to add to his collection. She personally doubted he even liked abstract, multilayer collage-style art like the Bradford, but she couldn't deny that it would be a good investment. They were selling it on behalf of a collector who was going through a divorce settlement, which meant Nate had gotten it for a good price.

A knock sounded downstairs and she jumped, spilling the glass of water she was holding. Faith cursed and tipped the rest out, crossing the room to collect her small case. She had a couple changes of clothes, jeans and a cute top as well as a dress, both outfits she could wear with the heels she had on if she needed to. She hated surprises and she especially hated the idea of being unprepared for an entire day of being with Nate. And the fact that he'd left a message for her saying they'd be out of the town for the day and that she might like to pack a few things had her even more antsy.

The knock sounded again and she walked slowly toward the door, opening it even though she was certain the smarter thing to do would have been to keep it shut and go hide in her room.

"Hi," Nate said, stepping back instead of filling the entire doorway.

"Morning," she replied, pleased she'd dressed up now that Nate was here. He was wearing a tailored black suit with a soft pink shirt open necked beneath it, and he looked so damn good it actually annoyed her.

"You look"—he held out one hand and scanned her with his eyes—"stunning. Very professional."

"If you'd told me where you were taking me, I'd have known how to dress."

"Believe me, your cute little skirt and leather jacket ensemble is perfect."

The corners of Faith's mouth twitched, desperate to break out into a smile, but she tried her hardest to refrain. The last thing she needed was to start thinking about Nate like that again, or make him think that anything more was going to happen between them.

He reached past her and took the case, lifting it rather than wheeling it, and walking back to his SUV.

"I wasn't sure how much luggage you'd have, so I thought I'd bring something big for transportation."

She fake-laughed. "Ha-ha."

Nate's grin was infectious and she found it impossible not to smile as she hopped into the passenger seat.

"You're taking me somewhere in the plane, aren't you?"

He started the engine, then turned to her. "Yes."

Faith stared him straight in the eye. "And where are you taking me?" she asked.

"I'll tell you that once we're on the plane."

She leaned back in the seat as he started to drive. "If you're trying to impress me with the fact that you can just whisk me off somewhere . . ." Faith didn't even know what to say. She'd told him that this sort of thing only made it more clear to her that they were from different backgrounds.

"I'm not trying to impress you with the plane," he said, eyes on the road. "I would have flown you coach, but none of the flight times worked, so this is just a means to an end."

"Bullshit," she said, laughing. "I don't think *anyone* could convince Nate fricking King to fly coach. No way."

He was silent for so long she almost reached over to poke him to make sure he was okay.

"You could," he finally said, his voice soft and low. "I reckon you're probably the only person in the world who could make me do anything, aside from maybe Harrison or little Rose."

Faith didn't have an answer to that. They stayed quiet on the short drive there, and when Nate jumped out and ran around to her side she let him. The airport was fairly quiet, and she followed beside him as he led the way into the terminal, his Range Rover being valet parked since it seemed they were only going to be gone until late evening.

"When's your painting being delivered?" she asked, just trying to make conversation and stop the stretch of silence that had formed between them.

"Ah, next week, I think. It's going to my office."

She nodded. "Great choice. I'll definitely keep my eye out for anything else by the same artist that will complement it."

Within minutes they'd walked through a door and were out on the tarmac and facing the King jet; to say it was not impressive would have been lying. Still, Faith refused to be all fangirl over Nate and his big bad plane.

A way too beautiful blonde waved, dressed in a tight-fitting suit, hair twisted up and off her face. As they got closer Faith could see that her makeup was flawless and she was easily the most attractive flight attendant Faith had ever seen. Although she hadn't exactly traveled a lot, there was no denying how gorgeous the woman was.

"Please don't tell me you've slept with her," Faith muttered as he reached for her hand to lead her up the stairs.

"No."

"But you've thought about it?" she asked, wishing she hadn't. "I mean, I know you like blondes."

Nate chuckled, squeezing her hand. "Honey, I like all

women, but I certainly don't have a thing for blondes over . . ."—he paused and touched a lock of her hair— "incredibly stunning brunettes."

She forced her mouth to shut.

"But I'd be lying if I said I hadn't thought about sleeping with her. I met her before you turned up that day."

"Hey, at least you're honest." But if she was truthful, all it made her want to do was punch the blonde's perfect little white teeth from her painted pink-lipped mouth.

"You want honest?" He chuckled. "Every beautiful woman I meet, I wonder how good she'd look naked. But you've ruined me, darlin'. Nothing compares."

She burst out laughing. "Come off it, Nate." There was flattery, and then there was just . . . she had no idea what that even was.

"Good morning, Mr. King," the blonde said, gesturing for them to enter. "We'll be wheels up as soon as you're settled."

"Thank you," Nate replied, nodding and keeping hold of Faith's hand, barely acknowledging the attendant. "I'd like to make sure we have chilled water, the bottle of New Zealand sauvignon blanc I sent over earlier, and a selection of food. Once you have all that sorted I'd prefer not to be interrupted except in case of an emergency."

She looked taken aback but nodded politely. Faith forced herself to smile as she passed—it wasn't like she was the only woman on the planet attracted to Nate King.

"New Zealand wine?"

"Only the best, darlin'."

"You need to stop calling me that."

He stopped, let go of her hand, and crossed his arms. "You used to like it, if I remember correctly."

Faith blushed. When he'd used that sexy drawl in bed and called her all kinds of pet names she'd loved it. Now it just reminded her of what she couldn't have.

"So where are we going?" Faith asked.

"New York," he said simply, as if he'd just announced they were heading down to a local café for lunch.

"New York?" she spluttered.

Nate shrugged and sat back in his seat, gesturing for her to take the one opposite him. She sank into the soft leather, putting her purse on the seat and wondering how the hell anyone could afford luxuries like a private jet. With the exception of maybe movie stars.

"Why are we going to New York?" she asked, more composed this time.

Nate's stare was warm, his gaze fixed on hers, unwavering, as he looked into her eyes. Nothing about the way he held himself gave away his thoughts or his emotions. He had his legs spread wide, arms resting on his knees as he leaned forward.

"Because I've never met anyone as passionate about art as you and you deserve to see the best galleries in the country. Or at least one of the best."

Faith swallowed. Hard. Like she'd been stranded in the desert for days she was so dry. "Why? Why are you doing this for me?"

Her question hung between them, Nate's eyes still fixed on hers. She thought he was going to look away, that he was going to blink and avoid what she'd asked, but he proved that nothing scared him when he finally answered her.

"Because I love you." Her eyes had been leveled on Nate's lips, as she thought how soft and kissable they looked as he sat not saying anything, but she quickly raised her gaze when he said words she'd never, *ever* expected to come out of his mouth.

"Nate . . . ," she cautioned, not sure what else to say.

"I love you, Faith, and this is me proving it to you."

Nate sat back, unfazed by what he'd just told her, so damn comfortable in his own skin that it drove her wild.

"You can't just say things like that." Her voice sounded weak, like she wasn't sure of what she was saying, and she was. Only hearing him say it . . . She cleared her throat. "Is that what this is about? You trying to tell me I need to move back into your place so we can keep having crazy-good sex?"

He laughed, his eyes crinkling at the sides as he pushed his too-long hair from his face. It was so at odds with his suit, the hair that should have been cut a little shorter but was instead left to be unruly.

"Sweetheart, I'll take you in my bed *anytime;* that's a given. But I want a whole lot more from you than your bedroom skills."

"Ha, or lack of," she scoffed.

Nate as good as growled. "Don't talk shit, Faith."

Nate liked flirting with Faith. Hell, he liked doing almost anything with Faith, especially after not seeing her for so long.

"You know how to play backgammon?" he asked.

Her eyebrows shot up. "Seriously?"

He passed her a bottle of water. They were about to

take off and he was happy to get in the air. It was going to take a few hours, and the sooner they got there the better.

"I was thinking we could play. Or I could teach you."

"Teach me?" she asked, a wicked smile curving her mouth. "I think I'm just about done with you teaching me wicked things, Nathaniel."

"I love it when you call me that," he teased.

It was strange how they could go so long without seeing each other and then go straight back into talking shit and having fun. Which was why he liked her so damn much.

"Yes, I can play backgammon, Nate. You don't think that Sam was able to play so well against you without having someone to practice with, do you?"

He sat back. "You've got to be kidding me. I wondered how the hell he got so damn good. Son of a bitch!"

Faith was smiling. "He taught me, but I haven't played in years. I'm game if you are, though."

"Let's do it," Nate said, reaching for the board he had stashed away. His brothers hated playing, so he was damn happy to have someone to spar with. "And while we're playing, we can discuss all those reasons you claim we couldn't work."

"Ha," she said, clicking her seat belt on as they started down the runway. "So this is actually some kind of therapy session where I get so distracted playing backgammon that I end up telling you my life's secrets?"

He shrugged. "Could be. Or maybe I just really like playing backgammon and I actually give a shit about why you're so scared to commit to anything but work."

He set the board out, fingers moving fast to place the counters in their rightful places. His counters were magnetic, not like the expensive leather set he kept in the library at home; he took all games seriously, which meant he had no intention of risking the counters flying off the board in turbulence.

"So tell me again why you left me?" he asked.

She sighed, rolling a die in one hand. "Nate, you know I think you're a great guy, but this was never going to work. We've been through this. I'm not going to . . ."

"Make the same mistake your mom did. I know that," he finished for her.

"So why are you covering old ground when we could just be . . ."—she paused—"I don't know, enjoying each other as friends?"

Nate glared at her, trying to stay calm and failing. "Because you and I know that we're never going to be just friends again, not even friends with benefits. It might have started out like that, but it sure as hell ain't ending like it."

Her eyes were damp when she looked up. "I don't want to argue with you, Nate." She threw her dice, took the move when hers was the higher of the two. "It doesn't matter how I feel or how you think you feel right now. We can't be together as anything more than . . ."

"Fuck buddies?" he suggested.

"I wouldn't have put it so crudely, but yeah."

"Well, screw that," Nate said, staring at her and wishing he could just take her right there on the goddamn plane, kiss some sense into her, and just tell her how it was going to be, whether she liked it or not. "And by the end of the day, maybe you'll realize that I'm not the same asshole who broke your mom's heart. Okay?"

She swallowed; he watched the movement of her throat, the way she glanced from him to the board. "How about we just start with playing the game?"

He threw the dice. "Deal."

Chapter 19

BY the time they landed, Faith was exhausted. Just being with Nate was enough to drain every ounce of energy from her. She'd tried so hard to forget about him, to put him behind her and move forward with her life, but it had been impossible. Then somehow she'd seen him once and ended up running straight back into the lion's den.

"Do I get any clues yet?"

Nate chuckled, stretching as he stood. "You'll find out soon enough."

"This doesn't change anything," she said, reaching for her purse instead of looking at Nate as she spoke.

"It will," Nate replied, moving to stand too close to her. She could feel his presence behind her, hated that her body reacted so instantly to his every single time he was near.

She didn't say anything, not wanting to encourage him. She should never have gotten on the plane. Being with him was a huge mistake.

"It can't."

His hands were on her shoulders, resting there, warming her before making her turn. She resisted, but there was only so long she could stay strong and not give in.

"Nate—" she started.

He put a finger to her lips, silenced her as he watched her so intently, his gaze so kind and different from the way he looked at so many others. To some he seemed intimidating, powerful, arrogant even, but with her he'd always been gentle, kind instead of ruthless, loving instead of careless. Which was why he'd blindsided her, when all she'd expected was some fun between the sheets.

"I know why you're scared, and I know why you don't think this can work," he said, moving his hand to cup the back of her head, his other softly touching her face, tips of his fingers against her cheeks. "Just give me today, Faith; that's all I ask. If you tell me to walk away after today, I will. For good."

They were the words she wanted to hear, but they also hurt. Because deep down, part of her was desperate for him to fight for her, to prove that he wasn't what she expected from him.

"So where in New York are you taking me?" she asked as his mouth moved closer to hers. His lips mesmerized her, reminded her of the times they'd shared together, of what she was missing out on.

"To a gallery," he said, finally closing his lips over hers, so gently she almost couldn't feel them. *But she could.* His kiss was light and warm, and she tried to stay still when all she wanted was to throw her arms around his neck and make him kiss her harder.

But Nate was a model of self-control today, no doubt having everything planned, including how to make her beg for more from him.

"What gallery?" she murmured, touching her fingers to her lips as she stepped back.

"Midtown Ink," he replied, a smug smile on his face. "And we have it all to ourselves."

Faith's hand dropped. If she'd let it, her jaw would have, too. "They've closed the gallery for us?"

"Yes. For a high-level investor who wants time to get acquainted with his purchases, and his bright young star of a consultant."

"You"—she said, shaking her head, then leaning over to punch him on the arm—"are something else." She grimaced. "And you also work out way too much. That hurt."

He laughed. "Hey, while I was with you I got all flappy. It's a good thing that I'm working out again. Gives me something to do instead of roll around in a cold bed. Alone."

"Flappy?" she asked, ignoring his reference to bed. No wonder he'd been confident that this stunt would work in convincing her how fabulous he was. Only he was kind of missing the point. She already knew that he was incredible; she just didn't believe for a second that he'd want her long-term, and she had zero intention of putting her life and career, let alone her heart, on the line for a man who was ultimately going to lose interest in her.

"Fat and happy," he joked. "Get it?"

"Oh yeah, because you got *so* fat." Faith laughed. Why did he have to be so damn charming all the time, even making bad jokes?

The pilot announced they were able to depart and Nate collected her case and an overnight bag he had and nodded for her to walk ahead of him. She did, smiling at the flight attendant who only had eyes for Nate before descending the stairs. The weather was pleasant, not as warm as Texas but nice, with a slight breeze blowing. She was pleased she was wearing a jacket and that she'd dressed businesslike now that she knew where they were going.

"I have a car waiting," Nate said, wheeling her case behind them now they were on the ground. "Let's go get it and head straight to the gallery."

She followed, amused by the smug look on his face. She was dying to see the gallery, truth be told, and being flown in by private jet and arriving as his consultant was incredible. Faith had to hand it to him; he sure as hell had been listening when she'd told him her bucket list career-wise.

"What would you do if I told you I wanted to move here?" she asked. "If I love the gallery so much that I want to try to get a job in New York?"

Nate frowned, slowing down from the fast-paced walk he'd adopted. "I'd say the jet is going to need some extra maintenance and an additional crew for all the flying she'd be doing."

Faith bit down on her bottom lip to stop from smiling. He really was pulling out all the stops today.

The ride from the airport was relatively quick, given the amount of traffic they had to negotiate, and she was wide-eyed the entire way. She'd never been to New York, and it was everything she'd imagined. Busy, incredible, vibrant . . . and that was just the vibe she got from inside the car.

"We're here," Nate said.

"Have you been here before?" she asked, waiting for the driver to stop before pushing her door open, not waiting for Nate to do it for her. She wanted to get out and discover the city she'd dreamed about so often and never thought she'd see in real life before she was thirty.

"Once," Nate replied as he stepped out behind her, passing the driver some bills when he took their cases from the trunk. "I had a meeting canceled nearby a while back and I took a look around. Granddad always liked his art, so I was just seeing what they had."

Faith walked alongside him and into the building. She'd seen pictures on various Web sites, had always followed their exhibitions and reviews, so she knew exactly where she was and what she was about to walk into.

"Thank you, Nate," she said, reaching for his hand as they walked in.

He took the opportunity to stop her, keeping hold of her hand, his palm locked against hers.

"You don't even know what I have planned yet."

"It doesn't matter," she said. "I'm here, at the gallery of my dreams, and you've made it happen. So no matter what else goes down between us, thank you."

Nate had never done anything wrong, which was exactly why she found it so hard to be angry with him or pull away. It was merely her resolve to be stronger than her mother had been, to prioritize herself and follow her own dreams, and not get her heart broken into a million pieces along the way.

When they entered, the gallery was quiet. So quiet she could have dropped a hairpin and it would have sounded like a rock crashing down onto the tiled floor.

"Welcome. You must be Nathaniel King." An immaculately groomed woman on superhigh heels stepped forward, holding out her hand to Nate. "We're so pleased to have you here today."

Nate nodded and clasped the woman's hand. "This is Faith Mendes, the art consultant I told you about. Faith is also a personal friend of mine, and she's helping me to develop my personal collection."

Faith stepped closer and shook the woman's hand, smiling as they exchanged pleasantries.

"You'll find that the only staff on are here for security reasons," the woman continued. "I'll be in my office should you need me, and you have the gallery for the next few hours. Your table is waiting where we discussed."

Once she'd left them, Faith turned, studying Nate's handsome face. "Table?" she asked.

"I know how hungry that little stomach of yours gets," he joked. "I couldn't have us here until midafternoon without something to eat now, could I?"

"Trust you," she muttered.

"Trust me to what?"

"Manage to give me the one thing in the world you knew I wanted, and turn it into something romantic at the same time."

He laughed. "Hey, I'm not all that interested in art

unless it serves as an investment purpose, so there had to be something in it for me."

Faith walked on ahead, leaving Nate to find somewhere to place their cases and then catch up to her. She could hardly believe some of the works she was looking at, all by amazing established artists, the most stunning blend of contemporary pieces she'd ever seen in the flesh.

"Anything you like?" he asked, his voice lazy like he didn't really give a damn.

"I love everything," she said, sounding all breathless and unlike her usual self. "But you want my professional opinion, right?"

"Yes," he answered, touching her back as he passed, moving to the next painting. His lingering hand, palm flat to her back, only made her more aware of him. "I doubt the owner will be happy with me if I don't buy anything after insisting that I would."

Faith nodded. "Well, let's look through the entire gallery first; then I'll consider my answer."

They walked slowly side by side, Faith pausing to make notes in her phone every so often. She might not have even finished her post-grad degree yet, but this was the experience of a lifetime, and more important than any final paper. She'd dreamed of being an art consultant to the rich, and this was her first taste of it. Just because it was Nate didn't meant she wasn't going to take it seriously, especially when there was so much money at stake. She wanted him to genuinely appreciate her skill when it came to art—see her as more than a pretty face and fun bedmate.

* * *

"Please tell me you're ready to stop walking now?" Nate loved spending time with Faith, but after close to two hours of her walking painstakingly slowly through the gallery back and forth and hardly saying a word to him except for the odd comment about different brushstrokes and styles, and anecdotes about various artists, he was well and truly over art.

"I just want to—"

"I'm not buying if you don't agree to break for lunch," he insisted, knowing he sounded like a spoiled brat and not giving a damn.

She glanced at him, her face different than he'd seen it before. She'd barely noticed him since they'd arrived, her entire focus the artwork on display and taking notes.

"Where are we going?" she asked.

Nate smiled, relieved. "This way."

He took her hand and led her across the room and to an alcove. There was a table set up in the window, looking out to the city, and a painting that was apparently a big deal hung nearby, carefully positioned to shield it from the sun.

"Oh my god," Faith gasped, letting go of his hand.

Nate turned. "You like?"

"This is an original Erwin Olaf," she said, gesturing to the painting, "Are you kidding me? This is just . . ." She kept looking from the art to the table to him. "Nate, this is too much."

"It's for you," he said gruffly. "I did this for you, because I wanted you to know that everything you told me, everything you shared with me, wasn't just idle chat.

I care about you, Faith, and it was never my intention to hurt you."

She walked closer to him, reached for him, and placed her hands over his forearms. "But that's the thing, Nate. You didn't hurt me."

"So tell me the truth!" he demanded, voice strong yet kind. "You need to tell me what I'm up against."

Faith sat down, looking out the window, his gaze fixed on something he couldn't see, or maybe she was just staring.

"When I told you about my mom, I didn't tell you the whole story."

Nate sat down across from her, taking the wine from the ice bucket and pouring sauvignon blanc into their glasses. He nudged one closer to her, then sat back, wanting to give her space.

"So tell me," he said. "After everything we've been through, you need to tell me."

"The man she was in love with, he was from money," she said, turning back around so she was facing him. "That's why I don't want to be impressed by your material things, Nate, even though I'd love to be surrounded by nice things all the time."

He frowned. "I never tried to buy your affection, Faith. Not once. Hell, I wasn't even certain you'd want to come on the plane with me because I know how you feel."

"Some women, they chase rich men as if it's a career. My mom wasn't like that, but she did fall for the wrong man. He told her he loved her, and maybe he did, but in the end she was from one world and he was from another."

"This guy, he told her that?" Sounded like an asshole to Nate. "I don't mean to be rude, Faith, but I've been friends with Sam for years. I don't give a damn where anyone lives or how much money they have, so long as they can look me in the eye and prove the kind of person they are to me."

She took a sip of wine, the glass resting against her palm as she cradled it. "He promised to marry her; she was dreaming of a life with him and put all of her own aspirations on hold. Never went to college, lived in his home with him for years. And then his parents pushed him to marry someone from their own circle, didn't want him marrying a pretty little Hispanic girl with no money, and two months after he finished with her he was married to another woman with a baby on the way."

Nate gritted his teeth, hating what she was telling him. "For starters, I'm not that kind of man. I make my own decisions about my life, and my family have a different set of morals."

She smiled up at him, but he could see it was filled with sadness. "You might say that now, Nate, but things change; I know they do. You might find me fun and attractive now, but one day dating your friend's little sister won't be novelty enough."

Nate took a slow sip of wine, deciding he was better off drinking than losing his cool and yelling at her or shaking her to try to get some sense into her head. He leaned forward, discarding his glass and staring into her eyes, hoping she could see how damn frustrated he was.

"You honestly think that I think of you as some sort of novelty? That I just got off on sleeping with you because you were forbidden?"

She shrugged. "Isn't that what made it all so fun?"

He unfisted his hands and reached for her, forcing himself to be gentle instead of giving in to his frustration and punching the table. "Yes, the fact that you were forbidden added an element on fun to what we were doing, but it wasn't why I fell in love with you."

"You're not in love with me, Nate. It's just lust. I'm sure of it."

He fought not to laugh at the serious look on her face. "Lust? Are you kidding me?" This time he couldn't help but chuckle at her, holding on tight to both her hands now. "Lust was me screwing my way through too many women all my life. Love?" He blew out a breath. "I've never been in love before, Faith, but believe me when I say I sure as hell know what it is. For the first time in my life there is only one woman I want in my bed, and I also want her in my life, by my side. I want to wake up and know that the one woman I give a damn about is tucked up beside me away from all the evil in the world."

"Nate . . ."

He shook his head. "No, Faith. You don't get to tell me how I feel. You can tell me to leave you the hell alone, and I'll back away if that's truly what you want, but right here, right now, is a man telling a woman that he loves her. No strings attached, as simple as that."

He could see her breathing. Her mouth was slightly parted, her chest rising just visibly as they sat in silence.

"I can't be hurt like she was, Nate. I can't give you my heart and worry that one day you'll wake up and realize you don't want to be with the hired help."

"Hired help?" He laughed, holding up one of her

hands and leaning in closer to drop a kiss to her skin. "Are you kidding me?"

The look on her face told him she wasn't.

"Darlin', you were my pretend housekeeper for a few weeks. That doesn't make you the help, and even if it did, I don't give a fuck, to be perfectly honest." He sighed, wondering how he was ever going to convince her that his feelings were genuine. Hell, he'd had women begging for a commitment from him in the past, yet he couldn't make Faith believe that he wanted to be with her exclusively no matter what he said.

"Faith, you're going to make an amazing art consultant. You're a strong, capable, *beautiful* woman, and the last thing I'd ever want is to be responsible for crushing your dreams or your career aspirations. That's why I love you so much. You came to me for protection when you were vulnerable, but at the same time you're so damn strong and determined."

She smiled, just a hint of a smile, but an upturn of her lips nonetheless.

"Your brother is one of the state's best horse trainers in my opinion, so whatever you think about your background or your family not being good enough for me? That's just crazy talk."

"So what are you proposing?" she said in a low voice.

Nate had planned on having lunch first, but to hell with it.

"Funny that you ask . . . ," he murmured, letting go of her hand and standing. He'd discarded his jacket and put it over the back of his chair, but he reached into it now for the small box he'd tucked safely into his breast pocket.

Nate cleared his throat, suddenly not quite as confident as he'd been the day he went in to choose it.

"Faith Mary Mendes," he said, dropping to one knee beside her.

Her hand shot up to her mouth as she looked down at him, eyes wide.

"If this isn't proof enough that I love you and intend honoring my word, then I don't know what is," he said. "Marry me. Put me out of my misery and tell me that you love me, too."

She sobbed, a quiet, barely audible sob, hand still pressed to her mouth. "I love you," she whispered.

"Good," he said with a laugh. "And will you marry me?" He opened the box, annoyed with himself that he hadn't shown her the ring straightaway. "I wanted to get you something spectacular, but I didn't think you'd want something new. So I found an antique jeweler to work with and we finally found this."

The diamond was substantial, five carats, and it was set on a platinum band with pretty baguette diamonds to each side. The style was perfect for her slender finger, and when she lowered her hand from her mouth, shaking, and extended it toward him, he carefully slid the ring on.

"Yes," she whispered. "It's beautiful."

He stood and pulled her up with him, wrapping his arms around her. "Almost as beautiful as you," he murmured against her cheek, holding her tight.

"Are you sure you want this? That you—"

"Hush," he said, kissing her to stop her from talking. "I have never wanted anything more in my life."

They kissed, a slow, lazy kiss that could have gone

on for hours if they hadn't been in the middle of a gallery with only an hour to spare before they could potentially be surrounded by other visitors.

"I will never ask you to forfeit your career for me, even it means being apart," he told her, holding her body against his, her cheek to his chest as he rested his chin on the top of her head, in her silky hair. "Everything that is mine is yours."

"Really?" she asked, her voice barely audible.

Nate stroked her back. "Really."

"I'm sorry for being so stubborn," she confessed, leaning back in his arms and gazing up at him. "I just . . ." She didn't even know what to say, so overwhelmed by what was happening, by what he'd just asked her.

"Hey, your stubbornness is one of the things I love about you."

Nate kissed her again, before laughing at the rumble that came from her belly.

"I think we should actually eat this amazing lunch before we leave. I don't want you being undernourished."

"I'm not pregnant yet, Nate. You don't have to worry about my eating habits."

They both laughed.

"Is it so wrong to want you barefoot, pregnant, and under house arrest?" he joked.

"What happened to wanting me to pursue my career?" She pushed him back, but he didn't let her escape his arms.

"I want you any which way I can have you, Faith. So long as you're mine." He pulled her close.

"You still want my advice on which painting to buy,

don't you?" she asked. "I mean, after all the time I took making notes and deciding . . ."

"Darlin', we have to buy *something* today. Just remember that it's going to be for *our* collection, so make sure you choose wisely."

The slow smile that spread across her face was contagious. "Ours?"

"Faith, you're going to be my wife. Whatever we do from now on we do together."

She stepped away from him, clasping his hand and tugging him to his seat.

"Well, let's have lunch, buy this damn painting, and find a hotel to spend the night. I'm ready for some of this togetherness you're talking about."

His eyebrows shot up, and he winked as she took the silver lid off one of the dishes.

"Oh really?"

"Yes, and trust me, you'll need all your energy to keep up with me. So eat up."

"*All* my energy?" he quipped, taking his own lid off, not nearly as interested in the food as he was in the woman seated across from him.

"Yes," she said, picking up her fork but never taking her eyes off his. "And then some."

He laughed; then so did she, holding out her left hand at the same time.

"Are we really going to get married?"

"No. This was just some big scam to get you into my bed tonight."

"Well, it worked." She was still smiling and looking down at her ring. "It's perfect, Nate. I couldn't have chosen better myself."

"You're perfect. And the perfect girl deserves the perfect ring."

He'd never been one for big romantic gestures, but seeing the smile on Faith's face told him that he'd want to spoil her for the rest of her life just to see her face lit with happiness.

"To us," he said, raising his glass.

"To us," she murmured in reply, taking a sip and grinning at him over her glass.

Thank god he'd stopped being such an idiot and manned the hell up to his feelings. He'd been an idiot plenty in the past, but not chasing Faith and showing her what she meant to him would have been the biggest mistake of his life.

"You know, it should have scared me, the fact that you've been with so many women."

Faith stretched out on the oversize bed, the final rays of sunshine falling across the covers. *So much for flying out tonight.* Instead they were holed up at the Waldorf Astoria, in an extravagant room filled with fresh flowers to make it feel like home, as if they were already newlyweds without a care in the world. She might like to pretend she wasn't impressed by his wealth, but there were certain things that she was already starting to look forward to enjoying, and beautiful rooms and lazy afternoons spent in them were top of her list.

Nate stroked her face, his fingertips gentle as they caressed her skin like she was the most precious thing on the planet. "How about we don't talk about the other women I've been with."

"But it didn't," she continued, finding it impossible to keep her eyes open, relaxed and feeling like her limbs had turned to jelly after being in bed with Nate all afternoon. "You've been with plenty of women, gotten all that out of your system, and by now, I figure that you know exactly what you want."

"Yeah." He chuckled. "You could say that." He dropped a kiss to her lips, mouth moving slowly across hers. "Because all I want is you. In my bed, in my kitchen, on my plane . . ."

She giggled. "I kinda like the sound of all that."

"Well, good," he muttered, reaching for her left wrist so he could push her arm back onto the pillow and force her onto her back.

"The benefit of you saving your bed at home for me is that I don't have to insist you get a new mattress at least," she teased.

This time she was certain Nate growled; she heard the rumble in his throat as he stared down at her, his face inches from hers as he positioned himself above her, supporting his weight with his elbows.

"Enough talking!" he demanded.

"Or what?" she asked, wiggling beneath him, arching her back so her breasts were against his bare chest. "Haven't you had enough of me yet?"

"I knew you were trouble," he muttered, reaching for both her wrists so he could hold her down properly, his body heavy against hers now. "From the day I realized you were all grown-up and gorgeous, and then all over again when you landed on my doorstep demanding I take you in."

"You think I'm trouble?" she asked, sucking hard on

his bottom lip and receiving a curse from him in response. "I'd say that's the pot calling the kettle black."

"Oh yeah?" he murmured, taking her mouth against his and kissing her hard until she moaned. He softened it then, his lips going from firm to so, so soft.

"Yeah," she managed.

"I'll show you trouble, Ms. Mendes. Like you've never known in your lifetime."

She let him kiss her, loving that he was holding her down yet she felt safe as she'd ever felt with a man. "That'll be 'Mrs. King' to you soon."

"I know," he replied, slowly releasing her wrists so he could move down her body instead. "And I can't wait."

Faith gasped as he kissed her neck, then her collarbone, then teasingly plucked kisses around her breast. He might have thought she was trouble, but he was the one who'd gotten her into trouble way over her head. Only now she could see that for once in her life it was the kind of trouble she should have embraced rather than run from. All she'd ever wanted was to be happy, to know that what she was giving a man was going to be returned and then some. And with Nate she had everything. A man she'd admired since girlhood, who'd turned into jaw-droppingly gorgeous, yet with the business acumen to succeed in everything he turned his hand to, and he loved her. *He loved her.* Nate fricking King loved her, and she intended to bask in his love for as long as she could.

Epilogue

NATE was sweating. His suit felt like a wet suit, it was clinging so tightly to his body, like a plastic cling wrap that he couldn't escape from.

"I've found a fan," the wedding planner announced, hurrying in with the cord of an old fan trailing behind her.

"Great," Nate muttered, tugging his shirt out of his pants so he could hold the cord up. She went to plug it in, but Chase took over, bending down to push it in while Ryder angled the fan.

"It's not that hot," Ryder teased, standing in just his shirt and tie, suit jacket resting over one of the pews in the first row of the old church.

"Trust Faith for picking the only damn place with no air-conditioning."

"Hey, she wanted an intimate ceremony for like thirty people instead of some kind of circus for two hundred." Ryder shook his head. "I'd be thanking my lucky stars."

Nate shrugged. "I just want this whole thing over."

"Cold feet?" Chase asked, frowning as he crossed his arms and leaned against a seat.

"No," Nate said emphatically. "I just want Faith here in front of me, the ceremony to be over with, and us getting to work on the happily ever after part."

"In bed?" Ryder laughed and Chase joined in.

"I'm just too damn hot; that's the problem," Nate muttered. "Why couldn't we have just eloped?"

"Don't say it!" Sam called out, interrupting him. "I might be okay with you marrying her, but I don't want to hear anything about the two of you, or whatever the hell depraved things you want to do with her as part of that happy ever after."

Nate dropped his shirt and held out his hand to Sam. "Does the fact that you're here mean she's here, too?"

Nate's friend grinned. "Yeah, she's here. Looking pretty gorgeous." He looked Nate up and down. "I think it's about time you tucked yourself back in. Can't have my sister marrying a hobo."

They all laughed and Nate was pleased Sam was here. They'd known each other a long time, and it was good having him with his brothers alongside him. People started to file into the church then, just a handful of friends they were both close to. Nate forgot all about how hot he was as he greeted everyone, took his mind off the fact that he was about to get married as he chatted. Ryder had been right—a ceremony for a couple hundred people wouldn't have been anything like this, wouldn't have held the same meaning.

The minister appeared then, walking in with a big smile on his face and holding out his hands to Nate. The last time he'd held a service for the King family it had

been for Clay's funeral, and Nate was pleased to be seeing the minister for something happier this time, even
if he was wishing his granddad was there to see him get
married.

"I think it's time," the minister said. "Your bride is
ready and waiting for you."

Nate sucked back a breath and followed the minister, his brothers, and Sam, moving to stand alongside
him.

"This is it, big bro," Ryder said.

"And just like that, all three King bachelors are off
the market," Sam joked, making them all laugh.

Nate was about to say something back when the
words died in his mouth. He couldn't even remember
what had seemed so funny at the time. The string quar-
tet had started to play, a soft rendition of Pachelbel's
Canon in D Major; goose pimples trailed across every
inch of Nate's skin, a chill that he'd never felt before. The
last time he'd set foot in a church had been to say good-
bye to his mother, a fact that he hadn't shared with Faith
because he hadn't wanted to ruin their special day when
she was so excited about marrying in her local church.
His brothers had known, he'd refused every Easter and
Christmas to join them even as a boy ever again, and
he'd seen the surprise on their faces when he'd told them
where their ceremony was taking place today. But now
that he was standing there, it felt right. Like his mom
could be looking down over them, all the awful memories of saying good-bye to her replaced with waiting for
his bride.

And there she was. Nate suddenly couldn't hear anything else, couldn't see anything else except the woman

standing at the back of the church. Chloe walked first with Rose, the little girl giggling as she threw tiny pink rose petals, Hope followed and then Faith's friend Cara, but he only managed a quick smile to her bridesmaids. Today was all about Faith, and damn, was she incredible. Her smile took his breath away, emotion catching in his throat as she slowly made her way to him. Her father was seated in the church, she'd invited him, but she hadn't wanted him to walk her down the aisle, and Sam ran forward. He crossed past Nate, did what they hadn't planned but what sure as hell seemed right, and took Faith's arm so she didn't have to walk alone.

When they finally reached him, Nate was brushing away a tear from his cheek and clearing his throat, holding out both hands to Faith. She was dressed in a simple gown; it hugged her body, white and covered in tiny beads that caught the light, her shoulders bare in the strapless dress. She wore no veil, just a white flower in her long dark hair that was out and tumbling down over one shoulder.

"You look incredible," he whispered, unable to stop grinning like an idiot. "Faith, you are so beautiful."

Her smile was wide as she stared up at him, eyes filled with tears that mirrored his own.

"You scrubbed up pretty well yourself, Mr. King."

Sam cleared his throat then, getting their attention. The music was still playing, which meant no one else heard the low words leveled at Nate.

"Don't you ever hurt her, Nate. You keep your promise," Sam cautioned. "You love her and look after her until your dying breath, you hear me?"

Nate held out his hand to shake Sam's. "I promise

you, Sam. On my mother's grave, I promise that I won't so much as harm a hair on her head."

Sam smiled and paused to kiss Faith's cheek. "I wish you two all the happiness in the world. I never planned on getting this douche bag as a brother-in-law, but it could have been worse."

Nate laughed, but his eyes were only for Faith. The church was silent, the music gone and everyone waiting for them, but he didn't care. He held both of Faith's hands and stared down at her, amazed that somehow he'd met a woman like her who'd completely changed his life.

"I never picked you for a man who'd cry," Faith whispered, touching her forehead to his when he bent down.

"Hey, I never picked myself for a guy who'd marry," he murmured, pressing his lips softly to hers to make sure he didn't ruin her makeup.

"I don't mean to interrupt you two lovebirds, but there's some folks here waiting to witness a wedding."

Their friends all laughed at Sam's loud words, but Nate took his time, not intending on rushing anything about his big day.

"I love you, Faith," he whispered in her ear.

"Well, good," she said with a laugh. "Because I love you, too."

They finally turned, hand in hand, Nate almost laughing, the whole situation was so hilarious. How the hell had he ended up about to marry the one woman in the world he'd vowed never to touch?

"Friends and family, we are gathered here today to witness the marriage of Nathaniel King and Faith Mendes," the minister began, facing them as he spoke.

"I've come to know this happy couple very well over the past few months, and I'm confident that their union is one that will truly pass the test of time."

Faith squeezed his hand and he glanced down at her. There was nothing he wouldn't do to keep her by his side forever, no matter what.

Faith felt like she was walking on air. The entire day had been incredible. She'd never been the little girl dreaming of a white wedding growing up, but she couldn't deny that her wedding hadn't been the most amazing day of her life. Or at least one of them.

"Sweetheart, it's time for speeches," Nate drawled into her ear, making her shiver. The way he spoke to her, the depth of his voice when he addressed only her, it did something to her, made her feel content and challenged and special all at the same time.

"Do you still want to go first?" she asked, leaning back so she could look up at him.

Nate seized the moment, dropping a kiss to her lips. "Have I told you lately that I love you?"

"Mmmm," she murmured, reaching up for him even though she was upside down. "I think you might have, *Husband.*"

"This is something that arrived for you yesterday, Nate," Chase said. "The lawyer told me to wait until your speeches to give it to you. He said you weren't to read it first, just to stand up and open it."

Faith watched the exchange between the two brothers, wondering what it was all about.

"What do you think?" Nate asked her.

"I think it's probably something from your grand-

father, don't you think?" It was the only logical expla-
nation.

Nate shrugged, but she could tell it was troubling
him.

"Just open it, darling. Take a quick look."

Nate did as she suggested, running his thumb under
the seal and pulling out a handwritten letter. She could
tell from the look on his face that it was indeed from
Clay.

"It's a letter from him," Nate said, eyes slowly meeting hers, the letter in his hand still. "He wanted me to
read it on my wedding day." He paused, a smile kicking
up the corners of his mouth as he read further. "If I
married you."

"Me?" She laughed. "He must have known what we
didn't."

Nate took her hand in his and turned it to kiss her
palm before moving to stand beside her at the table and
tapping his spoon to his glass.

"I'd like to say a few words!" he said loudly, his
booming voice quieting the previously noisy room.

Faith looked at her husband, unable to take her eyes
off him. He looked incredible in his Dolce & Gabbana
suit, his tie long since discarded, white shirt open necked
and showing off a whole heap of tanned skin.

"I'd like to begin by saying how grateful we are to
be surrounded by our closest family and friends. We
all owe thanks to Faith for the intimacy of this ceremony." Nate winked at her and she smiled back, taking
a sip of champagne as he continued with his speech. "I
never believed I'd ever fall in love, yet here I am today
having declared my love for this one incredible woman

who managed to come along and knock the stuffing from me when I thought I'd lost her."

There were murmurs amongst their friends and Faith reached for his hand, needing to touch him.

"I've known plenty of beautiful women in my lifetime," Nate continued, scowling when a few of the guys sniggered, "but none who also possessed the brains and sass to keep me in line." He cleared his throat. "And it seems that even my granddad knew I'd met my match, if this letter I just received is anything to go by. He's the one person missing today who I wish could have held on long enough to see me married, but I'll just take a moment to read this aloud for the first time, as he wished."

Faith could see the tears glistening in Nate's eyes, heard the catch of emotion in his throat as he spoke of his granddad, and so she rose, slipping an arm around him and dropping her head to rest on his shoulder, to stand by him and support him.

"'To Nate and Faith, because I know that unless you've done something to muck it all up, son, that she's the only one you're ever likely to marry in this lifetime.'"

Faith laughed softly and held Nate even tighter.

"'You swore black and blue that you would never marry, but I always knew that one day a woman would come along that would challenge you enough to make you want to chase her. And when I saw you all bent out of sorts over Faith, I knew you'd finally met your match, because that's exactly how I was over your grandma. She pushed all my buttons, made me fuming mad half the time trying to figure out what the hell she wanted, but she was the only one for me.'"